T0161553

GET RICH QUICK

Get Rich Quick

PETER DOYLE

**DARK
PASSAGE**

A Dark Passage book
Published by Verse Chorus Press
PO Box 14806, Portland OR 97293
info@versechorus.com

Design and layout by Steve Connell/Transgraphic
Series cover concept by Louise Cornwall

Printed in China

ISBN 978-1-891241-24-6 (paper)
ISBN 978-1-891241-88-8 (ebook)

Library of Congress Control Number: 2004104407

For Maurice Doyle

GET RICH QUICK

A glossary of Australian slang can be found at the end of this book

1

FEBRUARY 1952

I took the early tram to Maroubra Beach that Saturday morning, instead of jogging down the hill, which is what I usually do. If I'd run, I'd have arrived ten minutes later and everything since would have been different.

At that time, early in 1952, I had been living at Maroubra for six months, in a flat on Maroubra Bay Road. From my front window you could see sand hills and part of the old speedway. Downstairs was a dago milk bar. There was a church up the road, two pubs, a Chic Salon, a ham and beef shop and an old duck who sold sly grog. Back over the hill towards Coogee were some blocks of flats, supposed to be Spanish Mission style, like in Hollywood, but the salt air had rusted out the steel in the hinges and window catches, and now brown stains ran down the stucco and joinery. Over this side were a few California bungalows, put there by spec builders before the war. Mostly it was sand, scrub, and snakes. It was a shithouse.

My landlord was one Laurie O'Brien. He lived in a two-story house around the corner. Laurie was a starting-price bookie. He also operated on-course, in the Paddock at Randwick. He was one of the best-known bookies in Sydney, pretty well liked, too, as much as anyone ever likes a bookie. Most of the time, he was my boss. I oversaw his phone room on race days and paid everyone off at the end, while Laurie ran the show on-course.

I'd taken up swimming laps a week before, and was up to a mile a day. The nearest place was Mahon Pool, a tidal swimming pool blasted out of the cliffs at the north end of the beach. That morning I was under a cloud. There are people who can handle a hangover but I'm not one of them. It was already looking like being a hot day. I felt sick and giddy. And so I'd taken the tram.

There was a single car parked on the cliff above, a dark blue Oldsmobile, but I figured I'd beaten the mob to the pool.

I didn't spot the body until I had my shirt off and was about to dive in. He was floating face down, the water around him streaked with red. He looked like William Holden in that film, except this fellow was big, and he wasn't talking about how he got there. The blood had berleyed up a school of little tiddlers, and seagulls were circling above.

I dived in, swam across to the body, and gingerly turned it over. It was Charlie Furner, friend, adviser, and salaried thug to Little Jim Swain. The previous Thursday, I'd threatened him in front of a dozen witnesses at Dovey's Gym, and now he was dead as a mackerel. Blood was still dribbling from a hole in the side of his head. The bullet had gone right through his American-made toupee. It was one of those rugs you can wear in the water. Pity he couldn't do a testimonial—they couldn't even shoot the fucking thing off.

I could have dragged him out of the drink, called an ambulance, the cops, his mum—and a priest, for that matter. But I didn't. I left the water, left the pool. The Oldsmobile was gone. I walked back up the hill to my flat.

From three hundred yards away I looked back and saw a police car pull up at the pool. They didn't see me. Ten minutes later I rounded the corner to my flat and saw a new black Ford parked out front, and two jacks entering the lobby. I kept walking, straight past. I hailed a cab down on Anzac Parade, told the driver to take me to Darlinghurst. He gave me a hostile once-over. He was an older bloke, and he had his returned man's badge on. I was still wearing sandshoes, singlet, and old trousers, carrying a gladstone bag with my swimming gear. Plus, I wore my hair Cornel Wilde style, which was not the style most favoured by old diggers. As if I gave a shit.

I paid him with the last ten-shilling note in my wallet and went upstairs to the flat in Flinders Street. I hoped she'd be alone. It was seven-thirty when she opened the door.

"Well, Billy, hello there."

Maybe she was glad to see me, maybe she couldn't care less. She looked me up and down. "You've adopted the casual look today?"

She was in a dressing gown, her fair hair hanging loose around her shoulders. Smiling slightly. She had a smoke going, a Camel. Not a lady's smoke, but it was a long time since anyone had accused Molly Price of being a lady. The Radiola was on—she kept the radio or gramophone going all the time—and Nat King Cole was singing "Nature Boy."

"Is Jim Swain here?"

"Rather indelicate of you to ask, wouldn't you say?"

I walked past her, into the flat. On the sideboard stood a bottle of sherry, a Pimm's, and a couple of inches of brandy in a decanter. I drank the brandy, straight from the decanter.

"Do you have any beer in the ice chest?"

"You're making an early start."

"My day got off with a bang. Charlie Furner is dead. Is Swain here?"

She shook her head, not smiling anymore.

"Molly, the bulls are at my place already. If they put a message over the cab two-way, they'll track me here in no time. I've got a hangover, I've got no money in my kick, and I still haven't had my swim."

"Did you kill him?"

"No. I think I've been set up. When I got to the pool for my swim he was already snapper bait. I've got to nick off for a while, sort this out. Can I borrow your car and a few quid?"

"Are you serious?"

The door was thumped loudly, an unmistakable copper door-knock.

I ran through the kitchen, out onto the back stairs. Molly called to me, tossed me her car keys.

"There's a five-pound note under the driver's seat."

I drove her little Ford Prefect out to Canterbury, listening to the radio, trying to think it all through.

Two days ago, I had gone to Dovey's gym to settle up with a couple of Laurie's punters. If I'd known Furner was there working out, I wouldn't have gone in, but I was already inside and doing business by the time I pegged him. When he saw me he started taking the piss. He conveyed to me Little Jim's opinion that I was a "cheeky bodgie prick who had shirked his war duty and now was bludging off women."

I sure didn't want to fight Charlie. I had been the 347th best fighter in Marrickville as a kid, and Charlie Furner was an ape.

"I hear you're still knocking around with that Molly tart. It's a wonder she has any time for you at all, you not being a darkie. Or maybe she's too doped to tell the difference." He winked at the gawkers nearby as he said this, and they guffawed obligingly.

He was referring to Molly's wartime activities. Like a lot of local girls, she had knocked about with Yanks. She used to hang around the Booker T. Washington Club up in Albion Street in Surry Hills, which was for the use of Negro servicemen. It was off-limits to white American servicemen, just as the Roosevelt Club at the Cross was off-limits to Negroes. The Booker T had a hot jazz orchestra and a juke box stocked with American records, which attracted plenty of local musicians, as well as people who liked jive dancing and didn't mind the Negroes being there. And quite a few of the local girls preferred the company of Negroes. They were better dancers, but it didn't stop at that. They had taught the girls a few tricks the other local girls didn't know, or wouldn't have done even if they had known.

Molly had even briefly shacked up with a Negro victualing sergeant. Stationed up near Singleton, he had found wild hemp growing, and had introduced Molly to the delights of reefer smoking. She was only eighteen at the time, but then, as now, she didn't give a shit what anyone thought about her.

Since the war Molly had been making ends meet any way she could. For a while she'd been a dancer at the Tivoli. Sometimes she entertained gentlemen of substance. Including, recently, Little Jim. He'd fallen for her, wanted to marry her. He escorted her to cabarets, nightclubs, and stage shows, bought her presents and all that sort of stuff, but she had refused to commit herself.

I had known Molly since the war, and we'd been lovers on and off since then. She said she wouldn't be tied down to any one man if it didn't suit her, and so far it hadn't. Swain thought the only thing standing between him and Molly was me, so he felt about me the way Mr. Eisenhower felt about Mr. Stalin.

I could handle a yokel like Furner bagging me and the woman I sort of loved; I could even handle the suggestion that she was a dope fiend. Shit, I'd developed a taste for the stuff myself. What I couldn't handle was him getting a laugh at my expense. Being made to look like a goose was death to a low-level lurk artist like myself. So when Charlie made the crack about dope I laughed along with the others, and as he turned back to his weights I threw my best punch at him. It glanced off his head. He was waiting for it, and turned back to me to launch a big swing, and I knew I was ratshit.

During my fumbling assault, I had stumbled on a fifteen-pound barbell on the floor between us. It had rolled in his direction. Now it caught his ankle, and threw him off balance. His punch landed ineffectually and he tripped forward, fell at my feet, and managed to hit his head on the other barbell. It was never going to get better than this. I growled, "You'll get a lot worse the next time I see you, you ugly mongrel, so keep out of my way or you're fucking history." Then I took my leave, smartly. My sainted mother had always told me that my need to have the last word would cause me bother.

I stopped for breakfast at a chew-and-spew near Newtown Station, rang Laurie from a public phone, and told him I was sick, which he didn't appreciate. He asked me where I was calling from. I said it didn't matter. I didn't tell him about Furner, not yet.

I spent the morning at a flat near Canterbury racetrack. Laurie owned it, kept it as an alternative base for his SP. Above a frock shop near Canterbury Station, it had a clear view of the straight and the finishing post. 2UE used to run a landline from this very flat; they called the races from there, back when the racing clubs banned radio stations from the tracks. Laurie still used it as a relay point for tick-tackers—stooges on-course who used hand signals to telegraph odds to parties off-course.

I sat down at the trestle table, picked up the nearest of the dozen phones, and called Molly.

"Waters was here," she said. Frosty now. Detective Sergeant Ray Waters, easily the most feared copper in Sydney. A man, a New Australian, had died under his questioning, from the combined effects of multiple bruising, a punctured lung, a ruptured spleen, and internal haemorrhaging. At the inquest, Waters stated he had fallen on him accidentally. He was cleared. People used to say, "Shoot me, flog me, run me over, beat me with a cricket bat but for Christ's sake, please, don't *fall* on me!" A returned serviceman, he hated young blokes, he hated lairs, hated dagos, Balts, Jews, queers, hated immoral women, hated American music, hated Freemasons, hated Japs and Chows, and commos. Most of all, he hated eligible men who had not served in the war. If he got hold of me, he'd have me confessing to the Shark Arm Murder and the Pajama Girl Case, as well as Charlie's murder. One thing about Waters, he didn't verbal. Didn't need to.

"What did he say?"

"He said the moment hemp goes on the poisons list this year, he'll have me on a charge and see me slotted. He asked me if I was really a half-caste gin, since I liked to fuck niggers. He also asked if my father was still a bludging booze-artist, if my mum was still a drunken slut, and if my brother still copped it up the back door. Then he inquired as to the whereabouts of my gutless-wonder boyfriend. Other than that, he was his usual charming self."

"What'd he say about Charlie's death?"

"An anonymous caller informed Randwick police at six-thirty this morning that you had just argued with and shot Charlie Furner at Mahon Pool, and that the weapon was still in your possession. A second call told them you could be found here."

"I was followed. Jesus, but surely they can't believe an anonymous caller. Why don't they suspect *him*?"

"That's what I said to Waters. He said the caller said he was frightened of you retaliating."

"Yeah, well, if Waters gets hold of me I won't be retaliating on anybody. I'm sorry about all this."

"Yeah, great. When can I have my car back?"

"I'll ring you later. Today."

I'd been followed from Mahon Pool, to my place, to Molly's. The blue Oldsmobile. He could have followed me here. Thwarted when I left Molly's the back way, or else he figured I was pinched anyway when he saw Waters go in the front. Weapon still in your possession. I checked my gladstone.

A pistol was under my towel.

I walked around the flat wondering what to do. I tried a few phone calls but hardly anyone was home. At midday I was still pacing, smoking, and worrying. I rang Laurie.

"Shit, Billy, I wish you'd told me about Charlie Furner when you rang before. What happened?"

"Laurie, I haven't got the slightest clue. All I know for sure is that of all the people in Sydney, the only one that definitely *didn't* neck Charlie Furner is me. Who told you about it?"

"Waters was here, and so was Little Jim. This is a real mess. They're both sure you're responsible. I told them I didn't think you'd've done anything like this."

"Christ, Laurie, you didn't *think* I'd done it? You *know* I didn't. I couldn't."

"Now settle down. Look, I've always done the right thing by you, haven't I?"

"Yeah, you have."

"So just trust me to handle things this end, will you?"

"Yeah, all right."

"Like I said, I tried to talk them both around, but neither of them was ever inclined to think well of you. And the fact that you shot through, well, it looks like guilty behaviour, doesn't it?"

"I can't change that now. But there's no way I'll get a fair go from Ray Waters, so I'm not giving myself up. Listen Laurie, I need some cash to keep mobile while I clear this all up."

"What are you into me for already?"

As if he didn't know, to the shilling.

"Could be up to a hundred quid, I guess."

"You owe me nearly fifty quid back rent, and there's a hundred and sixty on your betting account. You've got to pull your socks up. How much do you want?"

"I don't know. As much as poss."

"I'll let you have twenty quid. But you better not come around here. I'm just about to head off to Randwick, anyway."

I told him I would be slipping back to the flat later on to get some clothes. He said what time. I said mid-afternoon. Could he leave it under the doormat? He said yeah, he'd send someone around with it.

That was typical Laurie. I'd worked for him off and on since the war. Back then I turned a dollar working a few different lurks. I delivered booze to nightclubs, did some black marketeering, and worked as a runner for Laurie—offloading big bets with other SPs, sharing the risk. All the while I was ostensibly employed in a little workshop in Redfern which made buckles and ferrules for kit bags and army boots. I paid the owner ten bob a week just to keep me on the books, so that if the Manpower Authority nabbed me, I could say I was doing my bit to keep the Japs out of Pitt Street.

Laurie used to be a Newtown butcher. In the thirties he'd run a pennies-and-threepences book for Newtown battlers, but during the war it came good, and he started making a lot more money from the SP than he ever had from lambs fry. He invested in blocks of flats around Coogee and Maroubra. He didn't make snags anymore.

Laurie had generally done the right thing by the local battlers during the Depression, and was a financial supporter of the ALP, but I'd never seen him actually risk a big quid, or make a donation that wasn't in some way to his own advantage.

I had no complaints. He'd always been pretty fair to me.

After I'd finished with Laurie, I rang Max. Max Perkal, piano player, guitarist, drummer, and sometime actor. You could have heard him on the radio a few years before as Zeke "Brumby" Perkins, the Yodeling Stockman; other times he'd been Sol Kanahele, the Smiling Hawaiian; or Bones Persil, blackface singer, noted around Joe Taylor's establishments for his blue rendition of "Open the Door, Richard." More usually he'd appear as Max Peck, leader of boogie-woogie dance combination Max Peck and his Pickled Peppers. If you tuned into *The Life of Riley* on Tuesday nights, you could sometimes hear Max playing the part of Ernie Pincher, the Riley family's sneaky landlord. Twenty-seven years old, half good at most things except punting, which meant he was always working and always broke. The last sensible thing I had done was lend him fifty quid three nights ago. His mum got him out of bed.

Yes, he had the money. Well, actually, some of it. How much? Maybe twelve quid. No, he couldn't bring it over, he'd have to take the tram, which he never did, on principle. I told him I'd come and get it, not to tell anyone he'd spoken to me, tell his mum the same. He said, Jesus, what sort of mess are you in?

I got to Max's place in Stanmore at one. The streets were pretty empty since the shops had closed and everyone had gone home. It was hot, the sun was very bright. I spent the drive looking out for policemen.

His mum let me in, went back to her form guide and bottle of beer on the kitchen table. The radio was on, announcing the late scratchings. A cig was burning in the ashtray. There was a pile of newspapers and magazines at one end of the table, more on the sideboard.

The whole family had long ago formed an addiction to the printed word, didn't matter much what it was. Mrs. Perkal and her late husband had run the news agency near Stanmore Station for fifteen years, until old Sam dropped dead in 1946. The older son, Morris, had been running the business since. Mrs. Perkal had never had much interest in the early starts and long hours, reckoned that's what killed Sam. Now she helped out during busy times, kept the books and read the mags, but was more interested in her weekend flutter on the gallops and the Wednesday night housie at St. Brendan's.

"He's in his room," she said, dropping back into her chair.

"You got a tip for me, Mrs. Perkal?"

"Yeah, don't listen to Max's tips."

"Come on through, Billy boy!" Max called from his room.

I went in. As usual it looked as though he was conducting a one-man paper drive. Magazines everywhere. *Downbeat, Music Maker, Time, New Statesman, Man, Australasian Post, The New Yorker, Trotguide, Sportsman*—everything. A mound of Cleveland Westerns and Carter Browns, Larry Kents, four or five Teach Yourself books, a few Penguin paperbacks. I was never sure how much of all this Max actually read, but he usually had something to say on any topic you cared to test him on.

"Over here, I'm in the wardrobe. Let me out, for Christ's sake!"

"What the hell?" I started over to the wardrobe in the corner, heard Max chuckling behind me.

"No, over here!"

I turned around, saw him standing behind the door, unshaven, wearing a tiger-striped dressing gown. I looked back at the wardrobe. His voice came again from inside. "Let me out! Let me out!" I pulled open the wardrobe door, saw a gizmo inside, a couple of spools on top, turning, an electric cord.

"It's a tape recorder." He walked past me, picked it up, set it down on the bed. "Jack Davey gave it to me. They're the new thing in radio."

"The fuck's it for?"

"Davey uses it to record five or six shows all in the one day, the studio plays the tape back over the air, maybe three weeks later. People think you're there in the studio, when actually you could be in Gulargambone by then. I brought it home for mum. She likes to record the races as they're called and play them back later. You can record the hit parade off the radio, too."

He rewound the tape, told me to say something, held out a microphone. I recited the first line from "Young Lochinvar," the only thing that came to mind. He wound it back, played it to me.

"That's me?"

"Sure is, comrade."

"Yeah, well, that's great, but I need that brass. I've got things to do."

"Yeah, sure." He picked his wallet off the dresser, took out the money, gave it to me. "What's the story? You look as nervous as the hare at Wentworth Park."

I told him. He smoked and listened. When I finished he shook his head slowly and said, "That's a bad, bad business." He reached behind the dresser and brought out a small bottle of Corio whisky, poured a nip into the empty glass on his bedside table and handed it to me.

"This isn't the one you put your teeth in, is it?"

"The scotch will kill the germs."

He took a quick nip straight from the bottle, wiped his mouth with the back of his hand. "I don't know who killed Furner. But really, no one will be all that cut up about it. The man was an animal, pardon my speaking ill of the dead. He took a blow torch to Greek Steve's testicles."

"Yeah. A charmer."

I stood up.

Max skulled the last of the bottle and chucked it in a bin. "So, you got any idea who did it?"

"No. You know anyone owns a blue Oldsmobile?"

"No, but I'll ask around, for what it's worth."

"Find out anything you can about Little Jim as well, will you? Any recent news, in particular."

"Sure. Ring me later."

He looked around the room for more money, found another couple of pounds in change, borrowed another fiver from his mother and gave it all to me.

It was even hotter when I hit the road again. There were no cars out. I drove down Broadway and pulled up at the Agincourt Hotel, just before Central. I bought three bottles of Flag Ale and drove on, under the railway bridges at Eddy Avenue, round into Reservoir Street. I found a park and walked back down to the Central Residential. All the terrace-house windows were open, and I could hear the same race being called on two or three radios.

I went to the fourth floor. The brown lino on the floor was lifting, and the ashtray at the top of the stairs hadn't been emptied since the war. I knocked on the door at the end of the corridor. Ken Howard was calling the tote odds on the race that had just run. I heard a chair scrape on the lino, a heavy step nearing the door.

"Yeah?" The door didn't open.

"Grafter, it's Billy Glasheen."

Nothing.

"Grafter?"

"What?"

"It's Billy, Grafter. Can you open the door?"

"What do you want?"

"Charlie Furner's dead. Open the bloody door, Grafter, for fuck's sake."

Grafter Nolan stood well over six feet. He was nearly sixty now, but had much the same build he'd had when the photograph on the wall at Dovey's was taken, back when he was a champion lifter. Now he stood there in his singlet, his hair still cut very short, combed and neatly parted high on his head. His face was pitted, his nose fleshed out, his cheeks red, leathery and bulbous.

"You'd better come in."

I followed him inside, into a small kitchen with a bedroom off it. There was a laminex table with a couple of chairs placed next to the window, a radio on the table, a *Telegraph* form guide spread open beside it.

I opened a bottle and poured us each a glass of beer. Grafter gestured me to sit at the table, said cheers when I passed him the beer.

We both took a mouthful and Grafter looked out the window at the street.

"So Charlie's copped it, eh?"

"Yeah, and Ray Waters is trying to frame me for it."

He nodded and took another sip. "So why did you come to me?"

I'd known the Grafter since I was a kid, back when I used to lug around a tray of Minties and Smith's Chips at the Stadium fights.

Grafter had been a kind of celebrity then, a muscle-man, fence, wrestler, thief. When he made his way to his seat in the front row at the Stadium the hoons would all cheer him: the pin-up of thugs and standover men. A couple of times he'd got me to run errands for him, gave me ten bob once for taking a message to a prostitute up at Darlo when the cops were watching her and him. I skited about it for months. Now he was just another old bloke in Surry Hills trying not to fall into the bottle.

"I'd like to get the mail on Jim Swain and Charlie Furner."

He nodded again and looked at me. "Yeah?"

"Like, how did they first team up?"

"That was in the war. I knew Charlie before the war, he used to wrestle a bit."

"But he didn't know Swain then?"

"No, probably not. I think they met in the army."

"Furner in the services?"

"He was trying to get out of trouble at home. He'd belted a bloke in a pub brawl and this bloke suffered brain damage. The family wanted Charlie charged. So he joined up, shot through. The idea of shooting blokes legally probably took his fancy, as well."

"But he teamed up with Swain."

"Yeah. They started stealing from American stores, selling the stuff back to fences. The Yanks had everything. You could make a good bob just trading in American cigs, if you wanted."

"I remember Swain from before the war. You must have known him back then."

"Yeah. He came up through the razor gangs. Ran a book up there at the Imperial. When he rorted an army commission for himself, he got Furner in as offsider and muscle man. The war in the Pacific was good to those two."

"So what happened after the war?"

"Well, Furner would have gone back to his pre-war profession, bashing SPs, robbing abortionists and prostitutes, whatever, but Swain figured that with the capital he had, and with Furner on-side, he could kick on in a big way."

I refilled our glasses and offered Grafter a Craven A. He shook his head. I lit one for myself.

"So Swain went back to SP?"

"Yeah. He built up his empire by standing over the little back-street and corner-pub bookies."

"With Furner bashing anyone who didn't play ball."

"They had other methods as well. Remember, your small bookie has always been vulnerable. He has to pay off publicans and coppers, and keep a look out for tea leaves like Charlie Furner. But above all, he has to keep faith with the punter. Which means he can never, *ever* be seen to renege on a legitimate pay-out. Do that once or twice and they're finished. So, you know, to cover their own arses the bookies lay off portions of big bets with other bookies—they sacrifice some profit but it spreads the risk a little. All done more or less informally, of course. What Swain used to do was send Charlie around to tell the bookies that in future they were to lay off their bets with Swain, and no one else. And then he'd knock them off if and when it suited him."

"I think I know the rest," I said. "Swain waits till he knows of a fixed race, gets a stooge to place a big bet with the bookie, just minutes before the race is run. When the bookie gets back to him, trying to lay off some of the bet, Swain says he can't take it, that he's already overextended, or some bullshit like that. Bingo, the bookie's fucked up, and Swain has his money."

"Good, isn't it?"

"I don't know why someone with public spirit hasn't put him out of business."

The Grafter chuckled, shook his head. "Jesus, Billy, you should know better than that. They're all the same, all the big bookies."

"Laurie's not."

He looked at me. "Isn't he?"

"What do you mean?"

He shrugged.

"Come on, Grafter, what do you mean?"

"Oh, I know, Laurie isn't a bash-merchant, but once Little Jim and Charlie started their shenanigans, there were a whole lot of small bookies went to Laurie for protection, and they were willing to pay for it. Swain's methods didn't hurt your mate Laurie O'Brien too badly at all."

I looked out the window. The sun had swung around now and was shining straight along Reservoir Street. A drunk was staggering up from Elizabeth Street, carrying a carton of beer bottles. He was singing, cursing. He stopped and called out to some kids on a billy cart, waving his fist, swaying.

I opened the second bottle and filled the two glasses.

"And there was no trouble between Swain and Furner?"

"Not that I ever heard of. Swain was quite happy for Furner to keep up his own standover rorts. Like a hobby."

"Prostitutes?"

"Yeah, tarts, other thieves, anyone with crook money."

"Furner was married, wasn't he?"

"That'd have to be one of the great mysteries of the age. Married a nice girl, Vi."

"But he was a root rat?"

"That's right. He used to force the tarts he was extorting to come across."

"Any thoughts on who might have wanted to kill him?"

The Grafter laughed. "Mate, the list of people who *didn't* want to kill him would be easier."

"When did you last see him?"

"I don't keep track of any of that crowd any more."

"Who could bring me up to date?"

"You could try the Jap."

I got up to leave. "Thanks, Grafter."

"There's something else."

"Yeah?"

"Not many people know about this. Little Jim and Vi Furner had an affair years ago, just after the war."

"Did Charlie know about it?"

"If he did, he never mentioned it."

"How long did it go on for?"

"Not that long. They ended it, but they say Little Jim was still a bit sweet on her."

I nodded.

"Here, take your other bottle with you."

"No, you keep it."

"I won't drink it. Take it."

I said goodbye, went out with the beer bottle under my arm.

At the door the Grafter said, "Don't let on you got any of this from me."

Downstairs, the drunk was sitting on the curb. He'd dropped his box and a couple of bottles lay in the gutter, broken. He'd pissed himself, was sitting there in the puddle. I went over to him.

"Where do you live, dad?"

"I'll go you, you bastard." He struggled to his feet and started shaping up.

"He's all right," a voice called behind me. A woman was leaning from a window across the street. "I'll send the young bloke over to get him later on."

"Are you sure?"

"Yeah, leave him there. I'm not letting him in like that. He'll be all right there."

I drove the Prefect back to my flat at Maroubra. A dry westerly was blowing across town, but a cloud bank had appeared to the south. The whisky and beer were sweating out of me. I opened the last bottle of Flag on the lip of the ashtray and took a gulp.

I parked down the street and looked around. I couldn't see any cop cars, so I went in. The front-door lock had been broken, the door left ajar.

I found the twenty quid under the mat. I showered and changed, put a couple of shirts and some underwear in my bag, and went to leave. I pulled open the front door to Ray Waters' red face, puffing after walking up the stairs. Despite the heat, he was wearing a blue serge suit and hat. He couldn't have run twenty yards, but could have throttled Charles Atlas if he chose to, so long as someone else was holding him still.

"Sorry, Ray, I can't stop to chat right now. Go in and make yourself a cup of tea, if you like."

I swung my bag as hard as I could into the side of his head, knocked him a foot sideways. I barrelled past him, almost got to the stairs, but he grabbed my shirt collar, swung his right arm around, caught me in the neck. It threw me back through the front door and across the timber floor. He walked towards me, reaching into his back pocket. He pulled out a cosh. The gladstone was still in my hand, snapped open. I fumbled out the revolver, aimed it at his face as he loomed over me.

"Like they say in the pictures, reach for the sky."

He stopped, but didn't put his hands up. He looked at me and began to grin. "Well now, young Mr. Bill Glasheen's got a roscoe, if I'm not mistaken. The same weapon used by a certain person or persons to cause a fatal injury to Charles Edward Furner this very morning."

"Move back, Ray!"

He shook his head like I was a naughty little kid.

"Now, I'd like you to put that down and accompany me to Darlinghurst Police Station to further assist me in my inquiries."

I pulled the trigger, blasting the shit out of a glass lampshade above his head. Glass pieces and ceiling plaster rained down on him. He stepped back. My ears were ringing and the recoil had jarred my shoulder. I got to my feet, waving the gun in his face. My hand was shaking.

"Now, just settle down. This behaviour won't help you at all."

"Yeah, well, excuse my manners just this once, Ray. Drop that sap on the floor." He let go of the cosh and I picked it up. Lead sinkers wrapped in leather. "Turn around, walk out the back." I directed him to the laundry downstairs, gestured him in. "There's some of my shirts there, you can give them a wash to pass the time. Pay special attention to the collars, if you would. Now turn around." I swung the sap at the back of his head, not too hard. He fell down, unconscious. I locked the laundry door, threw the sap in the garbage bin. He could shout for help when he woke up. Sooner or later someone would hear him.

Being a fugitive is a strange thing. I've seen a man wanted by the police drink all day at his local hotel, seen jail escapees at the races and football games, even on the street. They walk around, place bets, shake hands with people, and don't get caught. I read somewhere that Ben Hall and Frank Gardner, the bushrangers, used to attend Bathurst races under the noses of the traps. Without a specific tip-off, the police will very rarely track a man down, even when he's staying at the family home or his girlfriend's place.

But that knowledge didn't help me much. I drove back into town looking left and right continually, fearful of seeing anyone I knew. I stopped at a Greek in Darlo, bought some fish and chips and ate it in the car, parked in the shade in a laneway off Dowling Street, feeling like a Jap on Anzac Day.

The races were over, the unlucky punters were streaming back to Central Station and the city on foot. I watched them going by until I'd finished eating, then walked around towards the Beauchamp Hotel. It was less than two hundred yards from Darlinghurst Police Station, but it was where I had to go.

I rang Max from a phone box in Oxford Street. He was getting ready to go out to his professional engagement at the Hawaiian Club. He'd made a few calls.

"No one could tell me much we don't already know. Except one. Remember Tony Pettit? He used to swim with Furner down at the Domain Baths, and drank with him a bit down at the Coogee Bay. Well, he told me he heard Charlie and Little Jim quarrelled last week."

"What about?"

"Don't know. Another thing he said was that the widow won't be too distraught about the demise of her husband."

"A common sentiment."

"Apparently, his idea of a leg opener was a left hook."

"What about Furner rorting Swain?"

"Tony said he'd seen no evidence of that, but if Furner and Swain *were* drifting apart, a bloke like Furner would naturally see no percentage in not brassing Swain while he still had the chance. And loudmouth rube though he was, he had too much rat cunning to go bragging about thieving from Swain, if that's what he was doing."

"OK. That's beaut. Something else before you go. Can you hang on to that tape recorder thing? I've got an idea I want to talk about. Can I see you later on?"

"I'm finishing at the Hawaiian Club at eight-thirty. I can stop at the Rocket Range on my way to the Troc, if you like. See you there?"

I rang off and went into the Beauchamp.

The Jap was in the lounge, writing in a notebook, surrounded by men waiting to collect their dividends. He waved hello at me, indicated he'd join me in a moment. The Jap had run the SP in the Beauchamp for the last couple of years. Australian-born Chinese, Freddy Long had been called the Jap for as long as anyone could remember.

I bought a beer and sat down. The pub was full, roaring loud as men frantically drank as much as they could before the place closed at six, twenty minutes away. Freddy came over and sat down, a glass of scotch in his hand.

"Boy, I've been waiting for this." He took a big sip. "I never start until after I've settled up. How are you then, young feller?"

"Been better, actually, Fred. Charlie Furner's dead. The cops think I did it, which I didn't. I shouldn't be here, I'm going to bolt as soon as I can. I need some gen from you."

He nodded. "Sure. I haven't forgotten that business last year." When Fred had taken over as SP at the Beauchamp, Little Jim had sent Charlie around to put the proposition to him—to either pay Little Jim fifty percent of the takings, or close up business forthwith. Charlie had bashed the Jap to help make his point. The Jap approached me, asked me to talk to Laurie, which I did. Laurie offered his own deal to the Jap: for ten percent of the take, he would offer his protection, which the Jap readily accepted. Laurie spoke to Little Jim, told him the Jap was already under his wing, would he mind desisting. Little Jim went quietly, not wanting an open conflict with Laurie.

"Who would most want to kill Charlie Furner?"

"Everyone who knew him. He was a prick."

"His wife?"

"What about his wife?"

"What do you know about her?"

"Name's Vi. He used to bash her. She was scared shitless of him. Too frightened to leave."

"I hear she used to be sweet with Little Jim. Could they have got together to get rid of him?"

"Absolutely a hundred per cent no! She's a good, gentle woman who's had much worse than she deserves. And her and Little Jim finished years ago." The Jap looked at me, looked at the table. "I hear Little Jim's hot for Molly Price these days." He looked up at me, watching for my reaction.

"Where does Vi live now?" I asked.

"They—or rather, she has a place in South Coogee. Twenty Dudley Street, I think. But don't make any trouble for her, eh?"

I left and walked around the corner towards Molly's place. Parked almost out front was a blue Oldsmobile. Same one? Couldn't tell. No one around. A newspaper blown up against the back wheel, like it had been there a while. Felt the bonnet: cool.

I went inside. Molly was dressed up to go out.

"How's your day been, lover?" she said. I could smell reefer. The gramophone was playing some of the new jazz, the cool stuff.

"Well, I had a tussle with Ray Waters at my place. I had to put him out. Can I have a drink, and one of those funny ciggies?"

"Help yourself to the booze. Here." She took a roughly made rollie from her purse and handed it to me. I lit it, inhaled deeply, held it down as long as I could, then fixed a scotch, skulled it, then fixed another. I sat down on the couch, leaned back.

"I'm going out. You can stay here for a while, if you want."

"Thanks, Moll. That's great."

"Yeah, but you better not let my date see you. I'm going out with Jim Swain."

"Oh shit, Moll, why him?"

"He asks that about you. Wait in the bedroom when he comes to the door. Will you be here when I come home?"

"No. Here's your car key."

She looked at me a moment, didn't say anything.

There was a knock on the door, so I nipped into the bedroom. When I came out, she was gone. I had another scotch and read Friday's *Daily Mirror* while I listened to the other side of the record. The Historical Feature was about great scandals of Australian horse racing. I dozed off.

When I woke, it took me a few moments to realize where I was. It was eight-thirty and pouring rain outside. I had another scotch, relit the reefer and had a couple of puffs. I'd had some strange dreams. I looked at the Historical Feature again. When the rain stopped, I left.

Downstairs, the Oldsmobile was gone. It had just got dark, but the sky was clearing. A huge cloudbank was moving away to the northeast, flashes of lightning in it.

I hailed a hack, told him the Penfolds Wine Bar in Pitt Street, better known as the Rocket Range. Max was there, still wearing his Hawaiian shirt, a yellow thing with pictures of surfboard riders and palm trees on it. There were a few booze artists drinking silently at the bar.

Max looked at me, said "Ho, padre, how you travelling? Not so good, it would seem."

"No, I'm all right. Here, I've got something for you." I passed the remains of the reefer to him. He started singing: "*So light that tea and let it be* . . . Mighty neighbourly of you, brother. Now, what else? Is there any news better than this?"

"Much better. Now, pay attention. Do you remember Harry Solomons?"

"Yeah, the old race caller. When was it? '37, '38? Down in Melbourne."

"'39, it was."

"He used to do that thing, he'd call the race over the radio, in the morning, before it'd run. He'd call it the way he imagined it was going to turn out."

"That's right. The Phantom Broadcast, they used to call it. Very popular with the punters. I was just reading about it in the paper."

"Pity old Harry didn't leave it at that."

"Yeah, well, it gave him ideas, didn't it? He thought that if he could call a race *before* it'd run, he could just as well call it *after* it'd run."

Max nodded his head, didn't say anything for a moment. "I wonder if he's still in Pentridge."

"They let him out a few years ago."

When I finished with Max, I went across the road and booked a room in the Cosy Private Hotel. The bloke at the desk sold me a half bottle of Cutty Sark at double the price. I lay on the narrow bed and sipped from it. I tried not to dwell on Molly with Little Jim, probably back at her flat by now. The West End Hotel next door had a neon sign, flashing on and off, lighting up my room. I could hear a radio playing in a room somewhere, now and then a drunk cursing out on the street. At two o'clock a loud thump from the room next door woke me up. Other than that I had a terrific night.

Sunday morning, I had mixed grill and a pot of tea at the J & S Cafe, but I still felt like shit. I scanned the morning papers. There were reports on Furner's death in all the papers, but no mention of me. The *Sunday Telegraph* quoted Ray Waters saying the police "harboured very strong suspicions as to the offender's identity" and were confident of an early arrest and the prompt recovery of the murder weapon.

I telephoned Molly. She was subdued. "Is Swain still there?" She said not. I asked for the car again, she said OK, very cool. She said she was going out, she'd leave the car key on the front wheel. I said thanks. I got a handful of zacks in the cafe and went back to the phone box.

I rang the Jap. He asked if everything was all right. I said yeah.

"Listen, Fred, how many phone lines has Little Jim got going in? I mean, how many calls can he receive at once?"

"Up to fifteen, used to be."

"Well, can you find five or six people who bet with him who wouldn't mind making a few bob? They've got to be able to keep their mouths shut."

"I'll see what I can do. What have you got in mind?"

"Just a wild idea for a magic trick. I'll speak to you soon."

I rang Tommy McGrath, a post office techo who picked up a few extra bob looking after Laurie's phone lines. He'd been a signals sergeant during the war, had run the major communications link along the Kokoda Track and was mentioned in dispatches for it. I told him I had an idea I wanted to discuss with him. He said to come on out to his place.

Then I phoned Max's place, asked his mother to get him up. It's still the a.m., she said, no races today. I said would she get him up anyway. He came to the phone. I told him to be ready at eleven, I'd pick him up—and to bring the tape recorder with him.

Then I rang Laurie.

Max grumbled when I picked him up. He was wearing American sunglasses, hadn't shaved. I asked him how the job at the Troc had gone. Not bad, he said. Molly was there.

"Yeah, I know, with Jim Swain."

"Did you know they had an all-out shouting match? I thought they'd be asked to leave. Your name was mentioned. Then Molly left alone, took a cab. He stayed, got shitfaced, belted a bloke. Then he was thrown out."

I didn't say anything, and Max shut up, looked out the window.

We drove west along Parramatta Road, past the new car yards, onto Concord Road, across the Ryde Bridge. I turned right past the Home for Incurables to get to Tommy's street, which faced back down over the Parramatta River.

Tommy offered us a cup of tea, got no result, then offered us a drink. Bingo. His wife, Annie, got glasses and a couple of bottles of beer out, got her cigarettes and an ashtray, and we all sat down at the kitchen table. Their kids had gone down to the new swimming pool at Ryde, except for the youngest, who'd got polio the year before, when he was still a baby. Tommy and Annie took turns holding him on their laps while we sat there at the table.

We chatted for a while. I asked Tommy if he remembered Harry Solomons.

Yeah, sure he did, he'd read about it at the time—how Harry had delayed his call of one particular race, while his accomplices cut all the other radio stations' landlines. The race was run, but no broadcast went out. Harry watched the race start and finish, waited a minute, and *then* he called the race, but called it like it was truly happening then. All from memory. Meanwhile his cronies off-course had quietly placed their bets with bookies who were still taking bets, innocently waiting to hear the start of the race.

Tommy shook his head. "Yeah, it was a stroke of near-genius. "

I lit a cig, drank my beer. "I want to bring Harry's idea up to date," I said.

Tommy raised his eyebrows. "You've got a Harry Solomons?"

I shook my head. "We've got a tape recorder."

Max showed Tommy how it worked, then I told them both what I was thinking, then asked him about the layout of the land-lines.

"Back in the Harry Solomons days," he said, "four or five dif-ferent radio stations all broadcast the same race, and they all maintained their own landlines. Now, of course, with the inter-state races, there's only the one call. One landline. The post office maintains it."

I smiled at Tommy. "Makes it easier, eh?"

He nodded slowly. "The maps are at the post office. Not in my section, but I'll do some research."

Annie made some sandwiches and we stayed on into the mid-afternoon. I rang Laurie again at three o'clock, then Max and I shook hands with Tommy and Annie, and took our leave.

I drove back through town out to South Coogee, cruised past 20 Dudley Street. The blinds were drawn, but there was a sprinkler going on the front lawn. I parked the car, walked up to the front door, and knocked.

A woman in her late thirties came to the door, gave me a level look, and said, "Yes?"

I told her who I was. She paused, told me to come in, sat me down, asked me what I wanted, polite smile. She was neither friendly nor cool. Serious, good-looking, intelligent. I couldn't imagine how she'd ever hooked up with Charlie Furner.

I offered my condolences. I took a punt, decided to try the honest approach. I told her of my brush with her husband, my finding the body, the police being after me.

"Mrs. Furner, I don't want to upset you, but I'm deep in this mess. Would you have any idea who might have done it?"

She looked at me, was silent for a few beats, then spoke. "You have kind eyes," she said. "I'm sorry you had to get on the wrong side of my husband. Charlie wasn't a good man, and I've prayed for his death many times. Terrible thing to confess, isn't it?"

"Is it?"

"Yes, it is. Now he's gone, I don't know what to think." She started to cry. I touched her shoulder, feeling awkward. She buried her head in my shoulder, blubbing like a child. She smelled of booze, but not too much. After a minute she drew back, patted her eyes dry. She stood up and left the room.

A minute later she came back in, said she was sorry, she was very upset. I said that was all right. I asked her again about who killed her husband.

"Many people had cause to dislike Charlie. I'm sorry that you're involved, but I can't help you."

"Do you think Jim Swain could've killed your husband?"

"Will you leave now? I can't help you." She began to cry again. I made my own way out.

When I got back to the car, Max said, "Well?"

I lit a smoke. "Like the Jap said, she's had enough trouble already."

I drove to Molly's place and parked the car in the lane. I walked over to Flinders Street, took a long look around for coppers hanging about. It seemed clear, so I went around the back and listened at her door. The radio was playing, but there were no voices. I tapped on the glass.

She opened up. I gave her the car keys, asked if I could come in. She said OK, she didn't care one way or another. I put my arms around her, kissed her, told her I was sorry for yesterday. She held herself stiffly for a moment then I felt her kind of let go, and her body moulded itself to mine.

"I'm sorry, too," she whispered, and led me into her bedroom.

I spent the rest of the day at her flat. I kept peeking out the window looking for rozzers, but none came. We listened to her gramophone records. Later we cooked a meal together, then we smoked reefers, drank brandy, and listened to *The Life of Riley* on the radio. Max was on that night. He sounded like a kind of cross between Roy Rene and Jerry Lewis. Before we fell asleep, I told her, "This is a big improve on the Cosy Private Hotel."

But as Monday morning progressed, Molly's behaviour changed. She became preoccupied. At eleven she told me she was expected at her sister's place at Gosford that afternoon, that she was staying there for a few days, helping out with the new baby. I said yeah, all right. When she left at midday, we scarcely said goodbye.

I left by the back way and skulked back to the Cosy, drank the rest of the day away and all the next. On Tuesday evening, I put on my sports coat, stuck the revolver in my pocket, and took a taxi out to Little Jim Swain's house. He lived out at Blakehurst in a big, modern house, very flash. I told the cab to wait for me. I wasn't sure exactly what I was going to do, but when I walked up the path I leaned against Swain's door and kicked it hard. I waited a moment and then kicked it again. It swung open and I almost fell in.

Swain stood there and looked at me unblinking. At least fifteen stone and not an inch more than five foot six, mid-forties, hair brilliantined over the spreading bald patch.

"You're making a big mistake coming here uninvited. What do you want?"

"I want to talk to Molly, and I want you to tell me why you killed Charlie Furner."

He took a deep breath, sighed, and motioned me indoors.

"I'm not going to offer you a drink—you've clearly had more than you can handle already. State your business and then fuck off."

I drew the revolver and fired off a round. It hit the lampshade. I was getting good at this lampshade-shooting caper. This time I was braced for the recoil. Swain stood stock-still.

"Call Molly."

"She's not here, and that's God's honest truth."

"Question two, then. For twenty pounds: why did you croak Furner?"

"I didn't. He was my friend."

"You argued last week."

"So what? Friends can argue. It didn't mean anything. The man was completely loyal. He was my friend, and we buried him today and you're quite out of order."

"Yeah, well you blokes had a beautiful relationship and I can see how cut up you are."

Swain's fist felt like a two-by-four hitting the side of my head. He'd crossed the distance between us faster than I thought anyone could. Molly had said he was a great dancer. I was on the floor and he was taking the remaining bullets out of the gun. He was breathing noisily.

"Don't carry a gun unless you mean to use it. And don't walk into the lion's den with a bellyful of piss."

"Gee, thanks ever so much for the advice, Mr. Swain."

He handed the gun back to me. "What I told you is true. Now, get out."

"One thing. What kind of car do you drive?"

"A Customline, not that it's any of your fucking business." He opened the door. "Clear out."

On the way back to town I tried to make sense of it. Swain obviously knew I hadn't killed Furner, or else he'd have killed me. He may have been lying, but he could have shot me and told the police that I had come to his house drunk and brandishing a gun, with the intention of shooting him. The truth.

I told the driver to detour via Dudley Street, South Coogee, got him to park a few doors down from number 20. The lights were on. I walked quietly around the side of the house. I could hear voices, and music playing inside. The widow seemed to have recovered her composure. I looked in the garage at the back, saw the dark blue Oldsmobile. I went back to the cab, back to the Cosy.

I rang Max from the phone downstairs, then went to my scungy room. I was getting kind of used to it, like you get used to TB. I settled down on the bed, opened a bottle of Cutty Sark and disposed of the night. I woke at some point, it was light, I was thirsty and sick. I started in on the rest of the bottle, finished it, and got another.

"Hey, colonel, wake up. This is the big day. Come on!" Max was in my room.

I tried to stand up, fell over. "Give me the Cutty."

"Oh, shit, this is Wednesday. Remember? Tommy, Annie, the Jap, Canterbury, the tape recorder! Don't do this to me, Billy!"

"I'm a late scratching. We'll do it on Saturday."

"Saturday, bullshit!"

"I can't manage it. I'm history."

"What about Furner? I thought you were trying to find who iced him?"

"I know who killed him. But it doesn't help me. Can't do anything about it."

Max paced back and forth. "Christ, a couple of things go wrong and you fall apart. Wait here. I'm going for outside help."

I must have passed out again. Next thing I knew, Max was in the room again. I was on the floor.

"Here, swallow this." He pushed a small piece of cotton wool into my mouth. It tasted bitter. "You'll need another, I think." He put something on the floor, crushed it with the heel of his shoe, extracted another piece of cotton wool, cut it into sections with a penknife, gave a piece to me.

I slumped back against the bed. Max sat down, put one in his own mouth, took a swig of Cutty and lit a smoke. A couple of minutes passed and my heart started pounding. I could feel the blood charging around my body. It felt all right. I stood up.

"What was that?"

"The insides of a benzedrine inhaler. Now, you're still gone to Gowings, so don't make any decisions you might regret later. But at least that'll stop you from falling over. You better take a powder as well, you've probably got a monster headache."

"What's the time?"

"Eleven. There's still time. I spoke to the Jap. He's got his people organized. Tommy and Annie are ready to motor out to Campbelltown."

"I'd better clean up. Give me twenty minutes."

Max made two phone calls from the Cosy and then we walked around the corner to the Hawaiian Club. I flagged a cab while Max went inside. He returned with an amplifier the size of a suitcase, and we drove out to the flat at Canterbury. My heart was still racing, and I felt like talking, but I didn't want to say anything in front of the cabbie. Max was chewing gum, looking out the window and humming softly to himself.

I opened up the flat while Max bought some Coca-Cola and a couple of packets of chips. I turned the wireless on and Max put a microphone to the radio speaker. It boomed out through the amplifier. We listened to the first race from Melbourne. A wet track, a long shot got up. I turned it off again.

The phone rang at one o'clock. It was Tommy. He was in position at Campbelltown. He had tapped the Melbourne landline and rigged up a field telephone so he could talk to us. He and Annie were in a cow paddock, he said, out the back of nowhere. Too bad we couldn't be there, it was a beaut little spot. They'd had a job lugging the gear through the scrub, but everything was sweet now. He'd ring back fifteen minutes before the race.

Tommy rang back at ten to three. Max took the call. He kept the line open while I rang the Jap, told him everything was on, go for it. Shortly after, the phones started ringing—our stooges had got the go-ahead signal from the Jap. Soon we had six lines open. I laid the handpieces down on the trestle table, all of them off the hook. I turned on the radio. The fourth from Melbourne was scheduled for three-ten. The announcer was playing bits of music and reading advertisements, said they'd soon be crossing to Moonee Valley for the running of the fourth. At nine past three, the announcer in Sydney said there seemed to be a holdup in Melbourne, and they'd cross in a moment. Meanwhile, here was Patti Page singing "Tennessee Waltz."

Max grinned, gave the thumbs-up. "Tommy's cut the landline."

Max put his telephone handpiece to the microphone, Tommy's voice filled the room, loud and clear over the PA. "All right, you blokes, they're about to run," he said. "I hope your mob can hear this." He started counting backwards from twenty. At nine his voice stopped and then the race caller in Melbourne came on the line, "The starter's taken the button . . . And they're racing! Got them away well . . ."

But on the radio, Patti Page was still whingeing about her sweetheart and her best friend. Max turned down the radio and we listened to the race, while the rest of Sydney got Patti Page.

A horse named Rambunctious came in, another roughy. The race call cut out and Tommy came back on the phone line. "You get that, boys? You've got two or three minutes maximum now, so get those bets in before I reconnect."

I quickly checked that everyone had heard the call, and hung up the phones. Max put the radio back on. Patti Page had finished and now it was Eddie Fisher singing. But before it was finished, the song abruptly faded, and an announcer quickly said, "Crossing to Melbourne now." The caller's voice came on. "And they're racing! Got them away well . . ." It sounded convincing enough to me. With luck, the Sydney techos would put the interruption down to an unexplained hitch at the Melbourne end.

Rambunctious won all over again.

Max turned to me, wild-eyed, and said, "Copacetic!"

"Feel like trying it again next week?"

He shook his head. "If we *do* get away with this, it's a once-in-a-lifetime trick." He shook his head again, more slowly. "At least wait till next year before we try it again."

Max went off to meet Tommy. I tried Molly's number. She was in. I asked her how it was at her sister's. She said, where? You told me that's where you were going. She said, oh yeah, then started crying. I asked what was wrong, she kept crying. I told her I was coming to her place, she said no, she wouldn't be there. Then she said she was sorry, really sorry. I said for what? She said good-bye, she was going away, and then she hung up.

I tidied the flat and locked up at four o'clock. I turned out into the street and walked straight into a punch from Ray Waters.

I tried to pick myself up as Waters emptied my gladstone onto the footpath, but my arms and legs weren't cooperating. He picked the gun out of the pile of socks and underwear, pocketed it, then came over to me and stuck his fat finger in my face.

"I've had you, smart cunt." He kicked me. "You and that Yid banjo player keep out of my way. On your skates, now." I watched him walk away and wondered why he hadn't killed me.

Seven o'clock at Laurie's place. The day not so hot any more, a northeasterly breeze blowing off the sea, rattling the venetian blinds. I'd been there an hour, drinking with Laurie and Max, when the Jap arrived.

Laurie poured more drinks, brought them over on a tray to me, Max and the Jap, sitting on armchairs. Cheers, cigars, everyone happy. I'd bought a couple more inhalers at five o'clock. I was flying. My head ached a bit, and I had a black eye where Waters decked me, but I wasn't feeling much of anything.

"It all went so *well*," said the Jap, sitting back, cigar in hand. Telling and retelling the story. "Couldn't have been better. They all got their bets in on time. Swain senses he's been got at—Christ, half a dozen people ring his bookies up two minutes before the race is called, and place big bets on a roughy that gets up. Starting price 33 to 1. Word from Melbourne is that *no one* expected that bludger to win, so Jim can't figure it out at all, but he and his cronies daren't renege, or even hesitate in paying, or else they're finished. Well done, lads. Cheers." He held up his glass to me and Max.

Laurie said, "Bill, what was the name they gave Harry Solomons' rort?"

"They called it the Mandrake Broadcast."

"That's right, as in 'Mandrake gestures hypnotically.' It was Harry's little magic trick, except that it backfired on him. What happened there, he cut the wires too late or something?"

"Yeah, his pals were a bit slow, and listeners tuned to the other stations heard the race callers say the race had started, just before the lines went dead. Meanwhile on his station, Harry's saying, 'No, they haven't got 'em away yet, seems to be a holdup...' Then when he did call the race, five minutes later, people were suspicious. Since Harry was already well known as the champion at the phantom call, it wasn't too hard to work out what had happened."

The tape recorder was sitting on the coffee table. Max said, "Pity Harry never had a tape recorder." We replayed the race call a couple of times, heard Rambunctious come in again, and again. We laughed like lunatics each time.

Then Max moved the tape recorder, and the Jap emptied out a calico bag, full of bundles of ten-pound notes tied up with rubber bands. The Jap had paid off his stooges, twenty-five quid each—a couple of weeks' pay for most people. He'd had them each place bets of between ten and thirty pounds with Swain and crew, and at thirty-three to one, we'd taken Swain for about five thousand pounds.

Laurie came over and topped up my glass. "I'm sorry I couldn't have been more help to you on Saturday. I was worried sick about you. You don't know how relieved I was when you rang through on Sunday."

He strolled around the room, refilling glasses. "Now, let's get this settled up. The Jap and I discussed this, and we reckon a fair split for you and Max would be eight hundred each. You did the footwork, but the Jap and me went guarantor, and I provided the premises. And I'll fix up Tommy. How does that seem?" Laurie leaned over, counted out two groups of four bundles, and pushed them towards me and Max.

Max piped up before I could shush him. "That'd be great, Laurie."

"How about you, son?"

"Yeah, OK." I said. Same old story. One lot treads the grapes, another mob swills the wine . . . I glanced at Max. He collected his pile, walked over to the sideboard, started packing up the tape recorder.

Laurie spoke: "Now, remember, you're into me for two hundred quid—well, two hundred and twenty, actually. Do you want to settle that now?"

"Yeah, all right," I said.

Laurie took one bundle, put it back on his pile, and drew two tenners out of a second bundle.

"Good. Now, there's one more thing. To get you off the hook with the police, I had to let Waters in on it. He placed his own bet with Swain, but demanded two hundred quid on top. I paid him on your behalf."

"Didn't you at least try to bargain him down?"

"What could I do? He's closer to Swain than he is to me. I thought he'd be happy with a share, but then once he knew, he had us over a barrel. He could have crueled it for all of us."

Maybe it was true. I nodded, got up and poured myself another drink. Laurie took another bundle off my pile.

Max spoke. "So who killed Furner?"

Laurie and the Jap said nothing. Max turned to me. "So who? Give."

I turned to the Jap. "What sort of car do you drive, Fred?"

He looked at the carpet. "An Oldsmobile."

"A blue one?"

"Yeah, a blue one."

"Did Vi Furner kill Charlie?"

Fred looked at me seriously, and nodded slowly.

I went on, "I must've stumbled into it. You were still there, hiding. You set me up, put the gun in my bag. You rang the bulls. They beat me back to my place."

The Jap kept staring at the carpet, then spoke quietly. "I'm sorry, Bill. It was a spur-of-the-moment thing. I knew you'd get out of it, sooner or later. We needed to get away from the pool, for Vi to get home and collect herself before the cops came round to tell her her husband was dead. So yeah, we set you up, but we didn't think anything serious would come of it. We were just trying to get a breathing space for Vi."

He glanced quickly around the room, and blushed. "We'd spent the night together. We've been seeing each other for the last three years, since I started working for Swain. We were never sure if Swain and Furner knew or not. That night was the first time Vi hadn't gone back home. We went to confront Charlie. Vi knew he was swimming that morning, and she insisted on seeing him at the pool. We took a gun of his, just in case. When we got there, there wasn't any talking. She walked up to him and shot him, like that. Bang. We were leaving when we saw you jogging down the hill. We hid behind the dunny, watched you. Somehow, you didn't notice Charlie floating there. Then you did. When you dived in, I put the gun in your bag. Then we went up to the street, called the police from the public phone. It was the wrong thing to do. I'm sorry, kid."

"Did you know all this, Laurie?"

"Well, yes, I did. I found out on Saturday. But once it had happened, I was obliged to protect the Jap. At the same time, I was working behind the scenes to get you out of it, fixing it with Swain and taking care of Waters."

"And the Waters pay-off comes out of my cut."

"You're still well ahead, son. You're out of debt with me, plus you've got a couple of hundred quid. And of course," he smiled, "Furner won't bother you any more."

"Shit, Laurie, I could have made that much money working, for Christ's sake. And Furner was only having a go at me because I work for you."

Laurie straightened up. "Don't be like that. Think about it. Everything turned out all right. Given the situation, it couldn't really have been handled any other way. I'm sorry, son, but you'll have to accept that that's the way we're doing it."

That was that. We said our good-byes then walked outside, intending to go into the city and spend some of our money. Max was carrying the tape recorder under his arm. "We should've rung a cab from inside." He put the machine down, lit a smoke. I lit one, too.

"Yeah. Fuck it. I don't want to go back in there, though." We waited on Maroubra Road, outside Laurie's front fence, watching the traffic going past, looking out for a cruising cab. The sun was nearly down and the light was strange. From up there on the hill you could see the beach, the wooden surf club, the tram shed, the rifle range to the south, Mahon Pool to the north. Max spoke, but it was like I was thinking it.

"You can see it all from up here."

"Yeah."

Max looked around, threw his cig down. "You stay here with the tape recorder, I'm going down to the rank at the junction, get us a cab."

While Max was gone, I thought about the Jap's account of Saturday morning, pictured the view of myself down at the pool, leaving in a panic, running back up the hill, almost past this spot, and on to my flat around the corner.

I tried to figure how I could have failed to see the Jap and Vi following me in the Olds. I couldn't. I looked back towards the pool and tried to pick out the public phone they'd used to call the cops.

No phone.

I turned around and looked back at Laurie's place behind us. The Oldsmobile was here now, parked in the driveway, almost out of sight. Something happened in my gut, like butterflies in the stomach, and my heartbeat altered. Like Max said, you can see it all from up here. The booze and benzedrine were pumping through me. My mind was racing, but it was clear, really clear.

Max was back in a few minutes with a Red De-Luxe cab, and by then I'd figured it out. I told Max to hang on a tick. The hacky stood by the open boot, waiting for us to put the tape recorder in. I went over to him, gave him a quid, said sorry, we don't need the cab anymore. He put the quid in his pocket, said no problem. I turned to Max.

"How'd you like to earn some holiday pay?"

We went back to Laurie's front door. He was surprised to see us. I told him I just wanted to come in and ring a cab. He said, of course, I should have thought of that before, come in.

Inside, Max put the tape recorder down on the sideboard, I walked over to the phone. Laurie stood by the booze tray, the Jap was still sitting down. I half-turned to him.

"I s'pose I could've rung from a public phone, say the one down near Mahon Pool, eh, Fred?" I winked at him.

He looked at me, then quickly at Laurie.

"What do you mean, son?"

Max was ready.

I made to turn, then swung around and belted the Jap. I lifted the brandy decanter and smashed it on the coffee table between Laurie and the Jap. Max had moved around behind Laurie and had a headlock on him, not too rough, but enough to keep him still.

The benzedrine was really revving my motor now, and it felt good to be doing instead of talking. I picked up the big glass ashtray and hurled it through the picture window. Very dramatic.

The Jap was out of it. Laurie was silent, watching me. Max let him go, returned to the sideboard, opened and shut the drawers. He found a revolver in the bottom drawer, along with a cigar box. He threw the cigar box to me, put the gun in his own pocket, then went back to his tape recorder, started fiddling with it. I opened the box. It was full of loose five- and ten-pound notes. I put it on the table, next to the remaining bundles of notes.

Laurie tried to appear in control. "What the fuck is this about, son?"

I picked the Jap up, shook him, shouted at him. "*Bull*shit you rang the jacks from a public phone! Where, Freddy? Where's the fucking phone?"

The Jap didn't answer, just stared at me, his eyes wide. I pushed him back into the chair.

"You reckon Vi Furner shot Charlie, huh? Fucking crap. I think you shot him."

He looked at the floor, like a little kid in disgrace.

"I'll bet you quids I can tell you how it happened. In fact, I'll bet you this much." I picked up the bundles of notes from the table, stacked them in front of me.

Laurie was red in the face. He pointed at me. "You've gone way too far, son. Put that money back and apologize to Fred, or you're shit. I mean, you're fucking dead!"

"Laurie, I was fucking dead on Saturday."

"What do you mean?"

"I mean you're a dog, Laurie. So just shut your face." I turned back to the Jap. He'd given up. He sat with his head in his hands.

I took hold of his lapels and gave him another shake, shouted at him: "You fucking slime!" He was shit-scared now. Understandable, since I was yelling like a mental case. I let go of him and took a couple of deep breaths, went to the sideboard, picked up the other decanter and took a drink. Scotch. I passed it to Max, he did the same. I went back over to the Jap and stood so I could see both him and Laurie.

"This is how I figure it. You wanted to shack up with Vi, but both of you were scared of Charlie. Then you found out that Charlie had been rorting Swain. Correct?"

He said nothing.

"Did Vi tell you?"

He nodded.

"Then it occurred to you that maybe Swain might want Charlie out of the way as much as you and Vi did. You put the idea to Swain of killing Charlie, and he agreed. Nod if it's true, Fred."

He moved his head a fraction.

"I guess that means yes. OK, so Swain agrees. That gets rid of the Charlie problem for all of you. But you needed someone to take the blame. Swain suggested little ol' me, seeing how he hates my guts. You went along."

The Jap moved his head again. I took another gulp of scotch.

"So, you're betraying me, but this is for love, so what the fuck? How am I doing so far, Fred?"

He said nothing.

"Now, this is where it gets interesting." I turned to Laurie, who wasn't so red in the face now. In fact, he was quite pale. I turned back to the Jap.

"It's just like when Perry Mason explains to everyone what really happened."

Max said, "Come on, captain, get on with it. And pass me that bottle, for Christ's sake."

"Where were we, Jap? Oh, yeah, you and Swain then went to good old Laurie here, my mate." I strolled over and patted him on the back. "You told him what you'd cooked up, since you knew you'd need his cooperation as well."

Max whistled, shook his head, as if to say, *I don't believe this.*

"I'd like to think Laurie held out for a pretty fair sort of compensation for selling me down the river. Would it be indelicate of me to ask how much?"

Laurie said nothing. I looked at the cigar box, "Jeez, I wonder if this is the Swain pay-off. Don't tell me how much it is, I love surprises. Anyway, then you got Waters in on it as well."

I went over to the smashed window, looked down the hill to the pool. "So, Laurie knew I'd been swimming laps. Somehow you found out that Charlie was intending to swim at Mahon Pool that Saturday—I guess Vi gave you that. Headquarters was right here. Laurie observed it from this window. Jap ambled down to the pool, shot Charlie with his own gun. Maybe he had taken the gun with him, in case some seagull gave him lip, or maybe Vi gave it to you. Doesn't matter. Once you'd ventilated him, you waited for me to show, then you put the gun in my bag. You came back here, parked the car out of the way, lay low. You two watched me through your track binoculars, saw me leave the pool in a shit and a shiver. Laurie called Waters as soon as he saw you leave the pool. Waters had been waiting for the call. I should have been picked up back at my flat, maybe shot before I could say anything. The gun would have been found in my bag. Finito. But the wallopers got to my place half a minute too soon."

I turned to Laurie. "You probably guessed I'd go to Molly's, sent Waters on there. Then when I told you on Saturday arvo that I was coming home to get a change, you tipped Waters again, and he fucking near got me. You're a lagging dog, Laurie."

He said nothing.

"Sooner or later, Waters would've caught up with me. But then I rang up with the scheme to rort Swain, and you couldn't resist that, even though you'd betrayed me the day before. So you thought you could sit back, collect your payout from Swain, and rort him at the same time, while I did the work and took all the risks. And Fred didn't balk at swindling the same bloke he was conspiring with, once I'd given him the idea. How did I do, Fred? Did I get it right?"

The Jap said nothing.

"I guess that means I win the money."

I turned to Max, put on a Bob Dyer voice. "What'll it be, customers, the money or the box?"

Max laughed.

"I can't decide. I think I'll take the money *and* the box."

Laurie stood up and spoke. "All right, that's enough. You've got the shits with me and Fred, that's fair enough. But you don't understand. The fact is, Bill, that's the way business is conducted. You face new circumstances and you try to make appropriate decisions. But believe me, Bill, I was glad to get you off the hook again when I could."

He gave me a big sincere look.

"As for my consent, I thought that Freddy and Swain were going to go ahead with or without my consent. This way I'd still be in the picture, able to bail you out when the opportunity arose, which it did."

"Yeah, which it did after you sent Waters around to get me.

Maybe to shoot me."

"No, not shoot. As I said before, you make the best decision you can at the time. Now you're in the clear and financially in front. You'd have done the same if you were in my place, which you'll never be. The truth is, Billy, I don't even owe you an explanation. You want to play with the big kids, then don't cry when you get a bloody nose. The fact is, you've been tripping over your dick ever since I took you on. You're a mug punter and an unreliable worker, and you don't hold your drink well. That's it. You haven't got enough bricks in your wheelbarrow to pull this off. Now, last chance—give the money back, clear out, and that's the finish. Otherwise, both of you are dead."

Max spoke then. "Well, dad, don't blow your wig just yet. Hear this." He rewound the tape, ran it forward again. My voice came on, ranting like a maniac: "*Bullshit you rang the jacks from a public phone! Where, Freddy? Where's the fucking phone?*"

Max stopped it. "This goes on for a fair while," he said. "Wait a sec while I fast-forward it." He wound it on, hit the play button again. It was Laurie, saying, "*You'd have done the same if you were in my place...*"

"Well, it looks like we got it all down on tape. This is *my* little magic trick, Laurie. Like it? Now, Laurie, if Jim Swain, or any straight copper, were to hear this, you and the Jap'd be in a lot more bother than Harry Solomons ever was."

We packed up the money, both lots. Then we called our cab. Laurie just sat and watched us. On the way out, I said, "I suppose I've blown my chances of getting a reference from you, eh, Laurie?"

He didn't say anything.

We ended up with nearly six thousand pounds. We split it three ways, gave a third to Tommy and Annie. It just about cleared their mortgage. The gun was found the next day by police divers, in a rock crevice at the bottom of the pool. At the inquest, it was suggested that Furner had taken his own life. A suicide note was found. Vi Furner testified that the handwriting was that of her late husband, that he'd been suffering from nerves for some time. I gave her two hundred pounds the day before the inquest.

I asked her why she'd taken up with the Jap—out of the frying pan kind of thing? She said, don't judge him too harshly, he's a good man at heart. Yeah, and I'm Johnnie Ray.

I called at Molly's place a few times. She was never there. Three weeks later, when I called by, a bloke was loading furniture onto a truck. He said he was Molly's sister's husband. Molly had gone to America. She was living in Los Angeles, and she had no plans to return.

The Jap and Vi moved to Surfer's Paradise, bought a big block of land, subdivided it, made a shitload of money. Max took a Constellation to America, went to New York and Chicago. He made some contacts, booked Louis Jordan to play at the Sydney Stadium.

Naturally, I moved out of Laurie's flat, and into a joint at South Coogee. I never went back to Mahon Pool.

I didn't rush out looking for work. For a while there, I thought my money would last forever.

★ REPORT FROM AMERICA

LOS ANGELES. – Popular Sydney pianist Max Peck arrived in Los Angeles this week. Max told me he aims to see some of his all-time heroes while he is here. Top of the list, he says, is alto man Louis Jordan and his Tympany Five, closely followed by Nat King Cole.

(Australian Music Maker, June 1952)

WHISPERS AROUND TOWN

Sydney musician and "hep cat" Max Peck may be trading in treble clefs and score sheets for overdrafts and balance sheets. Word from Los Angeles, USA, is that Max has made contact with a number of top acts over there, with a view to organizing a tour of Australasia later this year. Max has been attending "Rhythm Reviews" all across the US, in such cities as New York, Cleveland, Los Angeles, and New Orleans, and he hopes a similar formula might find as much favor with our teens as it does with the Americans. Along the way, the already colourful Max has greatly increased his vocabulary with the addition of the newest slang words used by teens and entertainment people over there. Everything, says Max, is strictly copacetic!

(The Listener-In, January 1953)

RHYTHM & BOOGIE SHOW FOR SYDNEY STADIUM

Newcomer impresario Max Peck announced this week that contracts have been signed with an all-star lineup for the first of a series of "Rhythm Reviews."

In September, Australian audiences will have the opportunity to see some marvelous acts, none of which has previously visited our shores. Topping the bill will be Louis Jordan and his Tympany Five. Also present will be Slim Gaillard and his Flat Foot Floogie Boys. Special guests on the tour will be Ella Mae "Cow Cow Boogie" Morse, and Australia's own Blonde Bombshell of the Boogie Piano, Miss Dolores Del Rosa.

Miss Del Rosa–better known to her family and friends as Mary Howes–rose to fame (or perhaps notoriety) when she forsook the concert violin and a career which included work with both the Sydney Symphony Orchestra and the BBC Symphony Orchestra, under such conductors as Bruno Walter, Leopold Stokowski, and Sir Thomas Beecham. Now, as Dolores Del Rosa, she is rocketing to the top of the popular field with her special brand of Latin-American and boogie-woogie styles. Max Peck says she's sure to give the Yanks a run for their money at the first Stadium Show. If all goes well for our Max, maybe we'll soon be calling him "Max-a-million."

(Australian Music Maker, June 1953)

"All Tickets Will Be Refunded" Says Peck — Fraud Squad To Investigate

SYDNEY, Friday. Fraud Squad detectives are to investigate the business affairs of entrepreneur Max Peck, also known as Max Perkal. This follows the cancellation of his planned concerts at the Sydney Stadium.

Booking agents have claimed that Peck has failed to make money available to cover refunds on tickets already sold. Chief Superintendent Ray Waters announced yesterday that following representations made to him by "interested parties," the Fraud Squad would investigate the affair.

Meanwhile, Mr. Peck told reporters yesterday that funds were in fact being made available, but bank procedures had delayed proceedings. He said he expected the funds to be cleared today. Mr. Peck strongly asserted his own good faith in the matter, angrily denying that any funds had been wrongfully retained by him.

According to Mr. Peck, the concerts were called off when the top attraction, Negro entertainer Louis Jordan, fell ill last month. Mr. Peck told reporters yesterday that there was no truth to the rumour that the show was cancelled due to poor advance sales.

(Sydney Morning Herald, 15 January 1954)

PECK IN BANKRUPTCY COURT: "I OWE BOOKIES £5,000"

(Sydney Daily Mirror, 7 May 1954)

★ BOP AT BONDI!

Bloodied but unbowed, piano-pounder Max Peck is giving teenagers what they want, every Sunday afternoon at the Aloha Milk Bar at Bondi Beach. And what they want, Max tells us, is an endless supply of hamburgers, GI Lime, and "back-beat boogie-woogie Rock 'n' Roll." During his wanderings in the United States last year, Max had plenty of opportunity to see and hear firsthand what really "sends" American teenagers. "There are big changes on the American music scene. 'Sweet' and 'Cool' and even Dixieland are strictly squaresville with the Yank kids," says Max. "They don't go for Como or Fisher or Sinatra, fabulous entertainers though those men are. Kids over there are going crazy for simple, driving music with an easily identifiable beat. And believe me, some of these newer acts, many of them Negro and hillbilly performers, could really teach the old guard a thing or two about personality and showmanship."

Max says he became frustrated with EMI's policy of holding back new overseas record releases for anything up to a year, and then only releasing a later "cover" version of the original. To rectify the situation, he brought back a couple of suitcases full of red-hot singles, which he has installed on the juke box at his Bondi venue. These can be played when the band, led by the energetic Max, takes its well-earned breaks.

So far, the afternoon's record-hop-cum-rhythm-sessions have attracted an eager band of youngsters as well as a sprinkling of seasoned musicians who sneak in to hear the latest discs from the US. Max and his partner, Bill Glasheen, say they intend to open other venues in the western suburbs shortly.

(Australian Music Maker, April 1955)

Around Town This Week

Look out for the "King of the Bodgies," making a guest appearance at Max Peck's Rhythm Session at the Aloha Milk Bar this week.

Max Peck told us that Billy Glasheen, acknowledged as being Sydney's first genuine drape shape, "reet pleat" Cornel Wilde Boy, will be playing selections from his own personal collection of jive, boogie, and jazz records between sets at the Aloha this Sunday.

Dance addicts can tune into whimsicalities such as "Cement Mixer, Putty, Putty," new Negro songs like "Stormy Monday Blues," driving big-band music from the likes of Lionel Hampton, plus "rhythmized" hillbilly songs from Tennessee Ernie Ford and others, as well as the current popular choice among Aloha jivers, Bill Haley and the Comets' "Rock around the Clock."

(Sunday Telegraph, 20 June 1955)

Bondi Rhythm Club Meeting Place for Hooligans, Says Assistant Commissioner

(Wentworth Courier, 6 July 1955)

THIS I BELIEVE!

Australian society already has many onerous crosses to bear, such as the communist domination of our trade unions, the presence of Russian fifth columnists (who seem to have the gullible ear of the Australian Labor Party), and more recently the curse of the so-called "working wife." But it seems room needs to be made in our gallery of shame for a new tenant, the "boogie-woogie" bodgie. With his unmanly haircut, his garish clothes, his sex drugs (with which he will lace the drink of his consort, the "widgie," with or without her consent), and his raucous American-style "bebop jive," this fellow is an unwelcome addition to our society.

News this week of bodgie shenanigans at Bondi causes great distress to right-thinking Australians. While most young men are proudly completing their education, meeting their National Service responsibilities, and taking their place in Australian society, mature and optimistic in outlook, members of this corrupt little push of sneering knockers seek to undermine the resolve of all youth, flaunting their disrespect for the very things which so many Australians suffered and died for during the war.

The background of one of the ringleaders of the Bondi bodgie nest, who is now operating as an impresario of delinquent entertainments, well illustrates the nature of the caste. An able youth and of age, he avoided military service in 1945 while his fellows proudly went off to hasten the downfall of the Jap and the Nazi. After the war, he drifted into dubious employment on the fringes of the Sydney underworld. One bookmaker, a man of unimpeached reputation, did offer the hand of support and guidance to the youth, in the form of a well-paying and responsible job, only to be swindled by the man and his partner in crime, a musician and failed entrepreneur. Although the amount involved ran into some thousands of pounds, the bookmaker chose not to press charges against the ingrate, and now the same miscreant continues to practice his villainy.

This nearly 30-year-old "King of the Bodgies" gets about dressed like a would-be American spiv, affecting the sort of tasteless costume and hairstyle normally associated with the younger delinquent. Let all parents be warned of the dangerous influences which gather around their sons and daughters at these "rhythm session jive dances," and the moral turpitude of those entrepreneurs who derive income from the systematic corrupting of young Australians. THIS I BELIEVE!

(Daily Mirror, 13 July 1955)

2

AUGUST 1955

Monday morning, I'd gotten an early start. I had a watch, some American cuff links, and a Japanese transistor radio to hock. A week before, I'd had plenty of cash. By Friday night, I'd doubled it at the dogs, lost half of it at two-up the same night, won most of it back on the second race at Warwick Farm on Saturday, then lost it all on the last three races.

I'd been helping Max out at his Rhythm Reviews down at the Aloha Milk Bar on Sunday afternoons, which was turning into a modest but dependable earn. This week I'd made eighteen quid, of which I still had seven or eight, but that was only a quarter of the back rent on my flat. The landlady had given me till today to pay up. I'd asked her for one last extension, but she said I'd already had four last extensions, and that was it. Bailiffs today.

So I drove up to Taylor Square, to the Mont-de-Piété Loan Office. French for "mountain of pity," someone told me. Maybe you'd find a molehill of pity there on a lucky day, but don't hold your breath. The shop hadn't opened yet. The day was sunny, the sky dark blue, but it was cold under the awning. A couple of stiffs were waiting there when I arrived. They had something wrapped in a bit of cloth. The old mother's jewellery, some hoisted silver-ware, maybe some long-disused tradesman's tools. Enough for a heart starter, a punt, maybe a fuck. They looked at me, trying to decide whether to put the bite on me. I turned away. One came up to me. He was wearing an old brown gabardine, smoking a sodden-looking rollie. He had a returned serviceman's badge pinned on his overcoat.

"Spare a bob for a former digger, could you, son?"

"If I could I wouldn't be here, uncle."

"Get fucked, then." He moved back with his mate.

I watched a straight-backed old guy come along Flinders Street. Every thirty yards or so he'd stop, stoop down and write on the footpath with a piece of yellow chalk, then move on. When he got level with us he stopped again and wrote the word Eternity on the footpath in front of the shop. The stiffs and me looked at the well-formed copperplate script, with its decorative capital E and jaunty underlining.

The stiff who'd put the bite on me said, "You got a couple of bob to spare, have you, Arthur? We've been waiting here forever for this shop to open."

"You'd do better to consider the eternity which awaits you, friend."

"I've got my mind set on 10 a.m., when the Court House Hotel opens up."

The old man shook his head and strode off.

I turned back to the goods behind the window. Inside, two shopfronts were joined together. Sporting goods, fishing rods, and musical instruments one side; jewellery, electrical goods, and cameras the other.

I looked at the musical instruments. There were at least a dozen banjo-mandolins. Some salesman must have made a fortune selling the things. There were a couple of Hawaiian guitars and half a dozen ukes. I figured somewhere there must be a whole colony of down-and-out Hawaiian players. Maybe the stiffs next to me. I could offer them two bob for a rendition of "Sweet Leilani." Above the guitars was a shelf of brass and silver bandware. On the floor, a couple of bass drums. One of them had a picture of a red Indian on the front. Further into the shop were typewriters, some precision tools, and a trophy cabinet. Plated sports trophies, with little figures of golfers in mid-swing, swimmers poised to dive, bowlers stooped in mid-bowl, shields with names and years engraved. Triumphs gone to shit. Hymie, the pawnbroker, had told me they once had a Melbourne Cup in the store.

Looking in the window, I could see the Ford parked opposite in the bright morning sunlight. I knew the face. I'd seen him half a dozen times over the past two months—at the dogs, at the fights, a couple of times in the street, and twice near my flat, which was in a block up in Roslyn Street, in Rushcutters Bay. By the third time, I figured he was following me. Now he was looking my way.

There weren't that many possibilities. Either he was associated with Laurie O'Brien or Jim Swain, or he was part of the ongoing investigation of Max's semi-crooked business activities, which had involved me more than I'd have liked. Or maybe he was someone else with a grudge against me. There were a few of them around town.

If I was to bet, I'd say copper. He looked too much a squarehead to be working for Laurie or Swain. Shitty dark-gray suit, could be someone's leftover school uniform. Red hair, short back and sides, taller than me, my age, maybe a bit more. Thick-set, but not quite a typical copper's build.

The shop opened a few minutes after nine. Hymie apologized for keeping us waiting. I told him it had seemed like an eternity.

I let the old diggers go first. Turned out they had a gold chain in the cloth. They got five pounds for it. With my stuff it was routine. Hymie knew it would be redeemed, so he always gave me twenty pounds on it. He made out the pledge form. I signed it, he gave me the dough.

I left the shop and the redheaded watcher crossed the road and walked up to me.

"Excuse me, Mr. Glasheen. Could I have a word with you?"

"I'm pretty busy today. Got a board of directors meeting at ten, lunch at Romano's at twelve. What do you want?"

He held out his hand. "Noel Shoebridge."

I gave him a handshake, the kind of shake that indicated I couldn't give a shit. "Yeah, you know my name."

"Can I buy you some breakfast?"

"Do I have a choice?"

"You most certainly do, Mr. Glasheen."

"What do you want?"

He grinned. "I want to offer you a chance to make a little money and achieve some social good."

"I can take or leave the money, but I'm a sucker for social good. I'll give you five minutes."

We went to a cafe in Bourke Street. I had tea and toast. He had tea. He was polite. He told me that he'd observed me for some time now, saw that I was a person who could move easily among many different types of people. I said yeah, I was the darling of the social set. He said he'd also observed that I seemed to derive my income, such as it was, from a number of rather diverse activities.

I said, "Yeah, I don't like to get in a rut."

"No," he said, "clearly not."

"You don't talk like a cop. Who are you?"

"I represent a government organization. You may or may not

have heard of us. The name needn't concern you. I've been requested to make contact with you with a view to having you perform a small service for us. You will be well paid, and you'll find the task easy and without danger or inconvenience."

"Easy and well paid don't often go together," I said.

"Bill, I don't know how well informed you are on political matters." He waited a moment, looked to me for a response. I shrugged.

"The less you know, in this case, probably, the better. That's our policy, and we've found it's usually best that way. Suffice to say, the task we want you to perform is not illegal, in fact it's part—admittedly a very small part—of the ongoing measures the government takes to ensure the continuing security of the country. I should add that my organization is very favourably regarded by the current government, and its funding allocation reflects that high regard."

"I'm awfully impressed."

"Unlike the state and federal police forces, our organization doesn't have to beg for funds to carry out its work. Accordingly, there are plenty of opportunities in our organization for young men with savvy and commitment."

I didn't say anything.

He went on, "If you're not interested, I'll walk away right now, and you won't see me again. If you are interested, anything I say to you from here on in will be subject to the secrecy provisions of the Public Service Act, meaning you'll have to give an undertaking to place yourself under the same restrictions regarding secrecy that public servants are subject to."

"Is this an 'I Was a Communist for the FBI' kind of thing?"

Shoebridge smiled. "Nothing that dramatic, I'm afraid, Bill."

"What, then?"

"A simple errand. A delivery and a pickup, that's it."

"Why me?"

"Your name came to us originally through the Special Branch of the New South Wales Police. I can tell you that you were recommended by a very senior member of the force."

"Ray fucking Waters?"

"I'm not at liberty to confirm that, Bill. I can say that you were described as a resourceful and imaginative young man, with good social skills. And the ability to keep a secret."

I watched his expression closely, but he maintained a bland smile that gave nothing much away.

"I'm not a dog. I'm not interested. Thanks for the breakfast. Now, let's see you walk away."

"Our police contacts did suggest that your response might be along those lines. That's all right, Billy. But I should perhaps warn you that the police are keen to talk to you and your associate regarding certain matters. In fact, you'd be assisting them with their inquiries right now, had we not asked them to desist while we looked into the possibility of you providing an important service to our organization."

"Here we go. Which matters?"

"Mention was made of criminal behaviour at a young people's venue at Bondi with which you are connected. There have been allegations concerning a drug ring among the management and teenagers there. I understand they also wish to examine your financial records. Something about the sale of stolen goods."

I didn't say anything.

Shoebridge went on, "I understand it would be against your code to inform on anyone, and I absolutely promise you won't be asked to do so, or to spy on anyone. And I promise you there is no danger at all. There is absolutely nothing in all this that you need have reservations about. If I knew a cab driver I could trust, he could do this job—it's that simple."

"What exactly is it? Not that I consent to do it."

"In order for me to tell, you'll have to consider yourself subject to public-servant confidentiality constraints."

"Yeah, sure. When can I collect my pension?"

True, it wasn't much. Take a package to a bloke at Liverpool, collect a box from him in return. The guy was some kind of Yugoslav anti-communist. Shoebridge's mob wished to offer him support but couldn't be seen having any contact with him. Since I was known around town as a bit of a fixer and bagman, Shoebridge said, my presence could be explained away as some kind of minor-league villainy. The guy and his friends had an illegal distillery somewhere, brewed up some kind of wog spirit, which Shoebridge's organization didn't give a shit about. I was supposed to be buying a few bottles.

The address I had was in Casula, a half-arsed bit of scrub the other side of Liverpool, on a dirt road off the Hume Highway. I drove out past Warwick Farm, on through Liverpool. The turnoff was a few miles further on, just before the Crossroads.

I was driving an old Chev, a '38 model I'd bought for seventy quid earlier that year. I took it slowly over the potholed road, promising myself that one day I'd own a car that was less than ten years old.

The road took me past some paddocks up to a blue-painted fibro house. There was a chook shed out back, a small vegetable garden with a few bug-eaten lettuces next to the house, some shitty-looking cows the other side of the fence.

A fellow came out. He was maybe forty-five, fifty. Wore a red shirt, fawn trousers; unshaven, with brown hair slicked back like

Bela Lugosi's. One hundred per cent reffo. He came up to me, grinning, while I got out. He offered his hand.

"Hello! Bill! How are you? Please, please, coming in!" Like that. Everything was a terrific surprise, I was his best friend. He held out his hand. "My name is Bosco, yah."

He led me into the kitchen, which smelled of all sorts of things, none I could name. Bosco was grinning and nodding like a loony.

"Sit down, sit down! Please, have a drink."

He poured some clear liquid into two small glasses, gave me one, toasted me with words I couldn't understand, drank his down, then went on with his grinning and nodding, waiting for me to do the same. I did. The piss tasted like rotten fruit mixed with paint thinner. I smiled back at him. He refilled the glasses. Through the door was a kind of living room. There were four or five men in there, younger than Bosco. A couple of them were eyeing me suspiciously. There were rifles on the floor, .22s, and boxes of bullets stacked next to them.

The table in front of me was partly covered with foreign-language newspapers. There were more bullets under the papers. Bosco saw me looking at them.

"We shoot rabbits, yes!"

Yeah, Bosco, good for you. A few bullets were out of the box. Their tips had been scored in a criss-cross pattern, hollow-pointed. I looked at Bosco. "There won't be too much left of any rabbit you shoot with these."

"These are very big rabbits," said Bosco.

The bloke nearest the door heard it, translated it for the benefit of his buddies in the room. It got a big laugh. On the kitchen wall was a large piece of cloth, a checkered shield painted on it, HRVATA written underneath. The shield was placed inside a big U. He followed the direction of my glance.

"Croatia!" he said.

"Yeah, beaut."

I gave him my package. He gave me a cardboard box done up with sticky tape, and a bottle of his firewater. He indicated this was for me, personally, his very good friend. None of the others said anything to me when I left.

That was that. Shoebridge came to my flat late that afternoon, took the box from me, gave me twenty-five pounds and left.

I paid the rent, put a quid's worth of juice in the Chev, went to Angelo de Marco's in William Street and got myself a haircut, Cornel Wilde–style. At twenty-eight I was a bit old to be wearing my hair bodgie-style, but I reckoned I'd had it that way since I was nineteen, so why should I change now? It wasn't bad for business, either. The kids who came to the dance sessions at Bondi seemed to dig it, like they were among their own kind rather than a couple of old squares. Max tried to build it up like I was the King of the Bodgies. He told a reporter from the *Daily Telegraph* that I had been the first Sydney bodgie, back in 1946. In truth, there'd been plenty back then, except they were called different names: Woolloomooloo Yanks for one, or Burt's Boys, because we used to hang out at Burt's Milk Bar at the Cross.

Having long hair with a duck's arse wasn't going to get me a job in a bank, let alone an overdraft, but so far I hadn't had much need for either.

I paid Angelo for the haircut, then scooted over to Max's place.

We'd managed to piss away the money we'd rorted out of Jim Swain, each of us, like the song says, in our own peculiar way—me lairising around Sydney, punting, drinking, and not working, Max lairising around America, punting, drinking, and not working. The difference was Max used some of his as a deposit on a block of four flats in Llandaff Street, Bondi Junction. He put it in his mother's name, installed her in one flat, himself in another, rented out the other two to cover the repayments.

In conducting her life, Mrs. Perkal was guided by three core beliefs: red was a lucky colour when picking horses; her son, Max, was fabulously talented; and the Catholics ran the best housie-housie. So the old girl hadn't minded the move to Bondi Junction: Holy Cross Church was just down the road, and they ran one of the biggest housie games in Sydney.

When Max had gone broke after the aborted Louis Jordan tour, the bailiffs couldn't touch the real estate, and he'd managed to maintain a pretty good setup there at Bondi Junction. He had a second-hand Beale piano in the lounge room, a bar which was occasionally stocked, and a newish radiogram. People would drop in all through the day and night. Musos, jockeys, entertainers, radio people, dancers, bodgies, reefer smokers, lurk men, fences, girls of easy virtue, racetrack people, bookies, you name it. One night someone picked up the ringing telephone and said, "Perkal Towers. Can I help you?" The name stuck.

When I arrived, Neville Wran, an old mate of Max's from Fort Street High, was working at the coffee table in the lounge room. He and Max had been trying for the past few months to perfect a betting system, but it never seemed to quite get off the drawing board. Nev had worked on the track, pencilling for Bill Waterhouse, and knew the game pretty well. He had the table covered with papers, a slide rule, and an adding machine.

I shook hands with Nev and waved hello to Max and Mary Howes, Max's current squeeze and tenant of the downstairs flat. Mary, AKA Dolores Del Rosa, the Blonde Bombshell of Boogie Woogie, was a country girl from North Queensland who'd been classically trained as a concert violinist. She'd chucked it in to become Dolores Del Rosa, Pin-up of the Piano. Two weeks before, Max had rigged up a photographic studio in the flat and taken a bunch of photos of her. She had got herself up in a tight black evening dress that flashed plenty of cleavage, brushed her blond hair over one eye like Veronica Lake, then stood around in a variety of alluring poses while Max took pictures. Some of the shots were stuck up on the wall now.

I poured four glasses of the gnat's piss. Max didn't mind it, Mary hated it. Nev had a quick snort, then tidied up his papers, said he had business elsewhere.

Max and Mary had been playing records, picking up songs. Now they were at the piano, taking turns playing while the other sang. Max played and Mary sang "Don't Roll Those Bloodshot Eyes at Me." Then Mary played while Max sang "Hong Kong Blues."

It's the story of a very unfortunate colored man
Who got 'rrested down in old Hong Kong
He got twenty years privilege taken away from him
When he kicked old Buddha's gong

When it got to the part where the colored guy speaks, Max hammered it up, doing an Al Jolson routine. He'd done the Jolson shtick since he was a little kid. His aunties used to love it, and he'd lapse into it at the drop of a hat, though as an act it was getting pretty long in the tooth.

Won't someone believe
I've a yen to see that bay again
But when I try to leave
Sweet opium won't let me fly away

They did a duet on the keys, Mary playing the bass pattern while Max played up top, pulling stupid faces all the while. Then they swapped parts without interrupting the song. When Max accidentally kicked over the piano stool, they stopped. I told him that was the best part, looked like he meant it. He said cut it out—no one'll ever pay to see some idiot kick the shit out of the piano furniture.

At three-thirty a guy arrived. He was about twenty—short, fair-headed, had his hair done in a duck's arse.

"Billy Glasheen, John O'Keefe. John wants to do some singing with us down at Bondi."

"Yeah? What do you do, John?"

"I'm at the university at the moment," he replied. "Studying business. But I'm interested in the entertainment industry as well."

I gave him a glass of hooch. He didn't mind it, had another.

We drank on. After a while, O'Keefe sang a couple of songs. Not much good. He said he'd sung in the choir at Christian Brothers and at the Eisteddfods, but it was hard to see.

At five, Max cut up an inhaler and we each swallowed a piece. Max didn't want to give any to O'Keefe, but he insisted.

Max and I drifted into the kitchen, sat around while Mary and O'Keefe bashed out a song in the lounge room. The benzedrine did nothing for O'Keefe's voice, but he didn't seem to care, or notice. He was really throwing himself into it.

Max was talking about America, about music.

"The whole scene's about to change. There are big things bubbling under the surface."

"What kind of big things?"

Max smiled knowingly. "Who's the most popular entertainer among young people today?"

"The Prince of Wails, Johnnie Ray," I said.

"Right. Problem with Johnnie is, he can only really do that

torch-ballad shit. OK, so he sings differently from the mugs like Como or Crosby, but it's still that slow beat. In America now, that stuff only appeals to thirteen-year-old girls and poofters. But if Ray could sing this new Negro backbeat, crikey, he'd be king of the world. When the new sound arrives here, I aim to be prepared. If I could only find a handsome white kid who could sing boogie-woogie like a Negro, I could make, Jesus, a thousand quid, easy."

"What about Marlon Brando in there?"

He shook his head. "I'd get rid of him, but Mary feels sort of sorry for him."

I poured us both another measure of the nail-polish remover. "So can't you train him, or someone, for the part?"

"Mary says there's a kid in East Hills. Named Jacobs or Jacobsen or something. I'll give him a try, but the early indications aren't that good. I'll find someone, sooner or later. When I do, I'll take him to Jack Davey, get him a start on radio."

He drifted back inside, Mary came out and took his place at the bottle. I asked her about Max's entrepreneurial plans.

"Oh, he's full of ideas since he came back from America," she said. "You never know, he could be on the right track."

"Why doesn't he do it himself? He knows what's needed. He can play the piano. He's a natural. You two could do your duo thing."

"Well, Billy, I'll tell you something about Max Peck, master of the boogie-woogie piano." She poured herself and me the last bit of the reffo moonshine. "Now, Max—one of nature's gentlemen though he may be—is a musician of limited capabilities."

She saw my raised eyebrows. "Oh, sure, he can strum a bit of guitar or uke, but everything he plays on the piano is in the key of C—you know, he only plays the white keys."

"So what's wrong with that?"

"It drives musos crazy, and it gets pretty boring for listeners, too. No, Maxie isn't the boy for this job, though maybe he has enough smarts to find someone else who is able to do it."

I knew what she meant about Max's piano playing. A while ago, he had tried to teach me the basics of boogie-woogie piano, which involved a walking-bass pattern played with the left hand spread wide. If you just play in C, it's not really that hard, especially if you're hopped up on benzedrine. I never got any good, but sometimes I could half-impress a bunch of drunks in a pub or at a party, for about twenty seconds.

I recalled what Max's mum had told me. He'd been a shy fifteen-year-old when she'd sent him along to Buddy Wikara's Hawaiian Academy to learn the steel guitar, which the adverts promised would make him very popular at parties and such. It had worked, sort of. He had started playing around on the old pianola they had at home, learned some boogie-woogie, came out of his shell, auditioned for the Macquarie radio network, and got a start as a youngster with Jack Davey. In time, he became a semi-pro entertainer, and he still taught beginner's guitar at the Hawaiian Academy.

"So the talent search goes on. Max isn't too taken with O'Keefe in there. What do you reckon?"

"Max is right, sort of. The boy can't sing that well. But I'm not so sure. Sometimes he shakes his head around and messes up his hair when he sings, and it's, you know, different."

When I left, the three of them were at the piano, drunk as donkeys, singing "Goodnight Irene."

I was pretty far gone, despite the benzedrine, by the time I parked my car outside my flat. I heard car doors slam as I went inside, but didn't really register until I heard footsteps in the lobby behind me. I turned around at the top of the stairs and they were already on me. An old bloke, looked like Victor McLaglen only meaner, and a younger one, younger than me. They were from the same mold—big and thick, and both had a rotten tailor. That meant copper.

I was past putting up any serious resistance, but I was past common sense, too. I threw a punch at the young one as he reached the top step. It caught him unaware, took him backwards onto the older one. Both of them fell back down the top flight of stairs rolling over one another like Abbott and Costello. Bad move for me. I started yelling.

"Help! Thieves! Murderers! Thugs! For God's sake, someone call the police!" They sorted themselves out, came at me with more care. I shouted for all I was worth. The young one approached me.

"Shut your fucking mouth, cunt." He swiped me, lazily. I fell down, my head ringing. A door opened downstairs. The landlady. I thanked my guardian angel for having given me the presence of mind to pay the back rent earlier on.

"Are you all right up there, Mr. Glasheen?"

"Call the police! I'm being attacked!"

The young one picked me up, twisted my arm up my back and whispered, "Shut your mouth. We are the police, shithead!"

The older one stepped forward. "All right, Des, that's enough. Take him inside." He turned back to the stairwell. "Everything's under control here, thank you. Go back inside, madam. This is a police matter."

The young one rifled my coat pockets, found my keys, opened the door, threw me inside.

I picked myself up. "Cup of tea? Bonox? Ratsack?"

The older one closed the door, faced me. The younger one stood to my side.

"Sit down, Glasheen."

I did.

"What were you doing out at the wog's place today?"

"I beg your pardon?"

The young one hit me open-handed across the back of the head. "Answer the question, dipshit."

"Go root your boot."

He did it again, harder.

Victor McLaglen sighed. "All right, I'll ask again. What were you doing at the wog's place at Casula?"

"I take it you're referring to a New Australian gentleman. Sorry, can't help you."

"Who sent you out there? Give me a name."

"Bob Menzies."

"Smart prick." The young one drew his arm back. I had my hand over a pewter ashtray that was on the coffee table. It weighed a good three pounds. The copper wasn't expecting any opposition from me. He grinned at McLaglen as he prepared to hit me. I swung the ashtray round into his face. He went down. I was up and kicking him before the old one had made it across the room.

"Your mate's got rotten manners." I held the ashtray up high, ready to hit McLaglen.

"Settle down, boy. Assault with an ashtray is a serious offence." He bent over Des. "Come on, pick yourself up." He turned to me. "So you got that out of your system. My name's Downey, Bert Downey, but that's "Mister" to you. You'd better sit down, son."

I did, and Downey sat on the chair opposite me.

"Now, Bill, we observed you today driving into a property at Casula, owned by a Yugoslav migrant, one Bosco Udovic. You were carrying a package. You left a while later carrying a cardboard box. We traced your number plate. We are not at this stage contemplating charges against you, we just need to know what's going on out there."

"I bought some piss from him."

"What about the package you took to him?"

"Chocolate for his missus."

"What sort?"

"Cadbury's Roses."

"Big spender. What did you take away?"

"Just the piss."

"Did anyone contact you prior to this?"

"No."

Des was on his feet again, the side of his face swollen. "He's lying."

A loud knock on the door. Downey opened up. Two uniform coppers. God bless the landlady. The uniform asked what's going on, Downey said everything's under control, it's a Commonwealth matter. There was an inaudible exchange lasting less than a minute, then the uniforms left. Downey returned.

"All right, Des, let's go. Billy, we know you now, we'll be watching you. My advice to you is steer clear of the reffos. They're trouble—real trouble."

The next contact I had with Shoebridge was five weeks later, on a cold, wet Thursday morning. He rang me, asked to see me.

"Last time I ended up in all sorts of shit."

He asked what sort of trouble. I told him the whole story. He wanted a description of the coppers. He asked did they or I make any mention of him, I told him no.

"It's imperative that we meet as soon as possible," he said.

"Forget it."

"In view of what you've told me, and in consideration of your prudence in maintaining my organization's anonymity, I should tell you that I'll be requesting authorization from my superiors to offer you much more favourable remuneration for any further services you may perform. Our accounts section would be prepared to regard any meetings you and I have as chargeable. You get paid for meeting me for coffee."

"I'm not available."

"In that case, Bill, I must remind you that the same inducements I referred to at our previous meeting still apply. This includes the same punitive aspects I mentioned."

"You'll sic the cops onto me?"

"I certainly don't want to do that, Bill, but my superiors have instructed me to proceed along those lines, if necessary."

"I'll meet you, but not for *coffee*. Meet me at the Four in Hand in Paddo. Your shout."

He was there before I was. I ordered a double scotch. Shoebridge paid. He made me go through what had happened the other night. He took notes. Then he gave me seventy pounds and another package, told me to take it out to Bosco at Casula, only this time go at night. He thought it was terrific that I hadn't given him up to the cops, or whoever the hell they were.

I said yeah, I was a real hero.

My car was up at Barrack Motors getting new tires, getting the brakes done—had been there for a week because I didn't have the twenty pounds to pay for it. Rather than pick it up now, I rang Max and borrowed his Hudson. He said to drop it back later that night, he'd probably be at the Troc. After the evening broadcasts, the 2GB crowd kicked on, usually at the Troc or Romano's.

I went to Casula that evening, leaving town just as it was getting dark. The rain was really coming down now and I heard on the car radio that bridges at Liverpool and Windsor were out. It was snowing out Bathurst way. Max's car had a heater, so I was reasonably comfortable. There were very few cars on the road.

At Casula, I drove past the turnoff once, looking out for parked cars, but I saw no one. The dirt road out to the farm was covered in muddy pools of water, and the Hudson slipped around a bit.

Bosco was alone and three-quarters drunk when I arrived at six-thirty. He was wearing a grubby white shirt; a long greasy lock of hair hung over his face. A kero heater was burning in the kitchen.

Bosco poured me a tumbler of his lighter fluid and insisted I sit down and drink it before we did the swap. I just wanted to shoot through as soon as I could, but Bosco was adamant. I drank the piss, then another glass. Bosco rambled on, half in English, half in Yugoslav, and the rain beat on the tin roof. Seemed he didn't much like gypsies, thought they were dirty, godless animals. At one point he grasped my arm, started shouting about the communist-Jew devils in his beautiful homeland. Abruptly he stopped, leaned close, breathed his highly flammable breath over me, and whispered to me.

"In the war we are killing much vermin."

"Vermin?"

"Gypsies and Jew-communists. We fix."

"We?"

"Ustasha!"

"I what?"

"We will killing again so that Croatia will be free."

"Great, Bosco. Listen, I've got to go. Where is the box for Shoebridge?"

"Later, Bill, my friend. Please, drink."

He refilled my glass. I was getting plastered. Any more and I wouldn't be up to the drive. I excused myself, ran out to my car, got an inhaler from the glove box. After I'd cracked it open and eaten the cotton wool I felt better, even though my coat was sodden. I went back in, waited for Bosco to finish his spiel. He was still reliving the glory of World War II. When the benzedrine kicked in, I asked him, "Hang on, Bosco. How did you kill all these Jewish communists during the war? I thought we were with them and against the Huns?"

"Jewish communists are the great enemies of freedom and democracy. I fought with Germans."

"With? Not against?"

"With. Many Yugoslav patriots worked with Germans to rid Croatia of Jews. Now, we are planning our return, we will driving out Serbs and the Jew-communist beast."

"Does Shoebridge know you feel this way?"

"Mr. Shoebridge is a great friend to Croatian patriots in Australia. He gives us help."

The rain had eased by the time I got back to town, but it was freezing cold. I left the package Bosco had given me at my flat and went to meet Max at the Trocadero.

Max was sitting at a table with a group of people arranged around Jack Davey, who was holding court. Davey waved to me as I approached.

"Billy Boy! Come on over, sit down. What'll you have? Backing winners these days?"

"Plenty."

"That's the way. Come over here and sit down."

I'd first met Davey just after the war, at a baccarat school in Little Oxford Street. I had won that night, quite a bit, and was trying to figure out how to leave without getting a belting. In those days gambling clubs were rough joints, furnished no fancier than your average boxing gym, and the bouncers were just as likely to flog a winner as protect him.

Soon after, Davey had come in, bet for a while, done his dough, and then put the bite on me. I gave him twenty quid, on condition that he left right away and let me tag along with him. He agreed, and I got out with my money and health intact. He never paid me back the twenty. I met him again later through Max, when he started working with Davey on the radio. He liked a lot of the same things both of us did—like gambling, drinking, being a lair, and taking benzedrine.

When it came to money, he was a worse risk even than Max. He'd borrow a quid from a battler taxi driver, plumber, paperboy, anyone. Annie McGrath told me he'd botted a packet of smokes from her, back before the war, when she was a receptionist at 2GB earning less than two quid a week. He rarely repaid, but people seemed to feel privileged to give money to him. He was just as loose with money when he had it, tipping very big, but that was less often.

I shook hands with the crew—Peg, his secretary, his accountant, a couple of musos and their girlfriends, and a young fellow with buck teeth. I chucked the car keys to Max, said hello to Mary, and sat down. Davey said, "Billy, order anything you like, so long as it's not on the table already." The table was loaded with different bottles: brandy, scotch, wine, sherry, Pernod, Pimm's, champagne.

A waiter stood off to the side.

"Got any of that Yugoslav stuff, brother? Clear spirit, tastes like Estapol."

He brought a bottle of something, tasted sort of like Bosco's moonshine, a bit smoother, much sweeter. We drank and talked. Or rather, Davey talked. At one point he leaned over and said, so no one else could hear, "Listen Bill, old son, I'm strapped. You haven't got a ton, have you?"

It was hard to say no to Jack, but I could do it. Before I could knock him back, though, he went on: "Look, Bill, I know I'm a bit of a bad risk, but this really is a loan. I'll absolutely guarantee it, you've got my word. If I renege, you can have my car, Doretti Swallow."

For all I knew, he'd put his car up against half a dozen loans already. But I gave him sixty pounds, kept ten.

I said, "Jack, I don't know how you do it."

After twenty minutes his face went kind of pale. He looked across to his accountant and nodded slightly. Davey excused himself, whispered to the accountant for a moment and they both left the table, Davey saying he'd be back in a tick, don't anyone leave.

"What's up with Jack?" I said to Max.

"It's time for the drugs."

"Oh. Hey, tell me something. Who or what the fuck is *you starcher*?"

"Eh? Spell."

"I don't know. It's reffo."

"What kind of reffo?"

"Yugo. Croatian."

"Whoa, digger, hang on. Was that *Ustasha*?"

"Yeah, something like that."

He gave me a funny look. "You have business with them?"

"Not exactly. There's this bloke I was talking to, said he was one, or was in it, or it was the make of car he drove, or maybe it was his wife's name. I don't know, maybe he was giving me a tip for the gallops, he didn't make much sense."

Max shook his head "Well, if he is Ustasha, he's a certified ratbag. I'll tell you about them . . ."

Davey and the accountant returned to the table, and Max left off talking. Davey took his leave almost immediately. He shook hands with me, winked, and said to pop in for a yarn about horses—see him at 2GB anytime in the next few days. I said sure. I guessed he didn't want to talk about the money he'd snipped me for in front of the gang, especially the accountant.

The party was breaking up. Mary and Max put on their coats, and Max said to me in an undertone, "When you come down to the studio, I'll give you the mail on these Ustasha. If you're interested. And you should be."

I said all right.

"And for Christ's sake, don't bring your reffo mate with you."

I sat at the table with my drink. When they'd all gone it was just me and the buck-toothed bloke, and two girls. The buck-toothed bloke looked vaguely familiar, and I was about to ask him if he'd ever boxed with Jimmy Sharman's troop when he introduced himself.

"Chad's the name. I didn't catch yours." His hand reached out to shake.

"Billy Glasheen. How's things?"

"Not too crook, Billy, not too crook. I was on that *Amateur Hour* program last week, the grand finale, and they gave me first prize. So, I've got a thousand quid and everything's terrific, and I've teamed up with this hula dancer over here, her name's Dot, and she reckons I'm not a bad sort, says she wants to see more of me. I told her to hang around and she can see the lot.

"But I've got a problem. She doesn't want to leave her sister, Del, and Del doesn't want to come along as a gooseberry. So we need a likely bloke to make up the numbers. We're going to the Hasty Tasty for a hamburger, then maybe the Forbes Club, and then, if the girls are keen, back to my hotel room. So how about it, Billy? Want to tag along?"

Chad Morgan, the Sheik of Scrubby Creek, the Dinkum Dill

from Broken Hill, three-quarters pissed. Del and Dot, the hula girls, were half-pissed, and I couldn't tell anymore what state I was in. Del smiled semi-drunkenly at me. I told him, "I don't know, bud. It's been a bit of a long night for me already."

"Yeah, me too." He looked away. "I don't know if I can last the distance myself, but Dot reckons she can show me something the sorts over in France do, and I'm buggered if I'm going back to Childers without seeing it." Del and Dot were talking to each other in low tones. Del saw me looking her way and gave a quick wink.

I felt in my pocket. I still had two inhalers left. "Righto, Chad, ladies, let's go. But tell me, how are your sinuses?"

Later on, at his hotel suite, Del and Dot showed us their hula dancing, while Chad strummed along on his guitar. They weren't too bad. The hands tell a story, Del said. As the dance progressed it got more and more risqué, and I wondered how it went over at the RSL clubs.

The sisters had given Chad a real run for his money on the Amateur Hour, apparently, coming in a close second. Tonight they sang "She Taught Me To Yodel" with Chad, and they managed a harmony on the yodel. Then Chad took Dot's hand and led her into the bedroom, saying it was time to do the Hawaiian Mating Dance.

Later that night, Chad stumbled out of the bedroom, interrupting Del and me on the couch. Del's hand was lost somewhere in my fly and my hands were engaged about her person. The hands were telling a story. Chad sat himself on an armchair, oblivious to our carrying on, and muttered something about the trouser snake being in hibernation, and did I have any more of that go-fast. He said it was even better than a Bex powder dissolved in Coca Cola.

I didn't get to 2GB the next day. Del and Dot rose early so they could freshen up and get to their jobs by nine. Del told me a bit about herself over a quick breakfast in Chad's hotel room. She and her sister both worked for the government, in Repat, but they sang and hula-danced in RSL clubs at night.

Their surname was Keene. They had originally come from out back of Coffs Harbour, where their widower father ran a dairy farm that was slowly going bad. He drank. The brothers had stayed on to try to make a go of it, but the girls had bolted as soon as they could. They were working day and night and generally having the sort of time that would scandalize the bejesus out of the folks back home—but since their mum's death they'd been paddling their own canoe. I told Del to come down to Bondi the next Sunday, maybe she and her sister would like to perform. She said she might.

I left Chad's hotel room a little after the girls, intending to go home, shower, and change. I hadn't slept, and still had enough benzedrine in me to stay awake for the rest of that day at least.

Shoebridge was outside my flat sitting in his Ford. He said he'd just pulled up. He followed me inside and I gave him Bosco's package.

He had another delivery for me to make: could I go out to Bosco's place straight away? I pretended to be reluctant, but with all the crank in my bloodstream I didn't mind the idea of some activity, even if it was driving out to buggery to see the lunatic Croat. I told Shoebridge I'd need some cash up front to collect my car. He gave me fifty quid without hesitation, didn't ask what had become of the seventy he'd given me the previous day. I put on a kettle for a cup of tea. He said he'd like one.

When it had drawn, I poured us each a cup.

"That's a good strong brew," he said. "So Billy, how have your dance shows out at Bondi been going?"

"Not too bad."

"No trouble with riffraff?"

"No, not particularly."

"That's not what the police say."

"Is that so?"

"Of course, I know not to believe everything I read in the paper, especially when it comes from the New South Wales police. I'd like to hear your side of it."

"Why?"

"I'm interested, and I may be able to help you."

"It's no big deal. When we started running the rhythm club, the local cops approached me and my partner; they said that for a consideration they would give their blessing to the promotion. We paid up once, fifty quid to the local sergeant. After that, they wanted more. We told them to get fucked. Politely. Next thing there are articles in the local rag about hoodlums at the dances. Then the hoods actually started turning up there, thinking they'd been missing the action. But even that was OK, because they liked the music and ended up having a pretty good time. We haven't had any trouble at the dances at all. Mind you, I'm not sure what happens at the milk bars up the road after the show. Anyway, once the Cornel Wilde boys started coming along, we doubled our business almost overnight. Next thing, Eric Baume's doing his *This I Believe* bullshit. My guess is that he was in hock to a bookie named Laurie O'Brien, who happens to harbour a grudge against me, and O'Brien offered to wipe the debt if he slandered me and Max in his newspaper column. It's all bullshit."

"I see." Shoebridge finished his tea. "As you know, Billy, my organization takes, ah, a larger view of things, certainly a larger view than that taken by the police. I've been at pains to impress upon my superiors the importance of making contact with people of good will who are involved with youth. You may not realize it, but the enemies of the democratic system have plans in place for the systematic undermining of our youth. I know this sounds melodramatic, but our very way of life is under grave threat from concealed enemies. Billy, you and people like you are actually in a position to do a great deal of good. Or harm, for that matter."

"Ah, shit, spare me."

"No, I'm quite serious. Over the past ten years or so, my organization has been forging important links with the biggest investigating agency in the United States government, and we've recently been receiving some disturbing memos from them, on a range of topics. The reason I mention all this to you is that some recent reports have cast new light on the problem of juvenile delinquency and subversion of youth. I don't want to bore you, Billy, but I would like you to keep an open mind on this matter. I thought you might perhaps like to attend a confidential meeting between us, some important community leaders and some very high-ranking members of the American organization I referred to."

He saw me starting to shake my head, and came in again before I could say anything: "Of course, any cooperation you give to my organization in the future would be recompensed, whether in cash payments or other forms, such as commercial incentives, preferential treatment from government bodies and so on."

"Listen, you're talking to the wrong bloke. I'm a small fish, and I don't give a shit about politics."

"Don't underestimate yourself. You've managed to get Baume's back up, and you've come to the attention of Superintendent Waters, and of course, you're now regarded as a trusted operative of my organization. These are all credentials of sorts. Anyway, bear it in mind, Billy. I'll let you know when the meeting is on. Perhaps you can hold off making a decision until the time comes."

Shoebridge pushed his teacup away. "Now, to the business at hand. There's some stuff in the boot of my car. I'd like you to take it out to Bosco's as soon as you can."

He dropped me up at Barrack Motors. The delivery was two boxes. I took them out of Shoebridge's car, put them in the boot of mine. One was heavy, thirty or forty pounds; the other was a smaller package, not quite as heavy.

When we'd finished he leaned in my window and wished me luck. This delivery was extremely important, he said, so please treat it seriously. I said I would. As I took off I said, "Your man Bosco—he's a pretty strange character."

"Don't take too much notice of what he says. He's a great yarn-spinner."

It had just gone ten o'clock when I drove off.

It was cloudy and cold as I drove out along the Hume Highway. There were puddles along the road from rain the previous night, and a southwest wind was blowing. I pulled off the highway out near Warwick Farm and parked on a gravel road that ran out to a dump. I took my penknife from the glove box, went to the boot, and cut the packing tape on the bigger of the boxes. Wrapped in newspaper was another box. Inside that were small red and yellow cardboard boxes, labelled as blank ammunition for a .303 rifle. There was another package, tightly taped up, inside the box. It contained some sticks, each slightly bigger than a large cigar, wrapped in oiled paper. I took one of them out, peeled back the paper and dug my fingernail into the stuff, which looked and felt like plasticine. I rolled it back up and replaced it, and stood there at the boot for a moment. I'd come out in a sweat—a booze and benzedrine hangover. I wiped the sweat off my forehead, then carefully cut the wrapping on the smaller package. It contained a bundle of maps, which seemed to be of the Ingleburn, Campbelltown, Holsworthy areas, and some British Army booklets, marked Confidential, titled *The Uses of Explosive*. Underneath those was a large bulging envelope, which contained five bundles of ten-pound notes. There seemed to be about a thousand quid there.

I stopped at a hardware store at Liverpool, bought some packing tape, and repacked the boxes. My head had started to ache, right in the centre of my forehead. I bought a pie and a bottle of milk and drove the rest of the way to Casula, but I didn't drive straight in. I drove past the turnoff to the Yugoslav's farm, pulled into a gravel patch beside the highway, turned off the motor, ate my pie and drank the milk, and tried to figure if there was a possible rort for me here. I would have liked to talk to Max about it, but by now he'd be in the auditorium with Davey.

I chucked the milk bottle away and turned the car back toward Bosco's, swinging onto the road up to the farmhouse.

Bosco and a couple of his mates were waiting outside when I got to the farmhouse. There were two cars parked beside the house, old shit heaps like mine.

The two men standing with Bosco were wearing white T-shirts, with little chequered shields sewn on, like a soccer team. Bosco was unshaven and looked pretty crook, wearing a crumpled brown shirt and stained gray trousers. He nodded hello and tried to smile, but his heart wasn't in it. The young blokes pretty much ignored me, going straight to the boot of my car. They took the boxes and carried them inside the house.

Bosco turned to me and breathed some stale booze and garlic breath all over me. He leaned over close and said, "Last night, I drink." He shrugged and gave me a sickly grin. "Too much. I make jokes, just jokes." He watched me, waiting for me to acknowledge that yeah, they were jokes.

So I slapped him on the back, which made him wince, and said, "Yeah, sure, Bosco, no problem, jokes." And then I laughed and slapped him again, but I was thinking *you mongrel*.

He sort of laughed along for a moment, then nodded and said again, "Jokes," with half a question in his voice.

I would have liked to see who else was inside and what they did with the contents of the boxes, but for all Bosco's shit-eating, it didn't look like he was going to invite me in. I pointed to my throat and said, "Water?"

Bosco signalled me to wait here, he'd get some. When he was almost through the front door I skipped quietly up behind him and followed him inside before he realized what I was doing.

They already had the packages open on the kitchen table and a couple of blokes were putting the ammo in shoulder bags. There were guns everywhere, handguns and rifles, and the money was stacked in the centre of the table. There seemed to be ten or twelve T-shirted men in the house. One of them spoke a few rapid words to Bosco when he saw me walk in behind him, and Bosco swung around and put his arms out.

"Bill, please, outside, outside!"

A couple of the T-shirts were on their feet and advancing toward me. The one nearest me had a gun in his hand.

I put my hands up, gave him my biggest smile, and did an act like it was a cowboy movie and he was shooting at me, and I was ducking bullets, and then shooting back with the index finger of each hand, like it was all just fun and I didn't care a shit about the guns and explosives all over the place.

Bosco came to me with the glass of water. I drank it down and said, "I've got to be off, fellers. Take it easy. You got anything for me, Bosco?"

He gave me another bottle of Africa Speaks, but he was clearly preoccupied, and wanted me out of the place as quickly as possible. I strolled out with what I hoped was an insouciant air, but my legs were shaking so much I thought it must be visible. Bosco and two of the chocko thugs saw me out. I got in the car, gave the lads a friendly wave and drove off. But a quarter mile down the road, I pulled off onto a side track. I had a headache worse than any I could remember. I went into the bushes, spewed, then came back to the car and sat on the running board and waited for my head to clear.

I took a swig from the bottle, not a big one, and that helped. I was out of benzedrine.

The sun had come out, but a dry, cold wind was still blowing. I got in the car to get warm, and took another sip from the bottle.

I'd been there for about ten minutes, trying to collect myself, when I heard a noisy motor on the track, and watched as two khaki-painted trucks drove past, with army blokes at the wheel of each. They were heading out to the farm. They didn't see me parked on the side track. I started the Chev and reversed it even further down the track, stopped it again and waited.

Twenty minutes later, the trucks and one of the cars from the farmhouse drove out. I caught a glimpse of the T-shirt boys in the car and in the truck. After they'd passed, I got out of the car and walked over to the road, waiting until the sound of the vehicles died away completely.

I should have pissed off right then, forgotten about ratbag Yugoslavs and guns and bombs and creepy red-headed government men. But curiosity and a thousand quid took me back to the farmhouse.

I left the car and walked off into the scrub, figuring to get back to the farmhouse without using the road.

It turned out to be tougher than it looked. The scrub was thick, and still sodden from the rain. It took me twenty minutes to work back to the house, and by then my shoes were soaked and I had mud up to my knees.

I came to the farmhouse from the back. No one came in or out for the fifteen minutes or so while I watched, even though one of the cars was still parked at the back. I crept to within thirty yards of the house and lobbed a rock onto the roof. No one came out.

The door to the kitchen was bolted, but the bedroom window was unlocked. I climbed through it, stopped and waited. My heart was pounding, and I was suddenly busting for a leak. I'd never make a burglar.

Inside, the house was a mess, like a bunch of blokes had been living rough. In the lounge room were sleeping bags, clothes on the floor, empty booze bottles, full ashtrays, and dirty plates, with foreign-language newspapers and tit magazines lying around. In the kitchen, the ammo packets were empty, lying on the table along with a deck of cards. The booklets and money weren't around any more. In the laundry, I found a couple of crates of spirit, but nothing much else.

At the side of the house, there were two bedrooms I hadn't noticed before. The first one was almost completely dark until I switched on the light. The windows had heavy curtains of dark cloth. In the centre of the room was a large table with more dark cloth draped over it. On the table there were two daggers, laid across one another in a cross. To one side was a crucifix, and at the other side was a .303 rifle. There were two candles in holders which looked like they'd come out of a church. It was all laid out as if for a ceremony.

I turned out the light and went to the next bedroom. It was even dirtier inside than the lounge room, but looked a bit more permanently occupied. The windows were closed, curtains drawn, and it smelled of sweat, damp, stale clothes, and tobacco. It had a bed with gray blankets but no sheets. There was a wardrobe with a few shirts and an old suit. On one wall was a framed photograph of some old codger in a uniform, with one of those old-fashioned moustaches, like from World War I. On the other wall was another crucifix, with rosary beads hanging from it.

Maybe a woman lived here once, but it looked liked a bachelor's room now. There was a box of foreign-language books on the floor, but no money. The box I'd brought out was under the bed, with the gelignite still in it. Next to the bed was a little cabinet with a drawer and a cupboard. There were cigs and matches and some letters in the drawer. In the cupboard below was a wooden box, and inside that was the money.

I tipped it out onto the floor, and saw immediately that there was a lot more there than I had brought out this morning. I started doing a rough count of the money, then heard a voice behind me say, "Sir?"

I jumped liked a spastic, dropping the money I was holding. I looked up to see a small, foxy-looking guy at the door. He was wearing a dark beret, a dark-blue turtleneck jumper, and dungarees. He looked behind me, gave a small nod, then looked at me again, smiled, shrugged, and said "Sorry." And then it was nighty-night.

Nausea woke me. I was in the dark, lying down, cramped, on my side. I lifted my head for a moment, then went unconscious again. Thirst and cold woke me the next time. There was a pain behind my right eye when I tried to open it. I sat up in the pitch dark and felt around me. I was in the back seat of my car. I got out and dry-retched. The sky was not quite black, and I could see the silhouettes of trees around me, and a bit of a track. I took a step, slipped in a mud puddle, and fell forward. The cold water woke me up. I sat up and splashed some more water on my face. I went back to the car and found some matches in the glove box. My keys were in the ignition. On the front seat was another bottle of Bosco's piss. I opened it and drank a long couple of swallows, then took a butt from the ashtray, straightened it out and lit it. I felt in my pockets. My money was still in my wallet, the change from the fifty quid Shoebridge had given me. I flaked some dried blood off my neck, felt a lump on the back of my head.

When I'd finished the bumper, I started the car and drove off. I had no idea where I was or what the time was, couldn't even tell what direction I was driving in. I felt woozy, sort of detached from my body, which was how I always felt after a couple of days on benzedrine.

The track led on to a bitumen road, which took me to a lighted intersection. On the corner was a Golden Fleece garage, with a sign saying Wallacia Service Station. I was twenty miles from Casula.

I kept driving and eventually came to a sign which said Penrith, pointing back in the direction I'd come. I turned around. I reached the Great Western Highway half an hour later, slowly drove back to Sydney. It was raining and there was hardly a car on the road. A few cabs prowling, but hardly anyone on the street. The clock on the Peak Freans building said twelve-thirty. I was in my flat by one. I showered and went to bed, and slept through till the next evening.

I stayed in that night, Saturday night. I'd missed the races, and it seemed too late to try to catch up with everybody else's day. I went up the road to the Astoria Cafe and had a steak, then went down to the Piccolo Bar for one of those really strong cups of coffee. I went home and listened to the radio, didn't touch a drop, didn't take any benzedrine.

It was not so easy to take in all that had happened. The army trucks, the money, the gelignite, the little bloke in the turtleneck sweater, the biff on the head. It took me a while even to recreate the order it all happened in.

If the fox-faced bloke and his unseen accomplice were more of Bosco's goons, then I should've been in very deep shit. If he wasn't part of that crowd, then he was most likely a thief himself, in which case I was still in deep shit, since I'd be the first suspect if the money had been stolen. Bosco didn't know who I was other than "Billy," but of course Shoebridge had me pegged.

As I thought about it more, the strangest part was that nothing had happened yet. I'd been here asleep since the previous night, which would have given Bosco, Shoebridge, or the cops plenty of time to catch up with me.

I turned in before midnight and slept heavily, too fucked to give it any more thought.

Sunday was a work day for me and Max, with our Rhythm Show at Bondi running in the afternoon and early evening. We were using the dance hall in back of the Aloha Milk Bar, which was owned by Mick Camellieri. Mick was a Maltese who'd come to Australia before the war. His oldest son, Victor, was a bit of a bodgie himself, and a big fan of American music. Max had persuaded Vic to talk old Mick into reopening the dance hall, which hadn't been used since the thirties, back when there were a few dance halls in every suburb, and even large cafes had resident bands for Saturday afternoon or weekday dancing.

Mick had been leery at first, but at Vic's urging, he started making hamburgers and selling Coca-Cola.

Max had originally hired an AMI jukebox to use between band sets, so the music would keep up nonstop. We had Tommy McGrath rig up a record-player through a public-address system, so the music was really loud, which was the way Max had seen it done at record hops in the States.

At first, old Mick said it was too loud, he could even hear it out front in the milk bar. But the music berleyed up plenty of kids who spent their hard-earneds on hamburgers and drinks, and Mick thought that was all right. In fact, he moved the jukebox into the milk bar proper. It had an added benefit: now Vic didn't mind working in the milk bar so much, since his friends made it a hangout, so Mick saved himself a lot of grief yelling at his son to help out with the business. Max had even tried to get *Pix* to run a story about jive boogie-woogie music bringing a family closer together, but they weren't buying it.

Max was already there when I arrived just after lunch. He was having trouble getting the PA going, and kept pulling out leads and checking them. Mary was working out the program for the afternoon's show. I greeted them both and set about giving the room a sweep-out.

By two o'clock, things were set up. The three of us went out to the back lane and shared a reefer. Max had got it from an American seaman, a bloke we both knew as Chet, a Southerner who was also a big music fan. Along with the tea, he kept Max supplied with new records. I had other reefer sources, Chet being one of six or seven different travellers who supplied me. I sold the stuff on to musos, crims, prostitutes, and a few arty types.

A couple of times, Lee Gordon had rung me and asked me to get some stuff for visiting musicians; the previous year, I'd got reefers for some guys in Lionel Hampton's band, and on another occasion for Sammy Davis, Jr. I never made much money, but it covered the cost of what I smoked myself, and got me invites to some good parties.

When we'd finished the smoke, Max said, "So, what happened to you on Thursday? I thought you were going to meet me at the auditorium."

"A lot happened, most of it bad."

"Like what?"

"It'll take a while to tell. I'll save it for after the show."

"Yeah, all right." He took another drag of the reefer. "Gee, I love this stuff."

We had a good crowd that afternoon. Mary worked the door. We charged five bob a head, which was a little steep, but was what we had to charge in order to make a profit.

I started playing records at three o'clock, and the room was already half-full. Canadian jackets, like the one Marlon Brando wore in *On the Waterfront*, were all the rage among bodgies that winter. I could see a dozen of them in the crowd, red or green or even pink checks, plus some red cardigans. The girls were wearing tight slacks or jeans and mohair sweaters, with sleeves pulled up to the elbows, tits poking right out in front.

The band played a set that lasted from three-thirty till five. Max had had the old piano in the hall tuned, and he'd worked out a way of amplifying it by sticking a microphone inside. His band, the Pickled Peppers, was sometimes a trio, sometimes a quartet, depending on who was around at the time. Today he had a drummer and a guitarist, but no bass fiddle. The guitarist had one of the new Maton electric guitars, and Max was trying to get him to play in the style of Carl Hogan, the guitarist in Louis Jordan's band.

When the band stopped for a break at five, I took over as disc jockey. I had a half-bottle of Cutty hidden down behind the turntable, and I was taking discreet swigs while the records played. The dope had been pretty strong, and it went well with the whisky. Chet's latest records were going over great with the crowd. I played a record by Louis Prima and Foy Willing called "Vout Cowboy," then a thing called "Hound Dog," by Willie Mae Thornton. After that I played some of the new records we'd got from Chet: "Earth Angel," by the Penguins; "Work with Me Annie," by the Midnighters; and "Shake, Rattle and Roll," by Joe Turner.

Then I found a strange one. The name of the artist and the name of the song were the same. It didn't make much sense, and the rhythm was even stranger, like a bunch of tribesmen beating on their bongos. It was called "Bo Diddley"—and it was by Bo Diddley. Listening to it, I felt like I was right there in the studio with the band. It must've been the reefer, sometimes it did that to me—made me feel I was in there with the musicians. Whatever, the mood seemed to get to the dancers as well, they were really getting into it.

My gaze was drifting across the dancers when I saw the fox-faced bloke in the beret. He was standing near the back of the room. Half the kids there were taller than him, so I only got a glimpse, before the crowd closed over him again. I thought it might have been the reefer doing it to me, until I caught another sight of him, looking straight at me. He smiled and saluted, then I lost him again.

Later on, back on the door, I could check out everyone coming and going, but there was no sign of the beret-wearer. I asked a couple of the kids whether they'd seen him. They hadn't. They'd been too wrapped up in their dancing to notice anything much.

But one kid, Kevin something, had his leg in plaster because of a footy injury and had been standing at the side. He saw the beret—saw his mate too, a big bloke—and heard them talking.

Chockos of some kind. Hadn't seen them in the last twenty minutes, though.

When the band came back on at six, Mary did her duet with Max. It was clear even to a non-muso like myself that she could play circles around Max if she tried. Her singing wasn't up to the standard of her piano playing, but it was good enough. She sang "Cow Cow Boogie," "Route 66," and "Down the Road a Piece," while Max took over on guitar. The guitarist meanwhile switched to Hawaiian style, playing a new type of guitar, on four steel legs, like a set of vibes, with foot pedals underneath.

At half past, Del and Dot arrived, with Chad Morgan in tow, and then O'Keefe arrived a minute behind them.

After all the greeting and handshaking, the gang went in to see Max. Del sidled up to me.

She smiled and said gently, "How are you, lover boy?"

"Not bad. How about you?"

"All right. I wasn't sure whether I should come today." She looked at me curiously. "Wasn't sure how you'd react."

I gave her a quick peck on the cheek and said, "I'm glad you came."

"Well, I don't throw myself at just anybody, even if I did throw myself at you. Just count yourself lucky, that's all."

"I do."

I didn't really want to get into a heart-to-heart on the finer points of modern romance right then, so I told Del I'd catch up with her later. I took the door money out and stashed it in my car. On the way out through the milk bar, I asked old Mick if he'd seen anyone strange come through. He said, sure, about two hundred of them.

That was it. No beret. Back inside, O'Keefe did his Johnnie Ray routine, which went over pretty well, then Del and Dot sang. They were a big surprise to the bodgie crowd. They sang a hillbilly harmony, but with a boogie-woogie beat. They sang "Pistol Packin' Mama," and "It Wasn't God Who Made Honky Tonk Angels," then finished with "Shotgun Boogie." When they finished, there was half a minute of whistling and foot-stomping, along with shouts of "get your gear off!" Chad got into the act then. He got up and sang "Sheik of Scrubby Creek" and "Shotgun Wedding," and offered to take *his* gear off.

Then Max came to the microphone and told the crowd we were finishing up now, come back next week when the management would once again spare no expense in bringing them the most up-to-date songs and in-demand artists. Which made me laugh seeing how, apart from ten quid each to the guitarist and drummer, we hadn't spent a zack, unless you count the cost of my half-bottle of Cutty.

We kicked on back to Max's after the show. Mary played piano while Del and Dot sang, and I could see Max thinking what a great possibility the trio would be as a stage act. I didn't get a chance to talk to Max alone, and I lost track of it all after about eleven. Somehow I ended up back at my flat with Del, sneaking past the landlady's door.

By noon on Monday no one had tried to slit my throat, no coppers had come to my door, no mysterious little fellers in berets had hit me on the head, and no secret agents had come along flashing their license to kill, so I figured the business at Casula had blown over.

Del had shot through early Monday morning, and I'd spent the next couple of days taking it easy. I still had most of the money I'd earned from Shoebridge, plus a share of the money we'd made on Sunday night, which had been our most successful yet.

I'd gone to Dovey's on Monday and worked some of the poisons out of my system. I'd like to say it fixed me up, but it nearly killed me. I stayed in Monday night, slept well, and by Tuesday I was feeling sort of OK.

Which abruptly changed at ten o'clock when Shoebridge knocked on my door.

I didn't want to let him in, didn't want anything more to do with him.

I stood at the door and said, "Yeah, what now?"

"May I come in?"

"Why?"

"Really, Bill, do I need to press the point?"

He was showing more of the copper in him every time. I let him in, but didn't give him a cup of tea.

He didn't say anything about Yugoslav maniacs at Casula, or little blokes in berets. He wanted to talk about the entertainment business. He said he'd come specially to invite me to a private seminar being held on Thursday night, at the Metropole Hotel. It was to be attended by some high-ranking American gentlemen and some key people in his organization, as well as some other important types involved in entertainment, public relations, and journalism.

I didn't say it, but I thought it couldn't be that far aboveboard, if they were inviting someone like me along. He gave me the room number at the hotel, said it was starting at eight sharp, and that he'd like me to attend. There was an unmistakable threat in it, even though the wording was harmless enough.

After Shoebridge left, I got a call from Ted Rallis, a bloke I knew from around the race tracks. He worked as a bookie's penciller on the weekends, had a couple of greyhounds in his backyard, and made a bit of money flogging stolen goods. Every so often, he and his mates staged a dog substitution racket, running a good dog in place of a useless one, cashing in on the long odds. They couldn't do it too often and still get away with it, nor could they all cash in on every rort without alerting the bookies, so they took it in turns. Each one of them could get a couple of good collects a year out of it, to pay for the family holiday or whatever.

Officially, Ted worked as a labourer at Darling Harbour Goods Yard, but as far as anyone knew he'd never been there after the day he first signed on. He still collected a pay packet which he split fifty-fifty with a crooked paymaster down there.

Ted had rung me because I was one of the few people who *wouldn't* be at work on a Tuesday. He was going fishing and he wanted company. After all the rain, the fish were on the bite. He could've rung Max, who was also free that day, but Max had never taken to fishing—said it was like standing in a public phone booth, waiting for the telephone to ring.

I told Ted, sure, let's go fishing.

The day was sunny and there was no wind. Ted had a small boat he left down at Rose Bay on the little beach just east of the bay proper, and he was there before me. He already had the outboard in place by the time I arrived.

We pushed it in and motored off. Ted took us out to Sow and Pigs reef, a rocky outcrop in the middle of the harbour between the two shipping lanes, about a mile off Watson's Bay. At low tide, waves break over it.

We were the only boat there, all the honest, hard-working mugs being at their jobs. We moored on the heads side of the reef so the incoming tide would push our tackle back onto the reef. It was warm enough for me to take my shirt off, and the winter sun on my back felt great.

For a while, as the tide came in, it was pretty quiet. I dozed off a couple of times. We caught a few rock cod and chatted about racing.

At four o'clock, just as the tide was about to turn, we started up and moved around the other side of the reef, the harbour bridge side, and cast back at the reef. Just as the tide started moving back out, the bream came on, and by five we had a good mixed bag of bream and trevally. We stayed out there for a while after the fish stopped biting, watching the big Manly Ferries going back and forth while the sun went down behind the city.

It was dark when we got back to Rose Bay wharf, but hadn't turned cold yet. We cleaned the catch and went our separate ways, me to my flat, Ted off to give a greyhound a paint job for a coming substitution lurk.

I gave my share of the catch to the landlady, kept one nice-size trevally for myself, which I filleted and cooked up straight away.

I turned in that night without having a drink, feeling better than I had in a long time.

The next day I had another crack at Dovey's and did a bit better this time. I went for a run at Rushcutters Bay oval that afternoon, and turned in early.

Shoebridge rang on Thursday morning to ask me if I was coming to the seminar that night. I told him I would. Taking no chances, he said he'd pick me up at seven-thirty. He asked me to wear a suit—and not a zoot suit.

I didn't say much on the way there. I'd decided I was through with Shoebridge, fifty quid or no. But he was full of chat, ignoring my near silence. He said there were some very exciting opportunities opening up, and a great deal of work to be done in the entertainment field; and that he personally thought this was one of his organization's most important areas of involvement.

We went to a luxury suite on a high floor of the Metropole. There were fifty or sixty people there, some of them familiar faces, but no one I really knew. Eric Baume of *This I Believe* was there, although he wouldn't recognize me. There were a few younger blokes with short-back-and-sides haircuts. There was a buffet with drinks and biscuits and cheese, and a waiter doing the rounds. The people crowded around the drinks table I took to be journos.

I took a scotch. It was the good stuff. I stood there and drank another. After a few minutes Shoebridge called the gathering to order, asked us to sit down. He crapped on for a few minutes with the same sort of things he'd been saying in the car. I didn't pay much attention. Then he said something about how under the special circumstances this would be a strictly off-the-record affair, and by way of introducing the next speaker, we would refer to him only as "Colonel Sir William."

The good colonel carried on the same way Shoebridge had. He talked about the cold war, about the filthy godless Russians and their puppets, about traitors in our midst, as demonstrated conclusively by the recent Petrov Affair, about the need for vigilance. He said experience in other democratic countries had shown the pressing need for preemptive action by responsible organizations, and how it was now accepted that this action must often be undertaken independent of the government of the day, and would in some circumstances need to be expressly hidden from the members of the government, as many democracies were now under threat from covert communists and fellow travellers, elected in the guise of democrats, but owing allegiance to Moscow or Peking rather than Canberra or Westminster.

He went on like that and I switched off.

Off to the side of the room was another wing, where some

more people sat who I hadn't noticed before. There were three police types, except that they all had crew cuts and wore suits that didn't look locally made. Among them were two older fellows, one of them a short guy with a small-featured, pugnacious face. The other looked like Ward Bond. The short bloke looked familiar, but I couldn't place him.

I tuned in again to Sir William, who was winding up for a big finish. He was talking now about Australian Security's links with sister organizations in Canada, Britain, and, most importantly, the US. He said how terrific America was, how advanced their philosophy of law enforcement and security was. Then he started on about what a very special pleasure and a privilege it was, a rare opportunity, etc., etc., and I realized he was only the warm-up act for another speaker. Then the Ward Bond look-alike came to the rostrum, getting a big round of applause. Somehow I'd missed the name, or else he hadn't said it. He was a Yank. He thanked the colonel for his kind remarks, then launched his own spiel. I got the feeling he'd given it plenty of times before.

He said the Western world was at the crossroads, and everything we held precious and decent was under threat; our enemies were poised to destroy our institutions, our way of life, our morality. It was the filthy commies.

"But gentlemen, make no mistake. The front lines of this battle, of this deadly confrontation, are to be found not only in Central Europe, in Berlin, in the jungles of Indo-China, in the villages of Latin America, but in our own legislatures, our schools and universities, even our churches, our street corners, our very homes.

"Our leisure and entertainment industries, gentlemen, are particularly prone to infiltration by elements inimical to the very institutions we hold sacred, and within these we recently have found evidence of the most vile, reprehensible attempts to subvert and undermine the moral fibre of our young, to render them weak and deluded, disrespectful and restless, to seduce them to creeds of wantonness and abandon, to enslave them to addictive drugs and animalistic jungle music.

"Recent information received by my organization indicates that shady entrepreneurs are offering, under the disguise of 'satire,' propaganda that might as well have been penned by the apparatchiks of the Kremlin, given how it undermines our way of life.

"Newsstands right across the US, and I'm told, right here in Australia, carry so-called 'comic' books of a crude and insidious nature, which seek to inflame the lower drives and sick inclinations of impressionable youth, dwelling on ghoulish, macabre, and scandalous sexual subjects—subjects and story lines that frequently border on the satanic. These publications, sometimes masquerading as satire, make fun of family life and values, belittling and cheapening the old-fashioned virtues we hold so dear. Some of the most eminent psychiatrists and educators in America have gone on record to warn us of the dire effects these works can have on young minds, and a US Senate inquiry this year heard some very alarming evidence on the matter. Hitler was an amateur compared to the comic-book industry.

"We are all aware of the epidemic of juvenile delinquency that is sweeping the western world. The gangs that are appearing in the US, in Western Europe, and in Australia are not, as some liberal commentators would have us believe, just kids letting off steam. Rather, they display signs of a sophisticated, centralized organisational structure—from the motorcycle gangs of California to the street pickpockets of Naples, from the lunatic art students of Paris to your own 'bodgie' gangs. Behind them all we see the sinister hand of the communists. Whether it be the platitudes of the 'peace group' leaders, or the drug-crazed drivel of beatniks, the rantings of nonconformist pseudo-intellectuals, the naive pieties of leftist clergymen or the thuggery of street hoodlums, be assured, every one of these expressions gives delight to the men of the Kremlin.

"In the southern states of the US, we see attempts to replace wholesome American music with 'jungle boogie jive,' a deliberate attempt to confuse and enfeeble the otherwise clean, manly instincts of our young men, and seduce the decent, homely instincts of our daughters. And not just in the Deep South. Disc jockeys in Cleveland, New York, Chicago, and Los Angeles are foisting on the tender ears of young people Negro music of the most base type. Dancers at record hops and rhythm concerts have been observed by concerned parents and educators behaving in a trancelike state, as if under the influence of a narcotic. Sometimes narcotics are involved, but more often this state is produced by the hypnotic effects of the Negro jungle drum. No one objects when this jungle music is played only within the confines of low-life Negro dives. Gentlemen, if you'll permit me a vulgarity—I believe we are without the company of the fair sex tonight—we have a saying in the States that all that the niggers want out of life is tight pussy, loose shoes, and a warm place to shit."

A laugh went around the room, not that hearty. Some of the short-back-and-sides blokes looked distinctly uncomfortable. I looked into the wing where the other guests were sitting. The crew-cuts didn't crack a grin. The little pugnacious bloke also kept a straight face, but nodded his head slightly.

"That may be so, but young Americans, and young Australians, I'm sure you'll agree, will need to have a much greater appreciation of true values than that, and to possess much greater reserves of ambition and clear-mindedness.

"Documents obtained by our operatives outline International

Communism's ten-point plan for world domination. Item number seven on the plan makes mention of undermining the resolve of a nation by winning over its youth, rendering them effeminate and lazy through cultural infiltration, so that in the event of communist invasion, that country will be found incapable of defending itself. And I am sad to report that many deluded businessmen, all too frequently of the Hebrew persuasion, are the gullible tools of the conspiracy to undermine the moral fabric of the younger generation.

"Of course, the extent of communist infiltration in our movie industry shocked the world when it was exposed a few years ago. But quickly the fifth-columnists and fellow travellers, the pale-pink brigade, the bleeding-heart liberals and armchair intellectuals launched a clever counterattack, a campaign that sought to blacken the names of the very men who were leading the battle to expose the communists' perfidy. Now the communists, anarchists, Trotskyists, and their collaborators have turned to even more devious approaches, and we stand, gentlemen, as a staunch few, in readiness before the stinking tide."

He paused for a few seconds and looked around the room. The bloke next to me had his hand to his mouth, covering up a sly yawn.

The speaker put his hand on his lapels and dropped his voice. "Gentlemen, I can't stress strongly enough the importance of the role you have to play—as communicators, as journalists, as writers, as academics, as opinion-formers. In the past, we in law enforcement have concerned ourselves primarily with what people *do*, and left their spiritual and philosophical activities to the care of ministers and educators. But all of us, in our separate fields, must now concern ourselves with what people *think*. We must sharpen our own wits in order to remain one step ahead of those who would lead and influence the naive and gullible ones who all too often fail to see the perils that accompany the easy philosophies they adopt."

He went on, but I stopped trying to follow it. So did half the people in the room. A few jokers were looking at their watches, fidgeting, coughing.

The speaker finished up, asking for our support and help in fighting communist and antidemocratic propaganda in all its forms: in the press, in broadcasting, in community affairs, in public life. He thanked us and stopped, obviously pleased with himself.

Maybe the speech usually got him a big response, but it fell flat that night. A few people clapped like maniacs, but most of the crowd seemed a bit lost. I sure was. The applause was barely polite. The speaker waited for a moment; maybe he expected the applause to swell a bit, and he'd do an encore. Not so. The guy in front of me mumbled to the fellow on his right "Goose!" and a couple of people giggled.

The septic left the podium and shook a few hands. The journos were already back at the booze table getting stuck into the free stuff, while the squareheads were talking to Sir William. He led them over to where the Yank and his buddies were, around the corner. I drifted over and stood behind them as introductions were made. Something called the Congress for Cultural Freedom was mentioned a couple of times but it meant nothing to me. One of the crew-cut fellows saw me loitering and gave me a hard look.

I moved away and got another drink over at the long table where the journos had stationed themselves. They were getting louder by the minute, belting down all the free piss they could before the turn finished. I skulled a scotch, got a refill, and drifted over to the piano. I tinkled a couple of the keys with my right hand,

and even I could tell it was a beaut piano. I put my drink down and played my showpiece, my thirty seconds of boogie-woogie. The grand sounded so good I found I was really hitting the keys hard. I finished the piece and the journos let out a drunken cheer, a couple of them whistled. I started up my only other showpiece, which was almost exactly the same thing, only slow and bluesy. One of the journos, a fruity sort of bloke, came over and started singing along, in a sort of bullshit Negro style: *Big-legged women, ease your dresses down / You got something up there that'd make a bulldog hug a hound.*

After it finished, he took an elaborate bow while his mates ya-hooed, and then he mock-graciously directed the applause to me, his accompanist, like he was Dame Nellie Melba. I took a bow. Then I heard a fierce whisper in my left ear.

"Just what the fuck do you think you're doing?"

Shoebridge was apoplectic. Across the room the Yank and his Congress for Cultural Freedom mates had stopped talking and were staring at me and the journo, a couple of them literally open-mouthed. The smaller Yank was pointing at me and shaking his head. I could hear him paying out to the colonel, about how he was supposed to have vouched for everyone here, and who the hell were these rubes and degenerates. I turned to them and put my hand up in a placating gesture.

"Everything's OK, gentlemen. Rest assured, I was only playing the white keys."

That did it. The riff-raff let out a cheer. It was just like being back at school again, where you're showing off for the hoons, even though you know the teacher's going to have your guts for garters afterwards. Shoebridge clenched his teeth, and I thought for a moment he was going to thump me. He signalled to a couple of heavies and the three of them gathered closely around me. I saw the VIPs hastily taking their leave, as I was hustled out the other exit. Shoebridge stopped at the door as I was escorted from the premises. He didn't say anything. Behind him, inside, I could hear the journos boozily singing along to "Hallelujah, I'm a Bum."

"Like Larry Kent says, 'I hate crime,' as well you know, Bill."

"Yeah, I know you hate crime. But sometimes you have to do things you hate."

"That's it."

"And this is one of them."

He nodded slowly. "This is one of them."

It hadn't taken us a real long time to come up with the idea of robbing Bosco and his mates. After I was chucked out of the VIP get-together at the Metropole, I went back to Max's place. Mary and Del were there running through songs, putting together a little act. Dot had been expected as well but hadn't turned up. Del thought she was probably out somewhere with Chad. At one point Nev Wran arrived and did a bit more work on his charts while Del and Mary played music. He'd shot through at midnight, saying he had a law exam the next day. I offered him some benzedrine, but he said no thanks—he'd rather run on his merits.

Max and I sat in the kitchen drinking beer while I told him what had gone on that night at the Metropole, and everything that had happened, starting with the first run I did out to Casula.

At some point Mary and Del had come out and they listened in silence to the whole story.

Max filled in a few bits. He'd always kept abreast of current affairs, ever since the family had run the news agency. And he'd done a bit of checking after I'd first mentioned the Yugos at Casula. He said it sounded like they were members of Ustasha, a Croatian secret society. They were fanatically pro-Austrian—had been since the days of the Austro-Hungarian empire—and they hated the Serbs with a passion beyond all reason. The Croats were RC's whereas Serbs were Orthodox. During the war, many Croats had been pro-Nazi. After all, Hitler was an Austrian. The Nazis set up the puppet "Independent State of Croatia" with a guy named Anton Pavelic at its head. They'd helped out the Huns by running the extermination camps for them, taking the opportunity to settle all the old scores they could. Which meant sticking it into every Serb, Gypsy, Jew, or commo they could lay their hands on.

After the war, when the allies were rounding up war criminals—which meant concentration-camp staff in particular—Pavelic and his mates bundied. Like in Germany, suddenly there were no chiefs, only Indians, and not too many of them to be found. There were rumours that the top villains had received help from the Vatican and from Western intelligence in getting resettled in the Americas, Canada, and Australia. Pavelic, who wound up in South America, along with his network of old buddies around the world—mostly in Australia—called themselves "Ustasha," which meant "insurgents." Their aim was the reestablishment of the glorious Independent State of Croatia.

Whether every Croatian who pulled a knife and muttered "Ustasha" was really a card-carrying member or not, was a moot point. It was like the way an Italian, if he wanted to scare you, might let you think he was a member of the Black Hand or the Mafia or something, when in fact he was a nobody. What kind of secret society is it whose members will skite about it to any old yokel like me? Then again, maybe that's just the kind of dickhead that secret societies attract.

As for the chockos at Casula, I was willing to punt they were the McCoy. The guns, explosives, maps, and army trucks had been real enough. So had the money.

Max wasn't that impressed with any Croats to begin with. His family were Polish Jews, mainly of socialist or commo inclination. They'd been in Australia since before the First World War, when Max's grandfather had brought out his wife and two sons. He'd made a bit of money importing light bulbs, and later radio sets, but the gambling curse had been active even back then, and the old fellow had always managed to lose slightly more than he earned. He insisted on his sons getting an education, and both of them ended up working with publications. The elder son, Max's father, bought a news agency at Stanmore. He didn't drink, smoke, or gamble, but the younger brother did all those things. He was a journo, worked on the *Labor Daily,* and was generally active in labour politics. All the family had a big interest in current affairs, even down to Max.

Anyway, the family didn't have any relations in Yugoslavia, but they didn't feel too good about the death camps and Nazi collaborators, having lost plenty of kin in Poland.

So it wasn't hard for us to figure we owed it to Max's race and to the memory of his departed family members to rort the filthy Nazi scum of their ill-gotten gains if we could.

We'd started talking about it as a kind of joke, but the more we talked the easier it seemed. We could approach the house the back way, keep an eye on it until everyone went out, run in and grab the loot, and shoot through. We could certainly use the dough—I was living from hand to mouth and Max was an undischarged bankrupt. The Rhythm Club was still returning only chicken feed, a real job was out of the question, and so once more we were driven to crime, which we both hated.

Del and Mary joined in our loony scheming, and by the time we called it a night we had the money just about spent.

That should have been the end of it, but the next morning Del was talking like we were really going to do it. For the sake of peace I played along, gave Max a ring after breakfast, and then we went around there.

Max was still pretty keen and Mary was interested, although she'd never been involved in anything like this before. Del was really keen. She wanted to come out to the farmhouse with us when we hoisted the money. I told her she was crazy, and she got pissed off. At last I agreed, hoping she'd let it drop. But she didn't.

So that same day saw the four of us on the dirt track out behind Bosco's farmhouse, in Max's car, pretending to be picnickers, with a big bag of money in the boot and shifty looks on our faces, and each of us with enough benzedrine in our bloodstreams to outrun a greyhound.

It had been piss-easy. We'd packed up like we were having a day of picnicking and rabbit shooting. Then we'd driven to the Lands Department in the city and bought a survey map of the district, which marked a track less than half a mile behind where I figured Bosco's house was.

I'd borrowed a .22 from Ted Rallis, just to look the part. Ted didn't quite ask what I wanted the rifle for, but said, "I didn't know you hunted."

"It's for a kind of fancy-dress party."

"Really?" But he asked no more questions.

We all wore dungarees, loaded up a few sangers and a thermos full of scotch. Typical picnic group, except that it was Friday. Max and Mary sat in the front, me and Del in the back. I twice cut up and distributed more benzedrine on the way out there, which made us all feel confident but jumpy; so we swigged from the thermos to calm ourselves down again.

We found the track with no trouble. It was even better than we expected, because from the track we could almost see the farmhouse. We parked in the scrub, walked up a rise to a clearing, and we could see it all.

There were no cars in sight, and no signs of life inside. Some shirts and socks were hanging on a line behind the house, so I assumed Bosco was still around.

I did the same as I had last time, chucked a rock onto the roof to see if anyone was inside. No one came out.

We'd agreed just to have a look, then meet back at the car and plan what to do, but the go-fast had made me impatient. Fuck it, I thought. I walked straight up to the back door while the other three waited a couple of hundred yards back up the hill. I knocked, then I kicked it in. No point trying to cover our tracks, I thought.

The money was still there in the filthy bedroom. I wrapped it up in a grubby pillowcase I found on the floor and walked out, the sack over my shoulder like Santa Claus in reverse.

I ran back up the hill, hooting and yelling, calling out, "Let's fuck the hell off!" Max thought something had gone wrong and started waving the .22 around.

I ran straight past them to the car, still yelling, "Let's go, come on, let's go!"

They stared at me.

"I've got the fucking money!" I called, holding up the pillowcase.

We nearly made it. Max opened the boot and we put the money in. He put the rifle on the floor in the back of the car and we left.

A quarter of a mile down the track we encountered a car coming the other way and I knew it was trouble. We maybe could have bluffed it out but Max put his foot down and went for it. The other car was forced nearly right off the road, and I got a glimpse of

Bosco's face along with three of his goons as we went past. I don't know what they were doing on the back road—maybe they really were shooting rabbits.

They worked out pretty smartly that we were up to no good, turned their car around, and were on our hammer before we'd gone another hundred yards.

"That's Bosco!" I screamed.

They were blasting their horn at us to stop. We skidded along the dirt road and they couldn't get around us, nor could we shake them off. The way we were going, they'd follow us all the way back to Bondi.

Del said, "Listen, we've got to do something—either drop a browneye out the back window, or stop and talk to them. There's no other way." She leaned forward. "Hey, pull up, Max."

He kept driving.

Del turned to me. "They couldn't possibly know yet that we've got their money. Let's talk to them. It's the only way we'll ever get away."

"Jesus, she's right, Max! Pull over! But keep the motor running."

Max stopped. I bounded out of the car with a big friendly grin on my dial, as if to say, "Isn't *this* a wonderful surprise!" I walked over to Bosco's car.

"Ho, Bosco! How the hell are you?" I knew I was overdoing the hail-fellow-well-met business, but I was scared stupid.

Bosco was out of the car yabbering at me, along with two of his mates. One of them I recognized as the bloke who'd pulled the gun on me last time.

"Why are you here, Billy?"

"We're having a picnic—gee, we must be near your place! Aren't we?"

"Yes, Billy, you are going near our place. Your friends must get-

116

ting out of car. Come out, please." He didn't seem like a buffoon right at that moment. The goons were standing beside him.

When I heard the first shot, I thought I was dead for sure.

So did Bosco. Del, leaning out the car window, had blown out the front tire of their car, not a bad shot from where she was—a point not lost on Bosco. Now she had the .22 aimed at Bosco's head. The thugs were looking from Del to Bosco, waiting for a word from him.

"Aw, Bosco, now you've made her cranky." I shrugged my shoulders and made a face to Bosco as if to say "Women!"

Del got out of the car, holding the rifle to her shoulder like a pro.

"Let's not make her any more cranky, eh, Bosco? Move away from the car, please." Bosco spoke to his cronies and they slowly walked over to the right side.

"Del, please shoot the shitter out of the remaining tires." She did, without wasting a single bullet. I kept mugging apologetically at Bosco and the boys.

While Del kept the gun on them, Mary and I searched their car. Mary hadn't said anything, and she was looking pale, with her lips pressed tightly together. I was packing death, but trying to act like I thought this was all a bit of a lark. Max left the car, came over and turned out the fascists' pockets. I could see he wasn't thinking anything too charitable about them. He pocketed their wallets.

Mary and I found two rifles in the boot, which I smashed up as best as I could on a rock.

"OK, Bosco, we'll be toddling off now. I may as well tell you, since you'll find out soon enough anyway, I've borrowed some money from you."

He said something in Yugo, which was clearly the worst swear word the lingo had.

"Now, don't be like that. Believe me, I'll put it to good use. And Bosco, shit, I really hope I don't see you again. There are a couple of federal cops who are really interested in you. I think they'd like to send you and your pals back home, which I'm sure you wouldn't be keen on, you being a fucking Nazi war criminal. So keep the fuck out of my way, and that's the end, or else."

At that Max hooked Bosco a beauty, which knocked him down, with blood coming out of his nose and mouth.

Bosco looked back up at Max and said, "Jew!"

Max just said "Yeah, Jew," as he swung his boot into Bosco's gut.

We returned to our car while Bosco was still retching into the dirt, his buddies trying to comfort him.

Del, who still had the rifle on the Yugos, called out to them "Oy, you, Charlie! Take off your clothes!"

The rest of us stopped. Max said, "What the fuck is she doing now?"

Del waved the rifle at the Yugos. "You heard me, reffos—get your gear off!"

I turned back to them and said, "Go on, boys, better do it."

The Yugos hesitated for a moment, trying to guess just how serious Del was. The gunslinger spat and said something, and then made a run at Del. He was very fast, and by the time Del fired he was only a few feet from her. The bullet took the middle finger of his right hand clean off. So much for his career as a gunsel. He crouched over, howling like a werewolf, holding his right hand in his left. His recently separated finger lay in the dirt at his feet.

Del waved the rifle at the other two. "Sorry we haven't got any music to accompany you boys, you'll just have to imagine it. Now strip."

When they were all naked, Max gathered up their clothes and we got in the car. The gunslinger was sitting on the ground holding his hand, rocking back and forth, while the others were attending to Bosco, who wasn't in too good shape, either. Before we left, Del took the thermos of scotch over and gave the defingered one a swig.

First bridge we crossed, Max chucked the lads' clothes and wallets, minus the money, into the drink. We drove on.

There wasn't much talk in the car until Del said, "That was the worst thing I've ever done."

"He sure won't be sticking that finger up his date again," said Max. Then Del started crying.

"We've got the money," I said, but no one replied. "I don't reckon they can do anything much about it now." Still no answer. No one spoke for another ten minutes.

"All right," I said. "It's too much money. They'll be coming after us. They'll have to. What do we do?"

We counted out the take back at Max's. There was just over sixteen thousand pounds in total, hugely more than Max or I had ever rorted before. We decided we'd wait to do the whack-up till we knew for sure we were in the clear. Max took the money, said he knew just the place for it.

We had poured out strong drinks as soon as we got in. We took some more crank and tried to cheer ourselves up. The money sure helped. Del still didn't feel too good about shooting off the joker's finger, but with her share at over three grand, she was coming round fast.

Mary was still quiet about the whole business. At one point she said to Max, "A year ago I was playing violin under Beecham and Stokowski, and now I'm some kind of drug-fiend widgie gun moll. I'm not at all sure about this."

Max wasn't unsure. He was smoking a cigar, walking around like he was LJ Hooker, pouring drinks and talking faster than Ken

Howard calling the Doncaster.

"I don't see how they can get to us, at least not straight away. They don't know where I live. If they tell your red-headed government man that we've taken their money, sure, he knows where you live, but if you stay clear of there for a bit, well, what can they do?"

I thought, plenty, but I didn't say it.

I made some phone calls and booked into a guest house at Patonga. Del rang Dot, back at the boarding house in Lewisham where they lived, told her not to be concerned; she was going away with me for a few days, and should anyone ask, don't tell them anything. Del told her it would be better if Dot stayed well clear of the Rhythm Club on Sunday.

We drove to Narrabeen, parked the car out of the way, and took the bus the rest of the way to Palm Beach. We caught the twice-a-day ferry across Broken Bay, reaching the village of Patonga that afternoon. We spent Saturday lying low, keeping to the bedroom. There was plenty to keep us busy.

Later, we did a bit of fishing off the jetty and took a walk in the bush. We didn't talk to anyone much at the guest house, which was three-quarters empty anyway.

I rang Max on Saturday night. So far, no one had appeared looking for the money. He said not to forget tomorrow was Sunday, Rhythm Club day. I'd been hoping he might give the dance a miss this Sunday, I said, but Max said no way. I said OK, I'd see him at the usual time.

I hadn't been home since Thursday night—since going to the Metropole with Shoebridge—and I was reluctant to go home now, so Del and I went straight to Max's before going to Bondi.

We got to Perkal Towers at two o'clock. Max was still getting ready. He'd bet big the day before on the Randwick gallops; for once he had won and his confidence was up. Mine wasn't.

Mary wasn't around. I asked Max where she was.

He looked at the floor. "She's not coming today. She's still a bit upset about the fracas with the Ustasha. She's gone to stay with her auntie in Manly for a couple of days."

"Doesn't the money cheer her up? It sure does me."

"She says she doesn't want it."

"Bullshit!"

"Yeah, well, I hope she comes round. She earned her share of the whack."

Del said, "I understand how she feels. It was different the other night, when I was all fired up, you know, when you were telling us about those Croats and the death camps. But jeez, actually shooting a bloke's a different matter. That finger lying on the ground." She shook her head.

"The hands tell a story," I said.

"Mind you, I still want my share of the brass."

Max went to his room, getting ready to go, while Del and I sat in his lounge room, flicking through magazines. I was looking at a *Saturday Evening Post* when I came across it. I called out to Max like I was on fire.

He asked what I wanted.

"Look at this picture."

I showed him an article about the FBI, with a picture of its chief.

He said, "Yeah, so what?"

"That's the Yank who was at the Metropole!"

"Who?"

"Him!" I pointed at the picture.

"*Him?*"

"Yeah, him."

"That's G-Man Hoover!"

"I don't care if it's Jesus H. Christ himself, this bloke was at the Metropole last Thursday."

"He gave the speech?"

"No, this one was watching in the wings. Another bloke gave the speech. I don't think anyone said either of their names."

Max sat down on the lounge.

"Strike me lucky, J. Edgar Hoover in Sydney! Did anybody else there see him?"

"Not really. A few, maybe. I saw him being introduced around to some blokes from something they called the Congress for Cultural Freedom. But they were sort of keeping him out of the way."

"Did any of the press guys see him?"

"I don't think so. When he did make a brief appearance in the main room, after my little musical faux pas, the journos were all half-stung, and probably wouldn't have noticed even if the afore-mentioned Jesus H. Christ had turned up. Anyway, it was all off the record, which means they're honour-bound to keep it under their hat, doesn't it?"

"Sort of. You'd better tell me about this talk. Everything. We'll just have to be late for Bondi."

So I told him. Then Max rang his commo cousin, Andrew, who wrote for the *Tribune*, and told him to meet us at Bondi.

I detoured past Rushcutters Bay on my way to Bondi. Del went on with Max. We tried to persuade her to stay away for today, but she was having none of it.

I'd been wearing clothes borrowed from Max for the last two days and I really wanted to get back into my own threads. I drove down Roslyn Street twice, looking out for jacks' cars, but I couldn't see anything too unusually suspicious. Nearly everything in that part of town was slightly dodgy, and coppers were always pretty thick on the ground, but no one seemed to be watching the flat.

I parked down the street a way and went in up the back stairs. A note had been slipped under the front door. It read: *Contact me ASAP on FA 3671. Urgent!—NS*

This was the first time Shoebridge had given me any way of getting in touch with him. I dialed the number. A male voice answered: "Hello."

"Who am I talking to, please?"

"Who's this?"

"I asked first."

"Who's speaking, please? I must have a name in order to continue this exchange."

"It's J. Edgar Hoover here, but bugger it, I don't feel like talking anymore." I hung up.

I changed, took some benzedrine, filled an overnight bag with clean clothes, smoked half a reefer, and went out to Bondi—out to the biggest shitfight of my life.

Del was on stage when I arrived, singing "Saturday Night Fish Fry" with Max and the band. She had the knack of making the lyrics seem slightly blue, which crowds always love, especially when a good-looking sheila does it.

Max and the boys were getting into it, too. Max's singing was pretty how's-your-father, so when the band got behind someone who could really sing, their enthusiasm increased and their playing improved markedly.

Del sang the verse that goes "The women were jumpin' and screamin' and yellin', the bottles were flying and the fish was smellin.'" She winked when she got to the last part, and the crowd gave a rowdy guffaw. Sooner or later, I thought, we'll be getting a visit from the Vice Squad down here.

There was a pretty good crowd that night, the best yet. I waved hello to O'Keefe waiting at the side of the stage, shook hands with a few of the regulars and took over on the door, which Vic Camellieri had been minding for us. I gave him a quid and did a quick count of the dough so far. It seemed to be well over sixty quid already.

I looked around at the crowd. More than a few of the bodgies were already half-pissed. Normally we refused entry to anyone who was too far gone, but Vic had been letting in all comers. Even though it was Sunday, it was easy enough to buy piss from the night porter up at the Astra Hotel.

Max's cousin Andrew got there pretty soon after I took over the door. I gave him a teacup full of Cutty and told him to go enjoy himself, I'd catch up with him later. Last I saw of him, a widgie had dragged him onto the dance floor and was giving him close instruction on the correct line, bodgie style.

The band took a break and I ran the record player for a while. I played a few platters, surreptitiously smoked the rest of my reefer, sipped away at my Cutty, and gradually began to calm down, thinking we were home clear. Ha.

Back on the door a little later, I happened to glance out front into the milk bar, where the customers came in, past the counter and tables. I saw Noel Shoebridge walk in. He was dressed casual, like he was undercover. Undercover like a gorilla in a sports shirt. I walked away from the door, didn't even take the money from the tray beneath the counter, and tried to lose myself in the crowd. I went to the side of the stage and called to Max, who was playing, pointed at the door. He looked over, spotted Shoebridge by his red hair, and nodded back at me. He signalled for the guitarist to take over, and left the stage. O'Keefe took the mike.

Max joined me on the floor and said, "Where's Andrew?"

"He went for a walk on the beach with a chick."

Del turned up looking truly worried. Before she could say anything, I said, "Yeah, we know, the spymaster's here."

"Look again. The lads just walked in."

"Bosco?"

"Bosco, Fingers, the whole crew."

"Jesus, Mary, and Joseph," said Max.

Whoever first said that the best way to deal with a bully is to punch him soundly in the nose was a prize goose, and obviously had never come across a real bully. The way to deal with a bully is piss off. But sometimes you can't run, or can't run far or fast enough, and this was such a time.

I picked up a microphone stand from beside the stage and moved through the crowd, half-dancing as I went. I saw the Yugos gathered at the door, about seven of them. They hadn't seen any of us yet. One of them had already found the money behind the counter at the door and was slipping it into his pocket. I was about twenty feet from them, when a gap opened up in front of me. With the mike stand up behind me, I ran at them. I timed it pretty well, bringing the stand around as I got up to the knot of Yugos. Two of them went over with my first swing and another with the return. They were right out of it. I'm sure I broke at least one arm. I got another on my next swing, and had the other three backing off as I swung the stand around and around my head. I was actually starting to enjoy it. Then the mike stand slipped out of my sweaty hands. It went flying through Mick's triple-hung window, and I was left standing there like a mug.

I gave my most winning smile and said, "Jesus, Bosco, is that you? Well, I'll be fucked!" The biff that caught the side of my head felt like a Dodge truck, spinning me around, completely disoriented, until the first boot found me. I staggered back, hoping to get clear of the lads. Then I saw at least another dozen blokes had joined Bosco, some of them with pick handles and lumps of wood. I prayed that my part in this would finish real soon.

The whole show had so far only gone for ten seconds or so, and the dancers were just beginning to realize that a blue was well and truly on. I guessed Bosco and his mob intended to grab me and Max, take us away, and belt the tripe out of us until we gave them back the money. But they hadn't figured on the bodgies.

Now, most of the bodgies I knew would rather fight than fuck, and they'd rather drink beer than either of those. Out of deference to me and Max, and to Vic and his dad, the louts who came to our dances had observed an unwritten rule of no fighting in the hall or out in the milk bar. They knew the Bondi wallopers would close us down at the first report of trouble.

But all bets were off now. When the hoods saw me go down, it was on. I copped another biff, maybe from a Yugo, or maybe from a drunken bodgie, I couldn't tell. I crawled on my hands and knees over to the side of the hall and turned around to witness a different kind of dancing. Blokes were on the floor, sliding over tables, punching, kicking, headbutting. One of the Yugos had the mike stand now and was laying waste bodgies at a great rate.

Max was punching the shit out of Bosco, but it didn't seem to be having a whole lot of effect. I saw a girl kicking a bloke down on the deck with her stilettos. People were bleeding, holding heads, unconscious or semi-conscious. It was a riot.

The whack on the head, on top of the booze and drugs, had really disoriented me. I sat slumped under a table watching the brawl. There were at least forty or fifty people brawling now. I couldn't see anything of Shoebridge, but there were plenty of Yugos, and they were doing all right.

The order of events got a bit confused at that point. I crawled out from under the table, intending to get to the door, when I copped a hit on the neck from an axe handle, bouncing off somebody else's head. I went out again, even sort of dreamed for a moment—about the beret-wearing bloke, Shoebridge, Bosco, bodgies.

Next time I woke, I thought I could see Bert Downey and Des, the two federal cops, standing in the doorway. Unlike Shoebridge, they were dressed in copper fig, suits and hats. Normally, their appearance would have caused a stir, but no one was paying any attention to them. The two cops hesitated at the door, unwilling to enter the blitzkrieg.

The crowd closed over again and I lost sight of the cops. I crawled away from the door, back towards the stage.

I found Del crouched down behind the piano. I took her hand and led her down the stairs to the emergency exit. Mick had crates of soft drink stacked against it. I moved the stacks, opened the door a foot, and we slipped out into the back lane.

We walked around the block, back to Campbell Parade, across the street onto the esplanade, across from the Aloha, about sixty yards down.

Even from there you could hear the ruckus. Shouts, screams, oaths, breaking glass, and then sirens approaching.

A few people had stumbled outside, were sitting in the gutter, nursing injuries. A few bodgies and widgies who'd heard the sirens were scattering. I could see Mick king-hitting a Yugo out in front of the milk bar as the first wagon arrived.

Del said, "We'd better get out of here."

"I wonder where Max is."

A car reversed back down the road, burning rubber, stopped right in front of us. Max, cousin Andrew, and O'Keefe.

"Get in!"

Max's lip was puffed out, his eye was swollen, but other than that he was OK. He'd got out before us, had got to his car and started circling the block. He'd intercepted Andrew on his way back to the dance, then continued circling until he caught sight of Del and me.

We got in the car. I took stock of my injuries. I had a big lump on the side of my head, and a bruise on my neck, some sore ribs, but nothing was broken. Del was OK, hadn't been hit, but she was shaken up.

"Thank Christ you're here, Max. Now let's fuck the hell off out of here."

"Hang on, Bill, there's a problem."

"Yeah, I noticed. I'm not going back in there for anything."

"The money's in there."

"Forget it, it's gone. I saw some thieving Yugo fucker take it, pardon my Serbo-Croatian, Del."

"It's all right, I can see you're upset," she said.

"Not *that* money, Bill." Max spoke quietly.

Del and I spoke in unison: "Fuck!"

Del said, "You mean you had the sixteen grand in *there*? You said you knew a good place for it!"

"I did. I was going to give it to Andrew to look after. Communists are very careful with money."

Andrew said. "I don't know whether to take that as an insult or not."

"So what happened?" I said.

"I brought it along to give to him tonight. It was hidden in the piano. It's still there, I hope."

"We've got to go back, then. Jesus. We can't go yet, though."

Andrew said, "Drive back there. I'll go in."

"You'll be pinched."

"Maybe not. I'm an insurance assessor by trade. I can say I'm on the job."

He was dressed for the part, conservative suit, straight out of Martin Place, except for the sand in his trouser cuffs.

We pulled up in a street a couple of blocks away, and Andrew and I walked back to the Aloha. I halted at the corner while Andrew went in. There were two paddy wagons out front, and two cars, but the bodgies had all long since left—arrested, hospitalized, or they'd simply shot though.

Andrew came back ten minutes later.

"No money. Cops challenged me straight up, I told them I was doing a preliminary assessment for an insurance claim from Harry Landis Music Shop. They believed me. The piano's been pretty smashed up. Definitely no money. *Anyone* could have it."

"Except us."

We dropped O'Keefe at his place at Waverley and went back to Max's. I didn't even bother with my car, which was still at Bondi.

I rang my landlady. She was frightened. She said some rough people had been looking for me—New Australians, and very rude. They had insisted on searching my flat. I asked when; she said they'd left ten minutes ago. After them, the same two government men who'd been there before arrived. She said the government bloke, Mr. Downey, had left a phone number, would I get in touch?

She said the New Australians had left a terrible mess in my flat, and she hadn't been sure whether to call the police or not. She hadn't, waiting till she spoke to me. I thanked her, told her everything was all right, a small misunderstanding, I'd be away for a few more days. She was the most tolerant landlady I'd ever had. I made a mental note to get her a bottle of Porphyry Pearl and a hot mantel radio from Ted Rallis.

I told the others the Yugos had just been at my place. "That probably means they didn't get the money, which means they're still on our hammer. We're doubly in the shit."

"Does Shoebridge know about me?" Max had poured brandies for the four of us.

"He's never mentioned your name to me, but he knew all about the Rhythm Club, and he'd read the stuff you put in the paper. So, yeah, he'd have to know about you."

"Which means he'd know where I live."

"Maybe he never bothered to find out. Are you in the phone book?"

"Under my real name, Perkal. If he knows me from the press he'd only know me as Peck. But if he really is with the Security Service, he could find me easily enough. So it's probably only a matter of time until the coppers are banging on my door."

"Well, yeah, maybe. But maybe not."

"How?"

I lit a Craven A. "He was there tonight with the Yugos, but there weren't any other Security Service people with him. None that I could see."

"Right. So?"

"If we've really broken the law, he could have us all locked up."

"Yeah?"

"So why act like Jimmy Cagney?"

"What are you saying, that he's acting one out?"

"I don't know—maybe. The federal cops don't know about him, and they really *are* the law. Shoebridge himself is in with Ray Waters, but that's no guarantee that it's all aboveboard. The opposite's more likely true, in fact."

Andrew spoke then. "The Security Service are strange people, they're all mad king-and-country types, but often paranoiacs as well. They get plenty of money, though—they don't have to go through normal government purchase procedures. I've never heard of any of them being on the take, but with that much dough flying around, who knows? One thing's sure: you can't stay here."

"We sure can't go to my place."

"I think I know a place where we can all lie low."

Turned out Andrew had access to a whole network of safe houses and hideouts that the Communist Party had had since wartime, when the party had been outlawed. When Menzies started talking about banning the Party, they'd reactivated their underground in preparation. The referendum to ban the party had been lost, but the comrades were still playing it safe.

Andrew took us to a house in Bellevue Hill. It was pretty sparse, but had a few beds, a kitchen stocked with canned food, a radio, and a phone. Once we'd more or less settled in, we told Andrew the story. He was shocked that Max had been a party to a major theft. Max accused him of being petit-bourgeois, Andrew counter-denounced him as a lumpen opportunist. Max said who gives a shit.

Andrew lit up when we told him the J. Edgar Hoover stuff, though. He said it fitted with the philosophical turn the Security Service was taking: adopting American mass-surveillance practices, screening academics, teachers, public servants, and politicians for potential security risks—poofs, left-wingers, drunks, perverts, compulsive gamblers, drug addicts, habitual criminals. I said just about everyone I knew was at least one of those things.

The problem was how to make use of the info so as to squeeze Shoebridge and get the Ustasha and maybe the entire Australian Security Service off our backs. And get the money back. Andrew went off to confer with his party cronies, and the three of us drank ourselves into a semi-stupor.

Bodgie Rampage at Bondi

At least 30 people were injured in a wild melee at a Bondi jive dance last night.

Ambulances ran a shuttle service, delivering patients suffering from broken bones, head injuries, concussion, cuts, abrasions, and even knife wounds to Eastern Suburbs Hospital after over a hundred bodgies and widgies staged a wild brawl at the Aloha Milk Bar.

Detective Sergeant Ern Collins of Bondi police said it was one of the most violent disturbances he had witnessed in 25 years as a policeman.

So far 15 people have been charged with offenses ranging from assault to offensive behavior, but police believe they have not yet tracked down the ringleaders.

"Some of the people we arrested were local bodgies, but we also found a number of New Australians, Yugoslavs, in the thick of the fighting. We don't know yet what exactly the New Australians, most of whom gave addresses from outside the metropolitan area, were doing at the dance in the first place, or why the trouble actually broke out," said Sgt. Collins.

It is believed Federal Police were also on the scene. Today the Immigration branch of the Federal Police refused to comment on the matter other than to say that investigations into the incident are proceeding.

One unconfirmed report says the New Australians were members of a Croatian patriotic club based in Sydney.

Further muddying the waters, say the police, is the fact that many of the injured and arrested bodgies are themselves New Australians, of Italian and Maltese descent. Sgt. Collins said he was very eager to talk with the dance organizers, colorful Sydney identity Max Peck and his partner, Bill Glasheen, who so far have not been located.

(Daily Telegraph, 26th September, 1955)

Del went in to work at Repat on Monday morning. Max rang his mum back at the flats and told her he was all right. He got a call from Andrew mid-morning and went off to meet him. I spent the day reading the papers. There were no music or sports mags at the hideout, nor any westerns or detective stories, so I sat around smoking and reading old copies of the *Tribune*.

Late in the afternoon, Max rang to say they had a plan. He couldn't talk about it over the blower, so he gave me an address in

Riley Street, Surry Hills, and told me to come over straight away.

The address was a terrace house up near the new Housing Commission flats. I found three comrades there, along with Max and Andrew. The three were serious-minded chaps. They were curt, gee'd up.

First off, they had me dictate as much as I could of the talk I'd heard at the Metropole. I remembered quite a lot of it, to their surprise. They had me describe who was there. I gave a physical description of Shoebridge and then the Colonel, and the comrades nodded to each other, pleased.

Then I described the Yanks, told about recognizing the photograph of J. Edgar Hoover as the fellow I'd seen in the wings at the hotel room. One of the comrades took it all down as I spoke. Then they had me sign the statement, and one of them witnessed it and signed it as well, signing himself "Justice of the Peace," which struck me as funny, as we were already so deeply into illegal goings-on. The comrades didn't see it that way.

Then I rang the number Shoebridge had left, and this time got another person on the phone. I asked for Shoebridge, he said who was calling, I said don't give me the shits, he said he'd hang up if I didn't identify myself. I'd read that they could trace phone calls right to the phone you were ringing from, but it took time, so I figured maybe the guy was just stringing me along. I told the bloke I'd ring back in five minutes, that if Shoebridge didn't answer I'd hang up again.

When I rang back, Shoebridge answered on the second ring.

"So, Bill, things have got rather out of hand."

"Listen, silver-tongue, pay attention. Call the Balts off, we haven't got the money anymore, it was stolen from us. We all lose. Bad luck. Next, go to Surry Hills post office. There's a letter for you at the counter. It's a copy of a statutory declaration exposing the presence of J. Edgar-fucking-Hoover in Sydney, and the covert activities of the Congress for Cultural Freedom, and the collusion of the Security Service. If I ever see you again, copies go to the *Sydney Morning Herald*, the *Age*, and the *Tribune*, who'd just love to run the story. If I disappear, or anything happens to my friends, same deal."

"I thought you said you were apolitical."

"I got politicized."

I hung up before he could say anything else.

The comrades were dying to run the story, but I told them its value to me lay in its not being run, and if they ran it without my consent, I'd swear that the stat dec was a forgery.

Andrew and the comrades went off, leaving Max and me at the house. Max was acting mysterious. He reckoned he knew a way out—just do what he said, and it'd be all right.

We found Bosco's number in the book. The federal copper had told me his second name, Udovic, and the only trouble we had was guessing how to spell it.

Bosco himself answered when I rang. I said, "Bosco, how are you, son? Billy here."

He muttered one of those Slavic swear words at me, and I said, "Now, Bosco, settle down. Let's get together, see what we can sort out. But you must come alone, or else I won't see you."

"All right, Billy. I will coming."

"Yeah, good, Bosco, you coming. And, Bosco, don't bring any guns. There are no rabbits here." I gave him the address. I hung up and said to Max, "We're sitting ducks here."

He winked and said, "It's cool, trust me." Then we took some benzedrine, sat back, and waited for Bosco.

He arrived at four-thirty. He parked his car right out front. I was sitting in the kitchen, we had the front door open, the afternoon sun was shining down the hallway, and I watched as he got out of the car and approached the front gate.

Then he stopped and reached behind his back, under his coat, and pulled out a revolver. Max had gone outside a little while before, and I was alone in the kitchen, wondering what the fuck I was doing. I looked around me, and there was absolutely nothing to hand that I could use as a weapon.

I did what we'd planned and called out to Bosco, who probably couldn't make me out in the dark house. "Bosco, come in, this way." Thinking, Jesus Christ, this is it.

As Bosco stepped through the gate, two silhouetted figures slipped into view right behind him. A sap swung at his head and he went down.

They dragged him out of my view. I stayed in the kitchen, and less than a minute later Max came running into the house, excited.

"Come on, Billy, out the back, the car's out there! Quick!"

His Hudson was in the back lane. We drove away.

"So who the hell was that?"

"I'll tell you later. We've all got to clear out for a while. Mary's already out of the way. Ring Del at work from a public phone and take her away for a few days, anywhere. I'm going bush, too. Just trust me."

I did what he said. Del was getting ready to leave work when I rang. I told her the shit had hit the fan. She said what, again? What else could go wrong? she asked. I told her plenty, at least according to Max.

We picked her up, went to her boarding house for some things, then we went to my flat and did the same again. Then Max dropped us at Central, to get a train to the mountains. We made a trunk call to a guest house in Leura and booked in for a week.

I said to Max, this is another fine mess you've got me into. He said we should try to relax while we were away, enjoy the springtime up there, not to come back till we heard from him, but after a few days we'd either be in the clear or in jail. He was going to Newcastle, to a friend of Andrew's.

Max had raided his last-resort money stash, in his mum's flat, for his emergency hundred quid, which we split. As Del and I got on the train, Max standing there on the platform didn't look like a figure to inspire confidence. He was unshaven, haggard and hunted-looking from booze and benzedrine. In his gabardine overcoat he looked liked one of those Jewish refugees you used to see in the newsreels.

We didn't do too much bushwalking up there. It rained for three days, then a cold fog settled in for another couple of days. Del was pretty quiet through it all. Mary had shot through from Max, and I could tell Del was asking herself how the hell she got involved in all this, ending up without a zack to show for it. We were the bad companions she'd been warned about as a kid.

We borrowed some books from the council library—Del got a couple of Ellery Queens and I got Carter Browns and Erle Stanley Gardners. I read the papers every day, but there was nothing more about the Bondi fracas, except for an editorial in the *Telegraph* to the effect that all bodgies should be sent to military-style prisons for indefinite detention, and that jungle music and bodgie haircuts should be outlawed.

On Thursday we went to the flicks at the Savoy in Katoomba, the next town, and saw *The Postman Always Rings Twice*—not such a good choice for a couple of people hiding from the law.

Next morning, a message at the reception desk asked me to ring Max at the Carrington Hotel in Katoomba.

They put me through to his room. I asked what he was doing up here, and how long had he been here? Since yesterday, he said. I'd better come round to the hotel instead of talking over the phone.

We called a cab to take us to Katoomba, ten minutes away.

Max was booked into a big room, with a view over the main street to the Jamieson Valley in the distance.

Max was nervous and wouldn't give a straight answer to my questions. He asked us to sit down and have a drink.

We sat around a coffee table and had Remy Martins all round.

Max said, "Billy, Del, I'd like you to meet someone."

He went to the door, opened it, and the foxy-looking guy, this time without a beret, walked in.

"Del, Billy, may I present Igor."

The bloke bowed his head slightly and clicked his heels. "It is my pleasure to meet you."

He walked over and kissed Del's hand. Del gave him a big smile. I thought, Jesus, these New Australians can bung it on.

Then he came over and shook my hand and said, "I most regret my behaviour last time we met." That was when he'd bopped me on the noggin and left me out in the mulga, hung over and confused. Now he was grinning very slightly, like maybe he didn't regret it all that much.

He went on. "On that occasion, it was necessary to interrupt you, for your own good and for ours. My apologies. I trust you suffered no lasting injuries."

I looked over at Max and said, "Okay, I'll bite, who the fuck is this clown?"

Max half-whispered, half-mouthed something like, "He works for 2GB." I thought, so fucking what?

Igor said, "Bill, I am a friend. Let us leave it at that. Firstly, I must tell you that Bosco Udovic will not give you any more trouble."

"Yeah? Why is that?"

"He has been repatriated to his beloved fatherland."

"What's he doing there?"

"Awaiting trial."

"Is that so? What nationality are you?"

"I am Croatian."

"Like Bosco?"

He smiled at me and shook his head. "I am not like Bosco."

Max caught my eye and mouthed it again: 2GB.

I said, "For Jesus' sake, Max, I don't care if he works for 2GB or 2KY or the AB-fucking-C, what's that got to do with anything? I'm in the dark, this bloke has been spooking around throughout this whole business. He's not on our side, he's clearly up to no good, and I don't like any of it."

At that I hooked Igor. He went down, but not out.

I shrugged and said, "Sorry."

He got up smartly and said, "Billy, that is quite all right. Perhaps I should explain myself. Your friend Max has been trying to signal to you the name of my organization. Let me just say it's not 2GB, but . . . ah, well, let me leave it to you."

Del said, "Billy, I think he means KGB."

"Oh, shit."

I sat down and lit another Craven A, took a swig of brandy and turned to Max. "OK, so he does a beaut Peter Lorre. What good is he to us?"

"He has the money."

"He has?" I turned to him. "You got it with you, Igor?"

"No, but it is quite safe."

"So why are you here?"

"Max has pointed out that the only way we can conclude this affair is to reach an amicable arrangement. I agree with him completely."

Max came over to me, saying, "Excuse us a tick, Igor." Then he whispered to me and Del, "He's got the brass, but he's prepared to give it back. To us, I mean. Minus a cut."

"I don't trust him," I said.

"He has to play ball with us. We've got the goods on him. We can fuck him up completely."

I turned to Igor and said, "So where is the money now?"

"Do you know the Matraville Migrant Hostel?"

"Oh, Jesus."

"It is perfectly safe. If you like, we can go there now, yes?"

Max said, "Why don't we go together. You can all get acquainted on the way."

"That'll be ever so jolly."

We went in Max's car.

Max drove, Igor in the front seat, happy as a kid on his way to the Easter Show with his best pals. Del and I sat in the back. I smoked, sipped at the brandy bottle. I passed the bottle to Max, who took a drink and offered it to Igor, who refused.

There was a foggy drizzle falling. The road was slippery, and we saw no one much in the little mountain towns we passed through. The bottle came back to me.

"So, Igor, you say you're a Croat," I said.

"I am Croatian, not Croat."

"Pardon me ever so much. Croatian, then. I've heard you lot are all mad pro-Nazis."

"I am Croatian, but I am anti-Fascist, and I fought with the underground during the war."

"Whacko for you, you're a fucking hero." Del dug me in the ribs. "So why did you job me and leave me out in woop woop?"

"It appeared that you were about to take the money from Bosco, which would have been very unfortunate." He turned around as he said it, still with that smart-arse half-smile.

"Yeah, beating you to it," I said, thinking, you thieving prick. "So you'd been out watching Bosco's farm, same as the federal cops?"

"We kept an eye on activities at the farm, yes. But not while the police were there. We were there when you searched the place, and we went back later after the Bondi fight. Bosco was there, but his group had dispersed. We lost them."

"Pardon me a heap for having thwarted the KGB."

I went silent for a while, thought about what he'd said. "So tell me, are you acting for your . . . company now, or are you acting on your own?"

He paused for a long moment. "There is no simple answer to that question."

"Fuck that, I need to know who we're dealing with."

Del said, "Yeah, me too. Better give us an answer, Iggy."

Igor turned to us. "My parent organization has been, ah, unsettled for some time, and my own position was for a while uncertain. I made contingency plans." He stopped talking and stared out the windscreen.

"Yeah, so?"

Max came in. "Back in Russia, Igor's big boss, one Comrade Beria, got the boot, and all his pals ended up dead or in Siberia. Meanwhile, back here, Petrov defected from the Soviet Embassy and got a new start in Australia, courtesy of Mr. Menzies." Max glanced at Igor. "Iggy thought that might be the hip thing to do— follow Petrov's lead."

"So are you on our side now, or what?"

"And what exactly *is* your side, Billy?"

"The side of the free fucking world, you egg."

Igor smiled at me like I was a moron. "To defect is not a good thing," he said, then went silent again.

I said, "Are we supposed to put a shilling in the slot or something?"

But Igor remained silent. Max continued for him. "The Petrov business got complicated. Over in Russia, you denounce someone, and the denouncee gets thrown in the hoosegow, bang, simple as that. And it's not a jail like Malabar Mansion—it's a poxhole in outback Siberia, or up in the Arctic circle or someplace. See, that's what Petrov thought would happen here—he says, "Oh cripes, yeah, X, Y and Z, they're all fuckin' spies," thinking that's the end of them, they're history. But instead, him and his missus were asked to substantiate their claims in a court of law."

Igor took over. "And after all that, they have not been greatly rewarded. Petrov has been resettled in the area euphemistically known as 'Surfer's Paradise.'"

"A bit of swampy coastland over the Queensland border. Yeah, I know it."

"Indeed, I have heard that a parcel of land was bought from a speculator named Mr. Freddy Long, an old associate of yours."

"The Jap? Well, I'll be fucked."

"So I chose not to follow Petrov's lead. But I needed a success to demonstrate my loyalty to my new superiors. I was contacted by mutual friends. I decided to, ah, intercept Bosco Udovic and send him back to Yugoslavia, where he will be tried as an enemy of the people, and a paid stooge of western security. I will be commended. I have denounced my erstwhile controller as a supporter of Beria, thereby forestalling any such charges against myself."

"Remind me never to do business with you," I said.

Igor laughed richly.

Del said, "So what do you actually do in Australia? Officially, I mean. Are you a diplomat? Your English is too good for you to pass as a reffo."

"Thank you for the compliment. But I can speakingk like ze New Australian if you are vonting, no?"

"Crikey," I said.

"I am a genuine New Australian. I work on the assembly line at General Motors Holden at Pagewood. And I lead a small Croatian Nationalist Group, based at Matraville, called Free Croatia."

"An anti-communist group?"

"Of course. We have barbecues with the local Liberal Party candidate."

"Where do the federal police fit in?"

"They are reliant on moderate groups within émigré communities for their information."

"Which means you?"

He gave a big grin, and a continental gesture, as if to say, "Shit, eh?"

"Jesus, so they are mates of yours after all. Do they know about the money?"

"I certainly haven't told them."

I finished off the bottle and said to no one in particular, "This bloke's a smooth mongrel. It might all be true or it might be all bullshit. How would we know?"

Igor smiled at me. "Please be patient," he said. "Everything will work out."

It took over two hours to get back to town. We turned off the highway at Strathfield, past Canterbury Racetrack, through Mascot to Pagewood, then along Bunnerong Road, past the GMH factory. The hostel was half a mile further along.

It was a huge complex of Nissen huts, a wartime army base. Now with chain link fencing around it, a couple of crowded playgrounds and a few thousand migrants, it looked like a refugee camp you'd see on a newsreel. The whole site was set among scrubby sandhills and bits of swamp, right at the centre of a big arc made up of Botany Cemetery, Bunnerong Power Station, Long Bay Jail, and a rubbish tip. Guess it made the migrants feel pretty welcome.

At first I refused to go into the hostel itself, said it'd be crazy of us to walk into a Croat stronghold. Igor said it was no more a Croat stronghold than it was a Hungarian, Estonian, Italian, Serb, or even an English one, for that matter. He said we were mutually dependent, which guaranteed each side against a double cross.

Max didn't seem too worried. He said there were probably more federal cops at the hostel than anywhere else in Sydney. He patted his jacket pocket as he spoke, which I took to mean he was tooled up.

We drove through the gates and parked beside the second hut. Inside was a caretaker's office, a common area, and a communal shower block. There were a few chairs about in the common room, and fuck-all else. There were signs everywhere—no alcohol to be consumed on the premises, no gambling, no music after 8 p.m., no washing to be hung in the common room, no guests after 10 p.m. I said to Igor it'd probably be more convivial up the road at Long Bay.

No one paid much attention to us—a few more unshaven, shifty-looking characters among the throng. Igor led us down a corridor, through masonite partitions which went to a height of about nine feet. Above that it was open, so the rooms were actually not rooms at all, just enclosures. It was two o'clock, but there were plenty of people around, and voices wafted in from all over, unhindered by any real walls.

We went into a smaller corridor and then into a tiny room, with an iron-framed bed, a single-ring gas burner, a sink, a battered kitchen cabinet, a lowboy, an ancient fridge, a card table, and two stacking chairs. It made even the Cosy Private Hotel look flash.

Igor spread his arms, hands turned up in a gesture of apology, and said: "Chez Igor." He gestured for us to sit down.

He brought out a bottle of clear spirits and poured glasses for all of us.

"So where's the loot, Igor?" said Max, nervous now, his hand near his pocket.

"Please, Del, Billy, Max, don't be alarmed." He stood up, went to the door, and called out, "Stefan, please come here."

He came back inside with Fingers behind him. Max leaped up, waved his revolver at the two of them, and said, "Don't fucking move!"

Del and I were standing, ready to do whatever we had to, but Igor just smiled. "Please, my friends, sit down. Everything is all right. May I present Stefan Meza, my new colleague?"

Stefan nodded to all of us, and bowed slightly to Del. His right hand was heavily bandaged. He was scrubbed up, though, wearing a new-looking leather jacket.

Del reached nervously into her handbag for a smoke. Stefan whipped his lighter out and lit her smoke, bowed again. Del smiled back at him, despite herself.

"Stefan has ended his association with the terrorists. Perhaps, Max, you might put that away. Del and Billy, you will sit down, and Stefan will tell us his story."

Then he turned to Fingers and said, "Stefan?"

Stefan cleared his throat and began. "I am with Udovic for two years. We meet, we train, we talk. We are getting money from Shoebridge and donations from the church. Udovic tells us he sends money to freedom fighters, that one day we too will go to Yugoslavia to fight. He tells us he keeps only five hundred pounds in his house, for our group. Then you take money, and I am wondering if five hundred pounds is true." He turned to Del. "You are shooting my finger."

"Yeah, gee, I'm as sorry as anything about that."

He made one of those so-what-it's-no-big-deal gestures and went on. "So I am thinking, does lady shoot rifle for five hundred pounds? For love, for honour, yes." He smiled at Del. "For five hundred pounds, no. So Bosco says we must get money back."

He looked across to Igor, who nodded at him, gestured for him to go on.

Stefan lit a smoke. "Bosco talks to Shoebridge, and we meet him at Bondi, go to your dance. We fight. After you run away, we fight with bodgie boys and bodgie girls. I am angry—at you, at bodgies, at Shoebridge, and at Bosco. I see piano, and I am pushing it off stage onto floor. Then I find money. Not five hundred pounds."

"Did Shoebridge know about this?" I asked.

"No. I am not trusting Shoebridge any more. He is bloody bad bastard. I think Shoebridge and Bosco plan to take money."

Igor had poured Stefan a drink and he took a sip. "Then I see Igor. We talk. Igor makes many things clear to me, about Bosco, about Yugoslavia, about Australia. Now I believe the Motherland is best served by me joining Igor and his friends."

He looked across to Igor, who smiled, like he was saying, aw shucks, it was nothing much. "So Stefan decided to join my group," Igor said, "and we have received him with open arms."

"Is that the KGB or Free Croatia?"

Igor laughed, but didn't answer.

I could see it coming—a five-way whack-up, if we were lucky. The Yugos had the money, so our position was even weaker.

Max seemed to pick up what I was thinking. He turned to me. "It seems we're in a position of mutual dependence here. The way I see it, Igor owes us, since we enabled his advancement within the KGB and saved him from Siberia or worse. And we can still denounce him at any time, through the comrades, if he doesn't play ball. I imagine his superiors would take an extremely dim view of him keeping any of the money he found."

Max looked to Igor, who nodded in confirmation, maybe admiration. "At the same time, we owe Igor something, since he got rid of Bosco and won over Stefan here, who we might just need in case Shoebridge ever tries to get the money back, and we're forced to expose him as a scoundrel."

I thought, that'd be great, we go public against ASIO using the testimony of a commo spy and a would-be Nazi terrorist as our proof.

Max still had the gun in his hand. "So, we owe you *something*, boys." He paused, looking from Igor to Stefan and raising the gun again like he was ready to shoot someone. "But not that fucking much."

I came in. "You know, Max, I'm a bit sick of this bullshit. Why don't we just shoot these two fuckers, bolt, and forget about the money?"

"You know, that's not a bad idea, Billy Boy." He had started using the same voice he used when he played the bad guy on Smokey Dawson's radio show.

Igor didn't seem all that fazed, but Stefan was looking real jumpy.

Igor made placating gestures to Max and to Stefan, then said, "Max, Billy, Del, allow me to make a proposal. As I told you, I have recently taken a job at the Holden factory, and this is not much to my liking. I have managed to convince my superiors that my work could be better accomplished if I were to start a small business in the district, one which kept me in close contact with the émigré community. Rather perversely, my controller said that he would approve such a move if I was able to find a way to finance the venture myself. In a land of opportunity like Australia, he said, I should have little trouble in launching a capitalist enterprise."

"What did you have in mind, Igor?"

"I would like to start a travel agency, and later perhaps buy a television set. This would make me very happy."

"How much do you want?" I said.

"Two thousand pounds would suffice."

"What about the wild one here?" I said, nodding in Stefan's direction.

"Stefan is simply grateful for the opportunity to serve. However, a thousand pounds would be a suitable expression of gratitude for the services he has already performed, and compensation for the injury he has suffered."

Three grand. Not too bad, and it still left thirteen big ones for the rest of us. I looked across at Del, raised my eyebrows to signal *what do you reckon*? She shrugged, like *whatever you think's a fair thing*. Max nodded his agreement.

"Sweet with me," I said.

I never talked to Igor again, though I saw him once or twice going in and out of Balkan Travel, the business he opened at Kingsford. The last time I saw him, I was driving past in my new Customline just as Igor walked out with Bert Downey. Downey looked up and saw me, looked over the Customline, and doffed his hat at me.

Stefan I saw a few times. He went to visit Del a few weeks after the whack-up—he thought he'd put a bit of work in on her, I guess, but ended up falling for sister Dot. They got engaged after a while. Stefan Meza wanted to change his name to Steve May, but Dot made him hang onto the Stefan, said it sounded more sophisticated and continental. To me and Del he was still "Fingers," though, and eventually even Dot started calling him that. Their kids will probably end up calling him that, too.

Mary went back to London. She didn't want her share of the take, said she didn't feel right about it. Max eventually persuaded her to accept enough to pay the plane fare.

We gave fifteen hundred quid to Mick Camellieri, who refurbished the shop. He had his cousin paint a mural on the back wall, depicting a seaside scene, a kind of combination of Malta, Hawaii, and Bondi Beach, with Harbour Bridge in the background for good measure. He reopened the dancehall as a roller-skating rink, and made a packet.

I read in the paper in December that my old boss, Laurie O'Brien, had been done for a horse-substitution rort. Word around town was that he'd fallen out with Ray Waters in a big way. He went to trial for conspiracy and copped two years at Long Bay.

I didn't get back to see Jack Davey again until January, 1956. It was at the Macquarie Auditorium, early on a Tuesday afternoon. They were recording three nights' worth of Jack's radio quiz program, *The Ampol Show*. Max was playing in the band, and Del was singing a guest spot. Dot had pretty well given up the entertainment business in deference to Stefan's wishes—he believed that a wife should stay at home, not parade around performing lewd hula dances with men perving at her.

I'd been hanging loose. Max and I hadn't attempted to put on any more Rhythm Reviews, at Bondi or anywhere else. Max had his eye on the Leichhardt Police Boys Club for his next effort, but I was leery of having that much to do with police.

There was no urgency. I had money in the bank, and was still driving around in the new Customline I'd bought on hire purchase. When it rains, it pours, and Jack was keen to make good the sixty quid he owed me. He was temporarily out of cash, he said, but he knew how he could send a few quid my way. Would I like to go on the show as a contestant? He liked to keep a wide spread among the contestants, he said, a balance of men and women, old and young, old Aussie and new Australian. He needed a youngish bloke to balance out the numbers. I was on enough of a winning run to say, shit, why not?

The band played a song, then Jack joked with the crowd. Everything was recorded on tape, but none of the crowd-warming stuff would be used; it was too risqué for public broadcast. Davey was a great judge of filth, and managed to keep the gags right on the borderline.

Watching the auditorium from the wings was something. Old codgers, mums, school kids, good-looking sorts—faces lit up like you don't often see in a crowd.

The show proper started. When it was my turn Jack introduced me as a "commission agent," which was a meaningless term that SP bookies and lurk men sometimes used to make their work sound more legitimate.

My questions were all pretty easy, and my winnings were up to fifty quid when my final question came up.

Jack said "All right, Billy, for double or nothing, choose the correct answer. Croatia is (a) a disease of the brain which causes forgetfulness; (b) a region in Central Europe; or (c) a symphony written by the composer Igor Stravinsky. Which is it?"

I looked across to the bandstand. Max nodded at me. I remembered that he earned a little extra framing quiz questions for Jack. I laughed and gave him the answer.

3

SEPTEMBER 1957

I watched the Pan Am Constellation appear out of the clouds to the south of Botany Bay. I should have felt good about it, since I had a financial stake in the venture, but standing there in the cold, dry wind, I was full of misgivings.

You could smell smoke from the bush fires around Sydney, and southwest of the airport huge banks of it rose up to the sky, trailing right across the southern horizon out over the sea. There'd been a drought all year, and even though it was freezing cold, bush fires kept breaking out up and down the New South Wales coast.

There were eight of us there, sent by Lee Gordon to welcome the stars of his latest Big Show. Besides us, there were two junior reporters from the *Mirror* and the *Truth*, five uniformed coppers, twenty or thirty bodgies and widgies, and the Movietone Newsreel guys.

The plane taxied round to the terminal. When they brought the mobile steps into position and opened the door, I thought I saw the hostess swap raised eyebrows with the flight steward. She put her face back together and tried to smile as the passengers filed out past her.

The small herd crossed the tarmac, holding on to their hats, women holding down their skirts against the wind. Towards the back of the crowd, mixed in with the gray and blue woollen clothing, I could see flashes of more gaudy fabric—fake leopard skin, large red-and-white checks, blue sharkskin, a coat with tiger-stripe lapels, silver-flecked sports coats, women in satin slacks.

The respectable passengers hurried across the tarmac, separating themselves from the entourage of lairs, a few of whom seemed to be staggering slightly. As they drew up to the Customs Hall entrance, I saw at the centre a Negro with a pompadour haircut and thin moustache. We could hear his voice changing pitch erratically as his hands fluttered and his eyes rolled. He was wearing lipstick and mascara. It had to be Little Richard Penniman.

The coppers looked at each other and I heard one say, "Jesus, the Abo's queer!"

I was unable to do a head count, but the whole party looked to be eight or nine people short of the thirty or so we were supposed to be meeting.

The entourage disappeared into the Customs Hall.

I paced up and down, smoking cigarettes.

Fifteen minutes later, Little Richard and another Negro gent came out.

I walked up to Richard and put my hand out. "I'm Billy Glasheen. Welcome to Australia. My apologies, but Mr. Gordon has been detained."

"I'm pleased to meet you, Billy." He spoke in a subdued manner, and his hands trembled.

The guy next to him put out his hand. "I'm Charlie Connors."

We shook. Richard wiped his hand across his face, took a deep breath.

"Are you OK?" I said, "Is there anything I can get you?"

"Thanks, I'm fine. But I'd like to get out of here, if you please."

Charlie looked from him to me and said, "Damn, but it's a long way to Australia. We didn't have such a good flight." He leaned over so that Richard couldn't hear. "At least, Richard didn't."

"No? How come?"

"Richard's never been so far from home. He, ah, was looking out the window there, and he kind of thought the engine was on fire."

"Yeah?"

"Yeah. Last night, the engines were kind of glowing red, and Richard thought there were angels out there dancing on the damn wing." He looked back around at Richard, who had sat down on his suitcase. He patted him on the shoulder, turned back to me and said, "But it's OK, he'll be fine."

"All right then. Who's missing, Charlie?"

"Gene Vincent and them Blue Cap boys. They all got on the plane drunk—man, I mean, drunk as goats. They caused so much ruckus, they put them off the plane in Hawaii, said they were a danger."

"Shit!"

I had a list of all the artistes, and I'd worked out a schedule of who was to go in what car.

I made all the necessary introductions, teamed the musicians up with their drivers and saw them all off. That should have left Eddie Cochran and Alis Lesley, as well as the comedian on the show, one Marty Jay, plus his travelling companion.

Eddie and Alis were waiting patiently, but there was no sign of Marty Jay. I asked Cochran if he could see him anywhere. I had no idea what he even looked like.

"He ain't too well, sir. That's him over there with the blonde."

He pointed to a guy with horn-rim glasses, a check sports jacket, and a flattop, sitting down with his head in his hands. Next to him was Molly Price, my old girlfriend. She'd split for Los Angeles in 1952 when I was in trouble over Charlie Furner's death. I hadn't seen her, or heard from her, or heard anything about her since then.

For a moment I doubted it really was Molly. Then she stood up, walked over to me, and said "Hello, Billy." Like that Hank Williams song says, a picture from the past came slowly stealing.

She was a month younger than me, thirty this year, but up close she looked older than that. There were dark rings under her eyes.

"So, you got out of that hassle you were in?"

"Yeah. There've been a few since then, though. How are you, Molly?"

She shrugged her shoulders, bobbed her head slightly. The flat-top guy looked over at us and called out, "For Chrissake, when are we getting out of this shithole?"

"You're with *him*?" I asked.

Molly went back to him, took his arm, and led him over. "Billy Glasheen, Marty Jay."

"Yeah, great, charmed I'm sure. Let's blow."

"Rough flight, eh?"

"Just get the fucking bags and take us to the hotel."

Cochran looked away, Alis Lesley blushed, and Molly muttered, "Jesus, Marty!"

"Sorry, man, no offense meant."

"You're the comedian?"

Halfway into town, Marty spewed out the window of the Chev.

Molly patted him gently, then leaned over and said to me in a low voice, "Billy, I need you to do something special for us."

"Molly, I'm in the middle of the biggest rort of my life, there's a gang of thugs after me, and I've hardly slept for two days. Now, what is it you want?"

"Heroin."

Rock 'n' roll music had broken in Australia late in 1955, first with the release of Bill Haley's "Rock around the Clock," then later with Elvis Presley's "Heartbreak Hotel."

Max had seen it coming and had nearly cashed in. In February 1956, with my girlfriend Del Keene on vocals, he cut a tune called "Rocking Matilda" with "Mama, He Treats Your Daughter Mean" on the flip. The radio stations picked it up and it was a bit of a hit. Then they went on television.

Del was a big hit on the tube, but on her third appearance on *TV Disc Jockey* on Channel 9, she came undone. The credits were rolling and the cast were all together, smiling at the camera while the theme music played. A kind of custom had evolved, whereby Del would tell the cast a gag, to help them get a laugh going for the cameras. That day she told the one that finishes, "So the old bloke went back to the doctor and told him, 'For all the good those suppositories done me, I may as well have stuck 'em up me arse!'" Which was exactly the way I heard it—along with the entire viewing audience in their homes—after the fool in the control room accidentally switched on the microphone.

That was the end of her career. She'd been full of pep pills at the time, and decided there and then that she'd had enough city life, enough drugs, and enough of me. She moved back to Coffs Harbour. Max's career ended as quickly as it had begun. He went into a decline.

I'd got a start with Lee Gordon as "road manager" with his first rock 'n' roll show, with Bill Haley, the Platters, LaVern Baker, Freddy Bell and the Bellboys, and Joe Turner. The fancy title meant driver, general gofer, and supplier of reefers and amphetamines to Lee and to the stars.

In late August 1957, I had nothing much on. One Monday morning, Ted Rallis came to see me at my flat in Barcom Avenue.

He was keyed up. He had a rort on, wanted me to get involved. I said no. He said, this is as near to foolproof as you can get.

Two weeks before, a gang of tea leaves had hoisted forty thousand pounds worth of jewellery from J. Farren Price in the city, by excavating through a PMG tunnel into the vault. It was Sydney's biggest ever jewellery robbery, and it had been in the papers every day since it happened. The police hadn't made any progress.

Teddy told me the thieves—a crew from Melbourne—had arranged beforehand to fence the stuff with him.

"So do it," I told him. "Why do you need me?"

"I'm short of cash. We agreed to ten grand for the gear but I can't quite manage that."

"Won't they trust you for the rest?"

"Nup. They want the money up front. They're really nervous. If I don't come good in the next two days, they'll go to someone else, and I'll be in the shit for letting them down."

"And how will you get rid of the gear?"

"I've got a bloke in New Zealand who'll take it, it's all arranged. He's got the dough to buy the stuff from me, he's waiting for me to lob."

"How much do you need?"

"Five grand."

"A lot. What do I get back?"

"This is the best, safest return you'll get anywhere, anytime, Billy. I'm offering you double on your money, same as I'm getting. Give me five grand today and I'll give you ten back next week, guaranteed. I'm not making any profit on your money."

Ted Rallis was a teetotaller and career villain I'd known since the war. He had a rep as being one hundred per cent staunch, and I trusted him.

But I was a thousand short.

"All right, hang around for a while. I'll make some phone calls."

I rang Max straight away. He was good for five hundred and said he could maybe get another five from his mum. Ted and I played cards at the kitchen table while we waited for Max to ring back. At two o'clock he rang, said he had it all.

Teddy did the deal with the thieves the next morning and came back to my place at twelve.

He tipped the bag of stuff out on the table. Gold and silver chains, necklaces, rings, five diamond brooches, a dozen strings of pearls, watches, and a whole bunch of loose gemstones.

"And this guy in New Zealand's going to give you twenty grand for this?"

"Yeah, I've already sent him an inventory of the stuff and agreed on the price."

"What about the Melbourne blokes?"

"They're out of it. They're halfway home by now."

"So now it's us in the hot seat?"

"Yeah, but you know what they say: if you don't speculate, you don't accumulate."

I drove him to Mascot Aerodrome that same afternoon.

A week later he rang me from the Sydney Airport, said everything had turned to shit, could I come and get him.

On our way back to his place at Randwick he told me what had gone down.

"I'd arranged it months ago. I was to take the stuff to Jack Kyle in Auckland. I've known him for years, he's completely reliable."

"Yeah, so what happened?"

"Jack was going to fly to Europe with the stuff. He had this false-bottom suitcase, it's a beauty."

"Just carry the stuff away, just like that?"

"The good thing about Jack, he was never pinched for *anything*, he had no record. He could do it. No copper ever looked twice at him."

"For Christ's sake, what happened, Teddy?"

"He died."

"What?"

"He died the day before I got there. Heart attack. He was sixty. His family was in mourning when I rolled up."

"Did he have any partners?"

"Yeah, his widow directed me to a bloke she said was his business partner, but my deal was with Jack. No way I'd give this other joker forty grand's worth of gear."

"So what did you do?"

"Came straight home."

"So where's the stuff?"

He tapped his port.

"Christ. What now?"

"I'll have to line up someone else to get it out of the country. It's far too risky to try to move it here."

But things got worse in a hurry for Ted, and for me as a result. A standover gang started operating at Darling Harbour Goods Yard, and by September it was in the papers every day. Ted had officially had a job there for the last few years. He split the phantom wage he got with the one-armed timekeeper in the pay office. It didn't come to more than ten quid a week, but it gave Ted something to put on his tax returns.

The standover gang's MO was to get ten bob a day, or whatever they could, from each of the hundred or so casual labourers put on daily. Blokes had been bashed outside the Trades Hall Hotel in Goulburn Street. But the press coverage and the police inquiry hadn't put the gang off their stroke, and every day there were pictures in the paper of blokes with broken noses and black eyes.

Ted should've been in the clear—he never went near the place. But some of the gang had made contact with the timekeeper, found out about the rort, found out about Ted, come to see him. They figured he was worth considerably more than the ten bob they were getting from the battlers.

Ted tooled up, called in a couple of favours from heavies around town, and moved his family down to Wollongong to stay with rels.

But he still hadn't moved the jewellery. He came to my place at Rushcutters Bay on a Wednesday night, with the stuff in a Globite schoolcase.

"Keep an eye on this, Billy. I don't want to risk getting rolled by the uglies."

"Ted, you're the one who's armed up, not me."

"What would you rather—something happen to me and we *lose* the stuff, or something happen to me and we *keep* the stuff?"

"Jesus."

"It should be OK. The rozzers will have these palookas at Darling Harbour out of action soon."

"Yeah, that's what we pay our taxes for, isn't it?"

"You want a gun?"

"Shit, no."

The following morning Lee Gordon rang me. He was already into me for two hundred quid. For a mad moment I thought he wanted to settle up. Instead he asked me to road-manage the coming Big Show, starting at the airport next Monday—pick up the stars and their hangers-on, take them to their hotel, and get them what they wanted, within reason.

I said yeah, I thought I could do it. He said great, could you get hold of half a dozen drivers? I said yeah. He said be sure to spruce up well for the job. "I don't want you looking like a bunch of hobos." I said, heaven forfend.

Two years before, Lee Gordon had been worth half a million pounds; now he was stony broke. His last few Big Shows, with Abbott and Costello, Betty Hutton, and Bob Hope had all stiffed. He'd made back some good dough with Bill Haley, but that had gone on debts. He was doing the Little Richard show on the cheap, meaning we'd be paid after he collected. Lee was used to the high fall. Word was that back in the States he'd made a million dollars and blown it again before he was twenty-one.

Turned out he was doing the whole promotion on the nod— he'd persuaded Pan Am to fly the show out here on a promise—the promise being that if they covered him now, he could pay back the thousands of quid he already owed them from the last few shows. Likewise the hotels, stadiums, and internal flight costs were all on tick. He'd also managed to scab some brand new Chevs from a hire-car company in William Street. I said, "Jesus, Lee, I'd love to know how you manage to run up so much credit." He said he'd tell me the secrets of his success one day, if he ever managed to climb out of this hole.

"I'll tell you this much, Billy. Handle them right and your creditors can be your greatest business allies—they have the biggest stake in your future success."

"I can personally vouch for that, Lee, me being one of them."

"And you know you'll triple your investment if this show goes well."

I rang Max, who I knew to be presently financially embarrassed, seeing how he'd invested all his and his mum's money in Teddy Rallis's caper. He was happy to do the driving job. He was a fan of Little Richard's records.

I asked Teddy to drive one of the cars. He said beaut, he'd like to meet Little Timmy. I told him Ted, it's Richard, Little Richard. He said, yeah, he knew. I arranged for his goon baby-sitters to drive three of the cars. Vic Camellieri took the remaining car. He thought it was great, wanted to meet Gene Vincent, told me he was certain Vincent was actually Maltese. "Just look at him," he said. "Maltese. Like Presley."

Busy week. That same Thursday night Laurie O'Brien knocked on my door. I hadn't spoken to him since Max and I had screwed him for six thousand pounds in 1952. I'd seen him once or twice at the races, but I'd been careful to keep well clear of him.

He stood at my door with an old suitcase in his hand.

"How are you, Billy?"

"The fuck do you want?"

"You could invite me in and give me a drink. I haven't had anything but home brew for the past two years."

"Laurie, you tried to get me killed, and I brassed you for six grand. To tell you the truth, I'm not too clear on the correct etiquette in this situation."

"Let's have a drink and try to figure it out."

"What do you want, Laurie?"

"I just got out of the Bay this very day. I've got nowhere else to go, Billy. Let me in, son."

"Christ. You'd better come in."

A couple of years before, Laurie had fallen out with Ray Waters, who was a Chief Superintendent by then. Waters had formed an alliance with Jim Swain, Laurie's rival. Waters pinched him for conspiracy to rig a race—substitute a good horse for a nag—which was like getting done for lying on a tax return—a bit illegal, but it went on all the time.

While Laurie was on remand, Waters repeatedly raided his SP premises until he went right out of business. He sold his house at Maroubra to pay his legal costs and to keep himself afloat. They set fire to his block of flats at Maroubra Junction. No one was hurt, but it was so obviously arson that the insurance company refused to pay up. Then Laurie copped three years for the conspiracy.

Swain and Waters had set themselves the project of taking over Laurie's business. Pretty easy with Laurie out of action, but six months later Swain keeled over dead from a heart attack in the dining room at Big Tatts.

Laurie told me about how he did his time. They sent him out to Oberon for a while. He spent the last of his money trying to keep himself comfortable in the nick. When that ran out, he started running a book, which only kept him in jail currency, cigs, and homebrew.

"So that's it, son. I'm up the creek."

We were sitting around the coffee table in my flat, well into a bottle of Cutty.

"What are you going to do?"

"I've got my plans, don't you worry about that."

"Well, what do you want from me, Laurie?"

"Can I stay here for a few days while I sort myself out?"

"I don't think so."

"I know I owe you, Bill, but please give me a chance. Come on, Bill, I know you're not the type to keep a grudge."

"I've got things on this week."

"I'll keep out of your way, I promise."

"Well, a few days, then, Laurie, but that's it. I don't want you thinking this is the People's Palace."

That night he drank himself unconscious, fell asleep muttering about something I couldn't quite catch. I threw a blanket over him and left the fire on.

When I got up at eight, he'd already showered and folded up his bedding. He'd made a pot of tea.

It was a cold morning and I took my cup of tea over to the front window, which copped a bit of sun at this time of year.

Thirty yards down Barcom Avenue, behind my car, a Hillman was parked with two men in the front seat. They didn't seem to be doing anything much.

Laurie was pretty spry. He took my cup away and washed it after I'd finished it. I asked him what his plans were. He said he'd say hello to a few people, maybe go see his brother across town in Lakemba.

"Do you want to take my car?"

"Really?"

"Yeah, take the car if you want."

"Are you sure?"

I looked out again. The two were looking at the flats, talking.

"Yeah, go for it."

When he left fifteen minutes later, the two blokes were still outside. Laurie took off in my Customline and they started up and pulled out behind him.

I waited half an hour then got the port full of hot jewellery from my room, tied it up with cord and an old belt, and walked down to Bayswater Road.

The morning was still cold. A southwesterly wind had blown in some scrappy low cloud off the sea.

I flagged a cab which had just turned out of the Red Deluxe base, told him to take me to Central Station, steam platform.

There were thirty cabs on the rank there, so I didn't get him to wait.

I put the case into a locker. The sign said the lockers were cleared out every Monday morning, so I had till Sunday night to find a better hiding place.

I rang Teddy from the public phone at the station. He told me nothing much had happened, good or bad. I told him about the car outside my flat. He said that was bad news, did I get their number plate. I said, no, I hadn't thought of it. He asked where the gear was now. I told him, he said good.

"But Teddy, how could anyone possibly know that I'm involved? For that matter, how could anyone know that *you're* in it?"

"The hoisters might have dobbed us in."

"But why would they?"

"They've got their money once. If they get the stuff back again, they're laughing. We're not going to the jacks to complain, are we?"

"But isn't it the Darling Harbour mob that put the wind up you in the first place? How do these mugs fit in?"

"Maybe they're connected. Maybe they heard something around the traps. Maybe they're cops. I don't know, Billy."

I rang Max, filled him in.

"Oh yeah, one more thing. Guess who arrived at my place last night, wanting a roof over his head?"

"Who?"

"Laurie O'Brien."

"What does that old prick want?"

"He got out of the slot yesterday. He says he wants to forgive and forget."

"Kind of strange, him arriving out of the blue, you with forty grand's worth of hot jewellery in your sock drawer."

"Might be coincidence."

"This is the same bloke who arranged to have you bumped off."

"We took his money."

"So what's that mean, you're even? Bullshit. Keep an eye on the old cunt. I speak partly out of self-interest here."

"Thanks a heap for the concern. Why don't you come around later on, say hello to him?"

"Yeah, maybe I will."

I walked east across the steam train terminal, down the stairs to the electric train platforms, straight through to Elizabeth Street. I bought a *Telegraph* and went across the road to the Oceanic Cafe. I ordered a mixed grill and read the paper.

There was a cartoon on page three, of a giant Chesty Bond lookalike, labelled *Australian Worker*, rolling up his sleeves and making a fist at a low-browed, thuggish-looking character labelled *Standover Rackets*. There was nothing at all on the J. Farren Price robbery. On the page with the movie and stage reviews, there was an ad for the next Big Show: *Lee Gordon Presents ROCK 'N' ROLL!* Little Richard had top billing. There was a photo of him with his arms spread, his head thrown back like a wild man.

I finished my breakfast and walked home.

If the Hillman had really followed Laurie, and if he'd noticed it, he didn't mention it that night. In fact he didn't say much at all.

Television had come in while he'd been at the Bay, and I had a 21-inch Kriesler in the lounge room. Laurie sat staring at it all night.

The next day was Saturday and the race meeting was at Randwick. I thought Laurie might go out there, to show the world he was back in the action, but he said he'd stay in if it was all the same to me. I said suit yourself.

I made a few selections from the *Telegraph* form guide that morning, then went up to the Mansions to place some bets and grab a counter lunch. I could have rung the bets through, but I wanted to get away from Laurie for a while, have a couple at the pub.

The Hillman was parked up near the corner. I walked past it around the corner and up Craigend Street. I stopped to light a cig after a hundred yards or so. Two blokes came walking up the road behind me. One of them had a crew cut. He had on a leather jacket; the other, a fair-haired bloke, was wearing a blue cardigan. Tough-looking lairs. The fair-haired one had a broken nose, maybe did a bit of boxing. I walked briskly up to the Mansions and saw them walk past the door. They didn't come in. I spent the afternoon in the bar, but didn't see them again all that day.

I rolled out of the hotel at five o'clock, half-stung, seventy quid ahead on the day's punting. I swallowed a couple of dexedrine pills, which straightened me up well enough, then went on to the Astoria for some dinner. I managed half a Vienna schnitzel and some strong coffee, then ambled back to Barcom Avenue.

Max was at the flat when I got there. He'd done his last forty pounds that afternoon, and needed some petrol and drinking money to get to a gig he had at the Manly Hotel. Since late closing had come in, some of the bigger pubs had taken to putting on floor shows. The publicans were playing it safe, though, avoiding boogie-woogie or rock 'n' roll combinations, figuring they'd only attract the riffraff.

Not that Max was too put out about that. When Del up and left town and left the music business, he sort of gave up on rock 'n' roll. His style of boogie-woogie piano played strictly in the key of C was looking and sounding a little old-fashioned for the young crowd, and though his guitar playing was passable, he didn't really twang it the way they did now. So he started up a Hawaiian act which he took around to the pubs and RSL clubs. The feature of the act was a couple of hula dancers who did a semi-blue dance routine—more like a striptease crossed with a belly dance than a hula. They billed it as "The Forbidden Dance of the Islands." Max gave the publicans and club secretary-managers a spiel he'd written himself, attributed to supposed anthropologist "Dr. Kutisarki"—from Cutty Sark—and another one attributed to Prof. Benjamin Zadrine, as in benzedrine, which authenticated the performance as being Polynesian native ritual with profound spiritual significance.

Max and Laurie were kind of sizing one another up when I lobbed. Max had found my piss, but Laurie seemed to be staying dry again.

"Back any winners?" I asked Max.

"I backed Narcolepsy. It ran so wide it knocked a pie out of a bloke's hand in the Leger."

"Bad luck."

"I'll say. I was fucking robbed. It should have won."

"So you still like a punt, Max?" Laurie said.

"Oh, yeah, I suppose so . . . a flutter now and then, you know."

"Why do you bet?"

"Why? What kind of question's that? I don't know, for fun, for profit, to keep bookies like you in fancy houses."

Laurie looked at him, a bit of a smirk on his face.

"I haven't got a fancy house these days."

"Yeah, well, the wheel turns, eh?"

"Exactly, Max. It started turning for me when you two rorted me. That was the first of a string of setbacks for me."

Max stood up. "Fuck you, Laurie, you brought it on yourself, you greedy old cunt."

"Yeah, I know. I'm not even angry about it. Not now." He smiled at Max.

"Did someone hit you over the head out there at the Bay?"

Laurie laughed. "Yeah, it must seem like it, eh?"

Max signalled me into the other room. I brought him up to date on the jewellery business, the blokes in the Hillman, my last conversation with Teddy. He bit me for twenty quid and some go-fast. I gave him a handful of pills and the money.

I'd discovered dexedrine only after it had been put on the restricted list two years earlier. During the Melbourne Olympics, a few of the athletes had got stuck into them. Later it was claimed some coaches were even giving them to schoolkid athletes. It had been in the papers—"confidence drugs," they called them. As soon as I read about them I knew they were for me. These days you needed a prescription, but I had a couple of tame doctors, old Doc Foley over in Glebe or Harry Bailey, who always obliged. I made sure I kept a hundred or so on hand.

As Max was leaving he said, "Keep an eye on that old mongrel."

Laurie had the TV on. I sat down.

He was silent for a few minutes. Then he said, "So you did all right today, did you, Bill?"

"Nothing too great. How about you, Laurie? You feel the urge to have a bet or two?"

He shook his head.

"Really?"

"Do you know why people bet, Billy?"

"What *are* you on about, Laurie?"

"I've given this a lot of thought, Billy. Go along with me for a moment. Why do people bet?"

"I s'pose it's like Max said: easy money."

"Yeah, but most punters lose."

"Well, for fun then. Judging form, assessing the odds, trying to work out which horse is going to win."

"You know why people bet?"

"OK, why?"

"Look at Max. He studied the form. He selected Narcolepsy. It's not a bad horse. But today wasn't its day. Max was certain it was going to win, though."

"Yeah?"

"He was so certain, he staked more money than he could afford on its winning."

"Not the first time."

"No, it's not. Max put his dough on it because he was sure he knew what the outcome of the race would be. He had a strong hunch, an intuition. He thought he knew what the future was going to be."

I didn't say anything.

"Who knows the future, Billy?"

"Who?"

"Did you go to a Catholic school?"

"Primary, yeah."

"Didn't they tell you that only the Almighty knows the future?"

"Why, is He handing out turf advice?"

Laurie shook his head seriously. "Does Max think he's God?"

"I wouldn't've said so."

"No, nor would I."

"So what are you saying?"

"You know any history, Billy?"

"Christ, Laurie, you're talking very fucking odd. What are you driving at?"

"I read a bit out in the Bay. I read about the monks in the Middle Ages, the magicians and head shrinkers in the Arab lands and in India, and the blokes who turned lead into gold. You know what drove them on, Billy?"

"Lead into gold might do it."

"No. The gold was just a trophy for them, like a certificate of attainment. It wasn't their main aim."

"What was, then?"

"They studied hard. They looked at the stars, they manipulated numbers, they cooked up chemicals, they fasted in deserts. They searched nature for signs. Why?"

"Why?"

"To understand the hidden order of things, to know the mind of God."

"This is very fucking deep, Laurie."

"What does your punter do? He studies form, gathers every piece of knowledge he can—track times, jockeys' records, trainers' records, owners' records. He's like a detective. Or a scholar. And if the tea lady's son-in-law's cousin's friend knows someone who lives in the same street as the owner, then whatever *they* reckon is added to the punter's store of knowledge. Later, he'll add any piece of scuttlebutt from the track—something overheard in the queue for the Tote, or something the old stiff at the turnstiles told him, or the paper boy—anything at all that serves the punter's illusion that he alone has pieced together the *real* truth about a particular race.

And he'll be as stupidly superstitious as he will be scientific—always careful to include every conceivable scrap of intelligence, including hunches, lucky numbers, lucky jockeys, astrology, everything."

"But every punter will tell you the races are fixed."

"That just adds another variable to the equation, another piece of essential knowledge to be gained, if possible. Who's trying and who's not trying, which horses are being pulled up, which horses are doped. Your punter doesn't mind the races being a bit rigged—it gives him another chance to separate himself from the mugs, one more thing he can be in the know about."

I poured myself another Cutty.

"You sure you don't want one of these, Laurie?"

He shook his head. "Your mate, Max. See how put out he was that Narcolepsy didn't win today?"

"Yeah. As you said, he lost money he couldn't afford."

"He doesn't give a stuff about the money. He's put out because the result—Narcolepsy getting beat—shouldn't have happened."

"What?"

"You ever read Plato, Billy?"

"The Greek bloke? Nah."

"Max is pissed off because in some way he believes that in the *true* scheme of things, that horse really won."

"Is this what you talked about out at the Bay with the other crims?"

"Of course not. I'll tell you something else. You know why people bet repeatedly?"

"I think you're going to tell me."

"Because they hardly ever win."

"Laurie, you've completely lost me." I got up, took a leak, put the milk bottles out, got some more ice from the fridge, came back in. Laurie hadn't moved.

"OK, then here's a simpler question for you, Bill. How come you're being followed?"

"What do you mean?"

"You spend some time out at the Bay, you know when you're being followed. Two louts in a Hillman. They followed me around for a while yesterday."

"Might have been jacks keeping an eye on you."

"Why would jacks follow me?"

"Because you're a notorious fucking villain, Laurie."

"They weren't jacks. I thought maybe they were following the car. Your car."

"Laurie, I think you're off your head."

"Then they were here again today, they followed you up the street."

"Coincidence."

"Nothing happens by accident."

"OK, then you tell why you picked *now* to turn up at my door, Laurie."

"That's exactly what I was wondering. Maybe you can tell me."

"Christ. You're fucking touched, Laurie."

I went out after that, stopped by a few pubs, had some bets on the trots, ended up with a sheila at the Astra Hotel, kicked on to a party later. I came home Sunday morning and Laurie was out, for which I was thankful.

At lunchtime, I rang up Max and Ted to confirm the chauffeur gig for the next day. I told Ted about the louts in the Hillman.

"Yeah, I think I've seen them, too. A snowy-haired bloke and a feller with a crew cut?"

"Snow and Crew Cut, that's them. Did you recognize them?"

"Yeah, they were at my place once. The wife saw them, told me.

That's when I packed her and the kids off. It's got to be the same ones."

"What do you reckon we ought to do, Teddy?"

"Well, they obviously know you're involved. Looks as though they're just keeping an eye on things. Has Max seen anything?"

"Not that he's mentioned."

"The stuff's safe for the time being. We'll just have to wait and see. If the louts are still hanging around in a couple of days, we might have to have a talk to them."

Laurie came back that night and sat down in front of the TV again, watched *Pick-a-Box*. He was sitting there drinking tea and smoking cigs as I was going out.

"Do you believe in luck, Billy?" he asked.

"Jesus, Laurie, don't start again."

"I shared a cell with a Chow for a while. Chinese people believe that Luck is kind of a basic principle of life, did you know that?"

"They're maniacs for a punt."

"This Chow bloke, who ran a gambling club and a brothel, reckoned he knew the exact moment his luck deserted him. The dragon is their symbol for Fortune."

"Is that right?" I was at the door, waiting for him to finish.

"Yeah, that's right. When the luck's going your way, it's like you can't go wrong. You surprise yourself. Like there's something else working for you, something you don't know about."

"Yeah?"

"Like riding a dragon, the Chow said. But dragons are difficult animals. If you take the dragon for granted for even a moment, just a second, it'll turn on you. That's what he told me. The dragon turned on him."

"Yeah?"

"That's right."

"So?"

He looked at me and shrugged slowly.

There didn't seem to be anyone in the street when I left, and I didn't notice anyone following me as I drove down to the rail terminal.

It was bleak at Central Station. A couple of chats were sleeping on a bench underneath the McWilliams sign, an empty bottle of Invalid Port at their feet. Above them, neon drops of booze trickled into a neon wineglass. A few soldiers waited on another bench for a train going somewhere unexciting. There was an aboriginal bloke with a battered port, an old couple, and a young woman with a tiny child sitting near one another, all bent over against the cold wind blowing through the station. A couple of uniformed coppers were ambling in from the other end.

I got the bag of jewellery from the cloak room at the end of the hall and walked back to the car. The driver of the first cab on the rank looked up at me hopefully as I came out. I went past to where my car was parked, put the stuff in the boot, and drove back to Darlo.

When I got home I thought at first that Laurie had turned over the flat. Drawers were pulled out, bedding messed up. My clothes and records were on the floor, appliances pulled out, my fishing gear chucked around, the tackle box emptied.

I found Laurie sitting at the kitchen table. His eye was swollen nearly closed, the side of his face was puffed out, his lip split.

"Christ! What happened?"

"They were here."

"Who?"

"The blokes in the Hillman."

"Oh shit! Crew Cut and Snow?"

"Yeah, those palookas."

"What did they say?"

"They said 'Where's the stuff?'"

"What did you tell them?"

"What could I tell them?"

"I'm sorry about this, Laurie."

"I've copped worse."

I got some mercurochrome from the bathroom and applied it to Laurie's face. It made him look even more beaten up.

"Better stay out of sight," I said. "You'll frighten the kiddies."

"I've got to go out for a while. Can I borrow your car?"

The jewellery was still in the boot.

"I'll drive you wherever you want to go," I said.

"All right, let's go, now."

I took Laurie over to Redfern. He went into a house in Pitt Street, was there about ten minutes, came out with a paper bag, said, "OK, let's go home."

Back at the flat, he tipped out the bag on the kitchen table. Two pistols and a handful of bullets.

"Oh, shit, Laurie."

"Now, don't be like that. This is one occasion when you really do need one of these. Do you know how to use it?"

"What's to know? You pull the trigger."

"Yeah, that's basically it. You better take this one. It's a Luger."

He gave me the bigger of the two. I've never known anything much about guns, never shot rabbits or any of that shit. The only time I'd used one was a few years before, when I'd had cause to wave Charlie Furner's murder weapon around for theatrical effect.

"All right, Laurie."

"We see those cunts again, we'll sort them out."

I didn't say anything else. It was pretty clear to me Laurie only had one oar in the water.

I put the roscoe in the pocket of my Canadian jacket, but it fell out again. I tried it the other way, handle first, but then the barrel was sticking out pointing up at my head. I tried sticking it in my pants, but it was pointing down at the wedding tackle. I thought that must be why they always wear trench coats in the gangster movies. I put the gun in the underwear drawer of the dresser and went downstairs.

I got the port from the boot of my car, brought it inside, and put it under my bed. They'll never find it there, I thought.

Teddy rang. He'd just got home to find his house had been broken into and messed up. He'd been out for three hours. I told him my news.

"That shows us two things, at least," he said.

"What's that?"

"Laurie's probably not with them, for one."

"True. What else?"

"They're pretty fucking crude."

"That's for sure. What should we do?"

"Where's the gear now?"

"Here. But it's all right for the moment. Laurie's all fired up. He went and got some arms. He's ready for the OK Corral."

"Christ. You better bring the stuff with you tomorrow when we pick up Little Archie at the airport."

"It's Little *Richard*, Teddy."

"Right."

I rang Max, brought him up to date.

"We've got to do something with Laurie," I said.

"Like what?"

"He can't stay here. What about the spare flat at Perkal Towers?"

176

"Jesus. Laurie O'Brien, here? He's our sworn enemy, Bill, for fuck's sake."

"He copped a hiding on my behalf, Max. He was staunch."

"Gee, I don't know. With my mother in the other flat and all."

"It'll be all right. Look at it this way: if he gets necked here, the rozzers will be all over the joint. If they connect any of us with the jewellery we'll do at least ten years each for receiving, for sure."

"Let me think about it."

He finally agreed, and I drove Laurie over to Perkal Towers at Bondi Junction.

He went quietly. As I was leaving to go back to my flat he said, "I wouldn't rat on you again, Bill. You know that, don't you?"

The next morning, Monday, was cold and windy. The bush fires around town were burning fiercely, and you could smell eucalyptus smoke in the air, along with the dust and coal smoke. The air was so dry I was getting electric shocks off anything I touched. The wind had given me a headache. Or maybe it was just a dexedrine hangover.

I walked up to the Cross and bought the papers, read them over a cup of tea. The Russians had just launched Sputnik. They reckoned it would be going right over Sydney in a couple of nights' time. In America, they'd sent the army into Little Rock, Arkansas, where the governor was treating Negro schoolkids shabbily. The Russians said Sputnik would be flying over Little Rock, as a symbol of hope to enslaved people everywhere.

There was still nothing about the J. Farren Price robbery. I left my kero heater going all morning, it was that cold.

That afternoon, I was driving the crew back to the Hampton Court Hotel, with the jewellery in the boot of the borrowed Chev and

177

my old girlfriend nagging me to buy her heroin. We were driving along Dowling Street.

"Molly, I wouldn't even know where to get heroin. I don't know anyone who uses it, and if I did, I still don't think I'd get it. Christ, didn't you see *The Man with the Golden Arm*?"

"Don't turn square on us, Billy. This is serious."

"Is that's what's wrong with your pal Marty?"

"Yeah."

"Then he should lay off it."

"It's lack of heroin that's making him sick."

"What about you, Molly, do you take it, too?"

"A little."

"How come you're not sick?"

"I am."

"Shit!"

Eddie Cochran and Alis Lesley hadn't said anything through all of this. Marty was in the back seat groaning.

We got to the hotel and booked them all into their rooms.

The press filed in, then Lee arrived a little later, looking like a big shot, welcoming the artistes, pouring champagne, introducing radio announcers to the stars, arranging interviews. Turned out he knew Marty from years ago, back in the States. Once things were rolling, Lee signalled me to meet across the room, in semi-private.

"We gotta do something for Marty. He's dope-sick."

"Yeah, I know. He'll get better though, won't he?"

"Not in time for the show tomorrow."

"Sack him, then."

"It's not that simple. His girl's an old sweetheart of yours?"

"Yeah. Small world, eh?"

"Would you cop for him if it wasn't for the chick?"

"Listen, Lee, it's like I told her. I wouldn't know where to get that shit. And if you mean that I'm dirty on him and that's why I won't go hunting for dope, that's not it. Me and Molly were years ago, like back in the Dark Ages."

"Whatever, Billy, it's not my business. But you know, maybe you don't know your own mind on this."

"That's all right. Back in 1952, when I last saw her, it was 'she loves me, she loves me not,' and it finished up on the 'not.' For her, anyway. I got there later. I was off tap about it for a while, but not now. Not for a long time."

I didn't add that Molly and I went back to the war years, when we were both kids, learning fast, together and separately, and I could never really be neutral towards her, either.

"Yeah, all right. I can dig it. The chick has gone to their room. She said for you to drop in on her."

The Little Richard entourage had the top two floors of the hotel. I took the lift up there.

Molly answered when I knocked on the door to their room. She looked like a burnt-out Mamie Van Doren. She was wearing satin slacks, and had a blanket around her shoulders. The electric radiator was on full.

"Grab yourself a drink, Billy."

"Where's the clown?"

"Marty? He's in the bedroom. He's taken some pills to knock himself out."

"How'd you get mixed up in this shit, Molly?"

"In stages, I guess."

As I was looking at her, a sweat broke out on her face. Then she sneezed, once, twice, and again. She had a hanky to her face. Her eyes were watering and her nose was running. Then she started sneezing in earnest, maybe twenty times. She finished with a fit of coughing that turned into retching.

She flopped down on the armchair, drew her knees up to her face, and started crying.

She sat there shivering and sweating. I went over to her and put my hand on her shoulder. She recoiled like she'd been given an electric shock.

"Is this from the dope?" I said.

She nodded, her head on her knees.

"Christ, Molly. This is terrible. I'll see what I can scrounge."

"Really?"

"I can't promise anything. I'll try."

She stood up immediately, started brushing her hair. "I'll come with you. You got anything at all?"

"Some dexedrine."

"Give me some. Anything's better than this."

"Have you got any money?"

"Not really."

"How about Marty?"

"As if. But Lee's an old friend of his. He'll give you some."

"He's broke. If we do actually find any, I've got a few bob."

"This is very good of you, Billy."

"Listen, Molly, I'll try to get some for you. But first, before I do that, tell me: why don't you just kick it now, while you've got the opportunity?"

"It's not like that."

"No?"

"In a few days I won't be sick anymore, but there's more to it than the sickness. It's like you've got nothing left to live for. Nothing else counts."

"But in time, doesn't that pass?"

"It never passes. Not really."

Marty got up and tagged along. If we were going to find any dope, he wanted to be there when we did. We bumped into Eddie Cochran in the lift. He asked where we were off to.

"Just driving around," I said.

"Mind if I tag along? See the sights."

"We're not really doing the tourist route. More likely the dens and dives." I nodded in the direction of Molly and Marty. "You know. For them."

Eddie nodded slowly, then smiled. "That's OK, brother. I'll ride shotgun. Hell, man, you might be grateful to have me along as backshooter."

I didn't want to drive around town looking for drugs in a hire car, so I walked around the corner, got the Customline from outside my flat, and drove back to the Hampton Court. I took the Globite out of the Chev and put it in the boot of my car.

At four in the afternoon, I went into the Macquarie Hotel at Woolloomooloo. Marty and Molly waited in the car. Eddie had a beer with some bodgies who had recognized him, while I made inquiries with a couple of the crims there. No result.

We went to the Ship Inn, the Orient, then Monty's, all with no result. Eddie was recognized by the bodgies everywhere we went, had a beer at each place while I spoke to the fences and lurk men.

In the end, it was Eddie who got the tip on where to get dope. He was having a drink with a Scottish teddy boy, a seaman, down at the First and Last Hotel. He called me over and introduced me. The Scot, Andy, had asked Eddie if he'd like some reefer. He'd got hold of some dope in Sumatra, said it was the strongest marijuana in the world. I told him we were looking for heroin.

"No, I'd never touch that stuff. But some of the fellers on the boat do, and I know they got some here in Sydney."

"Who from?"

"Ask the old gray bloke. He put them on to it." He pointed to a fellow drinking alone at a table.

"Thanks. While I'm at it, I'll have some of that reefer if you can spare it."

"It's not rolled up into ciggies yet. You'll have to do that yourself. Can you roll a cigarette?"

"Yeah, that'll be all right."

"Just mix this stuff half and half with tobacco." He passed me a matchbox, I gave him five quid.

I bought two scotches and went over to the old bloke Andy had pointed out. He was a dead-eyed, unsmiling old codger. He still had his hat on, drawn low over his face. He must have been nearly sixty, but I wouldn't have wanted to scrap with him. He looked like he'd glass you in a second.

He took the drink from me, gave a slight nod which might have meant thanks.

We talked racing for a while, then yarned about the old days. He warmed up a little. Turned out he'd been a heavy before the war, a crony of Phil the Jew and Frank Green. I came clean about what I wanted, why I wanted it. He said, "It'll cost you."

"Yeah, I know the stuff's expensive."

"I don't mean that. *I'll* want something."

I gave him a five-quid note.

"Try the Chows."

"But who?"

"There's a bloke who runs the pak-a-pu in Dixon Street. Louis something."

"You don't mean Louis Hoon?"

"Yeah, that's him. If he can't get you some, there isn't any to be had."

"Thanks, dad." I bought him another drink and left.

I knew Louis Hoon. He was a Malayan Chinese, about my age, supposed to be out here on the Colombo Plan or something. He was a big gambler and a racegoer, which was how I knew him. I'd heard he was an occasional opium user as well, but they said that about every Chinese. I'd never heard of him selling drugs.

Eddie was half-drunk by the time we left, so I gave him some dexes. Marty and Molly were in despair, sniffing and sneezing all the while, complaining of the cold.

I drove to Dixon Street and parked outside the Come Luck restaurant.

I went in a side door and up two flights of stairs and knocked on a door. It was opened by an old bloke who gave an inquiring grunt.

I said, "Where's Louis?"

"No Louis."

I knew there *was* Louis. He ran his pak-a-pu from here.

"Tell Louis to come downstairs. I'm Billy."

The door slammed again and I turned around to go downstairs. It opened before I'd got out of earshot and a voice called out to me. I walked back upstairs and Louis Hoon gestured me in.

There were twenty or thirty Chinese men sitting in a large room. Louis took me into a side room, bare except for a couple of chairs.

"How are you, Billy?"

"Good, very good. You?"

"So-so. I haven't win daily double for very long time. What you want?"

"Louis, my friends from America are here. They are sick. They need something to make them OK."

"I don't know."

"They need something, Louis."

"This is very bad, Billy. Leave them."

"No, I can't, Louis."

"Who is friend, boy or girl?"

"My old girlfriend and her new boyfriend."

"Ah! Rich?"

"Not rich, Louis, but they can pay."

"OK, come with me, maybe we can find. Do you take?"

"No, it's not for me, just for them."

He nodded. "That's good."

He sent me back to the car and ten minutes later he came down himself, got in the front seat, and told me to drive to Surry Hills. I introduced him to everyone, first names only.

Louis turned to Eddie and said, "You sick man?"

"Not me, brother. Them." He pointed to Molly and Marty beside him. Marty smiled sweetly at Louis, gave him a friendly nod. Louis looked closely at him.

"You do this?" He pointed to the crook of his arm, jabbing his finger like it was a needle.

Marty nodded.

I drove up Campbell Street, across Elizabeth. It was dark now. People were walking up the hill from Central Station, going home. Others were going down to the station, leaving the small rag-trade factories and machine shops in the Surry Hills gully.

Louis directed me into Commonwealth Street and told me to stop. Some little kids were playing in the street. Nearly all the faces in the street were Chinese.

Louis went into a tiny terrace house. Ten minutes later, he walked out of a different house, three doors down.

He came back to the car and said, "Come."

Marty and Molly were out in a flash. I followed. Eddie said he'd wait in the car; he didn't care to go kicking old Buddha's gong.

Louis took us inside yet a different terrace and led us out the back through a smoky, greasy kitchen where an old guy was frying noodles. We went through a door to the left and into an almost completely dark room and then through a door at the other side. I figured we must be a couple of doors away from the house we started in. Louis took us upstairs and through another doorway, into a dim room with a tattered couch, a mattress by the wall and a low table in the centre. Magazine pictures of women—mainly Hollywood movie stars—had been pasted up on the walls.

Louis said, "Wait here. Give me money."

"How much?"

"Ten quid."

I gave him the money and he was gone. I could hear noises from all around us—a mother calling out to a child, somewhere else men's voices, talking rapidly and laughing loudly. And a regular, dull, thumping, like someone beating a carpet, except it went on and on.

Marty said, "I think that guy's taken your bread, man. What'll we do if he doesn't come back?" There was panic in his voice.

I didn't answer him.

An older Chinese man came into the room carrying a tin ash-tray and a candle stub in a holder. He lit the candle and gestured us over. He drew a particle from a paper package and put it on the ashtray and handed a straw to Marty. He held the candle under the tray and after a few seconds the particle began to smoulder. He motioned to Marty to inhale the smoke through the straw. Suddenly the particle, which was about the size of a peppercorn, started fizzing and darting around the tray as it liquefied before it burned. Marty inhaled, but he had missed most of the smoke which tailed off from the little rock. The Chinese guy gestured that he'd have to use the end of the straw to chase the burning particle around the tray.

"You chase the dragon! OK?"

Marty nodded. The guy put another piece of the pink stuff onto the tray and this time Marty got it all. He drew it down deep like it was reefer smoke and passed the straw to Molly. The guy dropped another particle down and she repeated the act. Then he gestured to me. I shook my head.

Marty sighed deeply and said, "Man, that's good shit."

He had another couple of turns and so did Molly.

They stopped their sniffing and coughing. Their skin took on a dry, dead look and their mouths sagged in a strange way. They'd stopped complaining, but to me they looked worse now than they had before.

We got up to leave and the Chinese guy gave the package to Marty and smiled.

He took us to the door, opened it, and Marty and Molly went out. As I went through the door, he gestured at Marty and said to me, "First, man chases dragon. Later, dragon chases man." Then he laughed.

Louis met us outside the room and led us a different way back to the street. We came out of a house around the corner in Ann Street. Good trick.

Eddie was leaning on the bonnet of the Customline, talking to some kids.

We drove Louis back to Dixon Street.

When he got out he said, "Good luck."

On the way back to the Hampton Court, Marty spewed out the window of the car again.

"What's wrong with him now?" I said to Molly.

"It's the shit doing it to him."

"I thought *not* having it made him spew."

"So does having it. It's a different kind of spew, though."

"Some people sure know how to have a good time."

Back at the Hampton Court, I went upstairs to see if Max or Teddy were still there. There was a party going on in the main suite. A bunch of women had been rounded up somewhere and a couple were dancing. One of the girls had her blouse off, dancing in her bra. Gordon was there, and so was Little Richard, walking around kissing the women, kissing the men. O'Keefe was there too, along with Catfish Purser, his drummer, and Vic Camellieri. They were all wide-eyed.

Gordon saw us all walk in, glanced at Marty, then called him aside. They both left the room. Molly went with them.

I couldn't see Ted, but Max was there whooping it up. He had a guitar out and was jamming along with a feller from Richard's band, who was bashing on the piano. Cochran picked up a bottle of champagne and joined them.

I interrupted Max, who told me Ted had split a while ago. I had a drink and circulated for a while, then went down to the Chev and got the Globite from the boot. I took it upstairs and put it in the hotel room where the stage suits and instruments had been stored.

I went back to the party, had another drink, then said my good-byes. I was nearly at the door when Lee reentered the room with Marty. Lee looked grey, his eyes were dim. He asked was I right for tomorrow? I said yeah.

Before I left he said, "And thanks for doing that for Marty and Molly."

"It's no big deal. Are you all right, Lee?"

"Yeah, I'm fine."

"Looks like you got bit by that dragon."

We were to drive the show to Wollongong the next morning. I rang Vic and then Ted when I got home to make sure they were still up for it. Vic was OK, and Teddy too, but he said the muscle men wouldn't be available, they had jobs to get back to. I said that was all right, I'd find some replacements.

"Actually, Bill," Teddy said, "it might be good to get out of town for a day or two with Little Whatshisname, keep out of reach of those blokes."

"We can't keep this up forever. Sooner or later, we've either got to get rid of the stuff or have a showdown with the mugs."

"I don't want a showdown. It shouldn't be too long. I'm working on a contact now. With a bit of luck I might be able to get rid of it in a few days."

"Thank Christ for that."

"Sit tight. Your mate Little Robert's a funny bloke, by the way."

"Isn't he just?"

I arranged two replacement drivers the next morning. Gordon was frantic. Marty wasn't coming, he said. The shit he was taking was stronger than what he was used to, and he was lying in his hotel room in a stupor. I said, some comedian: can't work stoned, can't work not stoned. Gordon said he did a new style of comedy, "sick" they called it, and taking dope was sort of part of it. I said I could vouch for him being sick, all right. I'd seen him do little else but spew out of car windows.

At ten o'clock, we packed up the stars and their gear—and the suitcase of jewellery—and took the Princes Highway out of town.

Past Sutherland there were big clouds of smoke from the fires still burning at Heathcote, Engadine, and Helensburgh. The wind was howling, with cinders from the fires starting more fires farther downwind, sometimes miles ahead of the original fire.

A couple of times we were stopped by police, because the bush fires had closed the road up ahead. Then we'd drive on through smouldering bush. At one point we could see a fire front a hundred yards or so from the road, with huge flames coming up a hill towards us.

Little Richard travelled in a car with Gordon, which Max drove, while I drove four members of Richard's band, plus Eddie Cochran.

Charlie, Richard's drummer, sat in the front on the trip down there. We passed a half bottle of Cutty back and forth, talking as we went.

I pulled into the petrol station at Bulli Pass. Charlie said. "Man. I gotta use the rest room."

"Yeah."

He hesitated.

"What's wrong?"

"Is there going to be, like, any trouble?"

"What do you mean?"

"I don't want to upset anyone, you know what I'm saying?"

"I don't get you."

"Back home, we go out to the boonies, we can't use just any rest room, can't walk into just any diner, without someone getting upset."

"A Little Rock type of thing?"

"Yeah, like that."

I wasn't sure what to say. If Charlie had been an Abo and this was out west, who knows?

"Jesus, Charlie, you guys are celebrities, for Christ's sake. They'd be honoured to have you use their dunny. Hell, for all I know, they'd probably dig it if you didn't pull the chain, know what I mean?"

After I filled up, I led the visitors over to Bulli Pass Lookout for a bit of "I love a sunburnt country" stuff. Normally, from the lookout there, you can see way down the South Coast, past Wollongong and Kiama and out to sea for miles. The fires were mainly behind us, and the wind was blowing from the southwest, so the air was clear up where we were; but below us, we could see a number of separate fires at the base of the escarpment, each with a big cloud of smoke trailing out to sea.

While we were there, the wind changed direction, began blowing more directly from the west, and smoke started drifting in around us, so we got back on the road.

We reached the hotel forty minutes later. We unloaded the baggage and went straight to the Crown Theatre. I took the musos backstage, found dressing rooms for them, made sure of the dinner arrangements. Gordon had lined up a local cafe to bring in a hot meal for the performers between the first and second shows.

While we were settling in, Gordon took Alis and Cochran to the local radio station, 2WL, for an interview to promote the show.

I took Ted aside and passed the Globite to him, so he could take a turn worrying about it.

Then I met up with Max, and we adjourned to the lane behind the theatre for a quick reefer. I asked him how the drive had been.

"Man, that Richard is a strange cat."

"Yeah, I saw him at the party yesterday."

"I don't mean that. He's going through some religious awakening thing."

"Yeah?"

"On the way down here, he was reading the *Telegraph* about Sputnik, how they reckon we'll be able to see it in the sky. He reckons it's a sign, that these are the latter days."

"Eh?"

"The end of the world, like in the Bible."

"Strike me lucky."

"Yeah, so when we drove through that fire, he was sure that this was it. Man, he was peering through the smoke and flames, looking for the Four Horsemen of the Apocalypse."

"Shit."

"He was saying he was through with rock 'n' roll, it wasn't God's will that he give himself over to riotous living. He didn't want to do the show. So Lee's trying to get him to have a drink, have a fuck, take some drugs or something, clear his head. Speaking of which, this is good reefer."

"Yeah, Sumatran. So what's happening? The show's going on, isn't it?"

"Yeah, Lee told Richard that he didn't see how God would want him to renege on his contract, break his word, upset a lot of people. He told him maybe he could use his fame as a way of doing God's work, show the kids that not all rock 'n' rollers were sinners."

"Did he buy it?"

"He's doing tonight's show."

The Sumatran reefer hit me. I became aware of musical sounds in the hall, as the band tuned up and did a quick check of the public-address system.

I reached into my pocket, pulled out a handful of dexes, and gave a few to Max.

The first show went on at five. O'Keefe and his band, the Dee Jays, opened the show. Gene Vincent and the Blue Caps still hadn't arrived from Hawaii. Gordon had hired O'Keefe's band to back up Alis and Cochran, but O'Keefe wanted to sing a couple of songs himself.

Gordon wasn't at all keen on the idea, wasn't interested in putting on any locals at all, but O'Keefe wore him down eventually. Gordon let him sing while the crowd were moving to their seats. He wasn't announced as part of the main show, nor was he paid.

O'Keefe just wanted to get in front of the local rock 'n' roll audience, and figured this was the best way. He'd learned a few tricks since the Aloha Milk Bar days. He'd give cheek to the audiences, which got him out of a lot of bother, especially with bodgie crowds. He'd come on, they'd boo him and yell, "Get off, you mug!" He'd tell them *they* were the fucking mugs for paying to see him. Then he'd tell them they'd paid because they loved him, the wild one. It sort of worked.

This time O'Keefe got his usual reception. He didn't seem to mind. Maybe the dexedrine helped. He was on stage for ten minutes. There was some thin applause when he left.

Cochran opened the show proper. He did "Twenty Flight Rock," which was a favourite of mine. The kids there hadn't heard much of him before, since his records had hardly been played on Australian radio, but he'd appeared in the movie *The Girl Can't Help It*, so he wasn't completely unknown. He played good guitar and moved around the stage a lot. Alis Lesley followed. She looked good, but musically didn't do anything special, just sang a few Elvis songs.

But Richard and the band really tore it up. They played louder and harder than anything I'd ever heard or seen. A lot wilder even than on Little Richard's records. Charlie belted the shit out of his drum kit. The crowd went troppo.

The second show was the same, but the crowd was even more into it. At the end of Richard's set the band kept playing, roaring, while Richard ran off stage and then came back on with an armful of booklets, which he threw into the crowd. Fights broke out as the kids all tried to get a booklet.

I was at the back of the theatre. When Richard finally left the stage and the crowd filed out, I stopped a couple of bodgies, asked for a dekko at the booklet. They were leery of handing it over. I assured them I just wanted a look.

It was a religious tract, published by the United Holy Southern Ministry of the Ten Commandments. The book was titled *Is This the End*? *What the Bible Tells Us about Signs in the Skies*!

I gave it back to the kids.

There was another party at the hotel that night. Some of the radio-station people were there, with their families, but as the bash got wilder they shepherded them away. A few of the girls from the Cross had driven down, and again there was topless dancing.

At half past twelve, I went into my room to get some dexedrine for Gordon. A couple were hard at it on my bed. Richard was sitting in the armchair next to the bed, just watching.

I got a bottle of pills from my case and made it to the door.

Richard called out, "Aw, Billy, don't rush away!"

The party went till late. I tried my room again at one. It was empty. I put the Do Not Disturb sign on the door and turned in.

In the morning it was even colder, but the bush fires along the coast were still burning. The paper reported that extensive snow-falls in the mountains and out to Bathurst had put out the fires up there. Richard was reading the papers over breakfast in the hotel dining room when I went in. I sat down opposite him. He was telling Charlie to look at the pictures of the snow and fire—wasn't this a sign? Charlie shrugged.

The front page of the *Illawarra Mercury* had a story on the show: *Little Richard "sent" teenagers!* There was no photo of Richard, but one of Eddie and Alis. It quoted Richard as saying his real ambition was to become a minister.

The other guests in the dining room stared at the group, particularly Richard. He was made up, his pompadour a good six inches high. He was camping it up more than ever this morning, exclaiming "Oh my oh *my*!" and "Oh, my soul!" at everything and everyone, his voice breaking into falsetto.

He made no mention of the goings-on in my room the night before.

O'Keefe joined us. He said "Richard, you really are something, man. That show was *gone*. Your clothes, your style—where do you get that from?"

"Why, Johnny, it's terribly charming of you to say that."

Charlie leaned over and said confidentially to O'Keefe, "You think Richard's something? Man, you should see Esquerita."

Richard and Charlie laughed fit to bust. Private joke, I guessed.

We left at nine. The next show was that night, in Newcastle. We were to drive there, wait, then take the entourage on to Williamstown afterwards. They would take a special flight from there on to Brisbane for the next show, while we would drive the hire cars back to Sydney.

Charlie travelled up front with me, while the rest of the band dozed in the back seat. I asked him how he felt about all this driving—six hours on the road between gigs. He said they did it all the time back home. I said that Richard was a strange chap. Charlie said yeah, he sure was one crazy nigger faggot, but a hell of a good boss to work for—paid good and showed respect to his musicians. I said what was the bible-bashing thing about. Charlie said, shit, it was nothing really, Richard had been under a lot of pressure lately. They all had—from all the recording and touring. The touring was fun, he said, but hard sometimes. There were plenty of chicks, but down south and even up north, most places they went the good citizens signed petitions to ban their shows, ban the records from the radio. They'd string Richard up if they could. I said yeah? He said sure. Hell, why do you think the newspaper back there ran a picture of Eddie and Alis, but not Richard, the star of the show. Because he's a brother, man, and because Eddie and Alis are cleanskin white kids, that's why.

We drove back through Sydney, but didn't stop except for petrol and a snack. Ted and Vic went with Gordon back to the Hampton Court to pick up Gene Vincent and the Blue Caps, who'd flown in the previous night. Gordon said he was going to try to get Marty Jay on his feet. We were to meet them all at the Newcastle Stadium.

Newcastle was altogether different from Wollongong. Newcastle was bodgie-ville. Driving through town, kids were whistling at Richard, banging on the car roof, begging for autographs. The old folks, of course, had never heard of Richard or Vincent or Cochran, but the kids were hip.

We parked the cars behind the stadium and took the gear in. The musos did a quick run-through.

Ted arrived at three o'clock with Gene Vincent and his band. Marty was there, looking not much better than he had before.

Ted came over to me, smoking a bunger and looking alarmed. "Where's Max?" he said. "We've got to talk."

I found Max and we all met in a storeroom at the back of the stadium. Ted was carrying the Globite.

"We've got trouble."

"What happened?"

"I stopped by my house to get a change of clothes. The place had been turned over, last night I guess. And there was a message for me to ring Laurie O'Brien, urgently."

"At Max's place?" I said.

"Yeah, that's right. Laurie had come around to my place, saw what had happened, left me the note. He left one at your place, too."

"And?"

"I rang him. Did you tell him about the rort?"

"Christ, no."

"Well, he knows we're holding the jewellery from the J. Farren Price robbery."

"He must have figured it out after he got bashed," I said.

Max said, "I knew the old fox was onto something. I told you, Billy."

"What does he want?" I said.

"He reckons he just wants to do the right thing. What he *did* say was that he'd made a few inquiries of his own."

"And?" ·

"According to Laurie, these mugs aren't acting on their own. They're a gang."

"Yeah?"

"It's worse. They *are* the standover mob from Darling Harbour, and they've got police backing."

"How does he know all this?"

"He didn't say, just got mysterious and said he still had contacts, not to worry about that."

"So do the cops know we've got the jewellery?"

"If the gang knows, then the cops know."

"Which cops?"

"I don't know."

I sat down on a dusty crate. "We're fucked."

"There's more."

"What?"

"They're here."

"In Newcastle?"

"Yeah. I had all the details of this job written on a pad next to my telephone. They must have seen it, figured that's where you and I had disappeared to."

"Doesn't mean they're here."

"I saw them. Twenty minutes ago."

"Where?"

"In a car outside. A bloke with a crew cut, another with slicked-back fair hair, a leather jacket. A couple more in the back seat I couldn't see clearly."

Max said, "They must know we're holding. Looks like we'll be doing the nasty swing from here on."

Ted looked at Max and said, "You tooled up?"

Max patted his jacket pocket.

"How about you, Bill? You got the gun Laurie gave you?"

"It's with my stuff somewhere."

"Then for fuck's sake, get it and keep it with you. OK, that was the bad news, here's the good news. I rang my contact, the next fence up the line. I think we can do a deal on the stuff. A pretty good deal at that."

"How good?"

"Better than if we'd done it earlier. The sooner it is after the actual hoist, the hotter the gear is. Now that the hoo-hah has died down a bit, the gear is worth more to a fence."

"We'll get more than we expected?"

"Don't know. But we shouldn't get much less. I don't want the word out that we're desperate to sell, it'd cruel our price."

"So what's next?"

"I'll take it to America, maybe in a week or two. We've just got to hold on to it, that's our big problem now. Tonight, Max, maybe you and I should watch the entrances to this place. We need to hide this stuff in the meantime, somewhere in the stadium. Got any ideas, Bill?"

"I'll find somewhere."

But the more I looked, the harder it was. If I carried it with me, I was a target for the thugs; if I stashed it in the stadium, anybody might find it. In the end, I put it in Richard's dressing room, behind the crate that held his stage clothes.

I bumped into Gordon outside Richard's room. He was keyed up. There was already a big queue outside, and this night promised to move the enterprise into the black, which was good news for all of us.

He pulled twenty quid out of his wallet. "Listen, Bill, I'm kind of caught up here for the moment. I need you do a run for me."

"What do you want?"

"Pyjamas."

"Eh?"

"For Richard. He wants five pairs of pyjamas. All different colours."

"Like five men's pyjamas?"

"Men's, chicks', doesn't matter. It's for the show. Bright as you can get."

I passed Ted on the way out. He asked if I had my gun with me. I told him yes, although in fact I didn't know where it was.

Eddie Cochran saw me leaving.

"Hey, Billy boy, where you going? More Chinaman's hooch?"

"Nah, a shopping run."

"I'll come with you."

We slipped out the back way.

A couple of years before, Max and I had tried to run bodgie dances at Bondi. But apart from a few hoods, no one had much of a clue what it was about. Back in the Aloha Milk Bar days, and before, the bodgies had been like a sect, like commo trade unionists, or female impersonators. Most people probably didn't actually know any bodgies personally, but everyone knew *about* them. Squareheads back then were still wearing mainly brown, gray, or navy-blue clothes, so the few bodgies about the place stood out. Drape suits, red or blue cardigans, black jeans, and ducktails for the blokes; tight sweaters, slacks, and ponytails for the girls.

But since then, Bill Haley and Joe Turner had toured out here, and there'd been movies like *Blackboard Jungle*. The squareheads would never go to a Haley show or see a rock 'n' roll movie, but plenty of teenagers had. Then Elvis Presley appeared on the scene. "Heartbreak Hotel" was played on the radio and Elvis's picture appeared in *Pix* and *Post*. The bodgies said, "Look, he's a bodgie, just like us." And that was the funny thing. He *did* look like a bodgie from Toongabie—like a cross between Boofhead and Tony Curtis. Except that his clothes were better cut than anything we could buy at Bennets or Gowings.

Now that the bodgies had the right music, the style caught on bigger than it ever had before. But I'd never seen anything like the scene outside the Newcastle Stadium that afternoon; nor had the coppers. Normally, you'd only see bodgies and widgies hanging around certain milk bars, listening to the jukebox. If there were more than seven or eight of them it was probably a blue. But now there were thousands of them, and no trouble, not yet anyway. Wollongong had been an OK crowd, but this looked like every bodgie and widgie in Australia had turned up. So had every cop: mounted, uniform, plainclothes. You could feel the excitement and expectation—maybe big trouble brewing, maybe just something really new and wild.

We walked out of the lane behind the stadium, a block away from the entrance. I said "Jumping Jesus, look at that!"

Eddie said "What, man?"

"The crowd! There's thousands of them. If they turn on a blue . . . "

"A blue?"

"A fight."

"Aw, don't worry, man, rock 'n' roll crowds don't fight each other, not when the music's playing. I've seen it like this plenty of times. They'll be a good crowd."

We found a Fosseys. I picked out five pairs of pyjamas, all different colours. The salesman wrapped them in a box, tied it with string.

On the way back, Eddie insisted on going into a milk bar, one with a jukebox. He got some change from me, put a couple of zacks in the box and played "C'mon Everybody" and "Going to the River," by Fats Domino. We drank a milk shake, played the pinballs for a while. No one said anything to Eddie, thinking he was just another bodgie.

As we turned back into the lane to get to the stage door, they jumped us. A fist swung around from behind me, caught me in the cheek. To my left, I saw Eddie get pushed over, onto the bonnet of a parked car. I turned around and stumbled back, just out of the way of a bodgie swinging something wrapped in a towel, heavy enough to be an iron bar. The one who'd pushed Eddie snatched the package out of my hand and ran off towards the entrance to the lane. The other advanced on me making long swinging arcs with the iron bar. I fell over backwards, heard a plosive "Oomph!" and looked up to see Eddie crash-tackling him. The one carrying the package had hesitated and was half-deciding to come back and assist his pal. I ran for him. He dropped the package and started to shape up. Then he thought better of it, grabbed the package, and started running. I caught his coattail and swung him around and into the wall. He went down. I gave him a quick kicking.

People in the crowd had noticed the fight, and there were already dozens rushing over. I picked up the package and grabbed Eddie, who was laying into the other guy.

We hurried, half-running down the back lane a hundred yards or so and back in through the stage door.

"I never heard of *nobody* being mugged for a few of pairs of pyjamas."

"Strange, isn't it?"

"Sure is."

Eddie dusted off his clothes and pulled a comb out of his back pocket, fixed up his hair.

We were still there huffing and puffing when Gordon walked past.

"Christ, Bill, there you are! I've been looking for you, man. Did you get the goddamn pyjamas?"

"Yeah." I handed him the package. "Look after them."

"Thanks. Now listen, there's a problem. Marty's all fucked up."

"That's news?"

"I want him to perform tonight. This isn't like Wollongong.

That crowd's jumpy as hell, man. I really want to send a comedian out there first, settle them down."

"Won't O'Keefe do?"

"Very funny. You still got the pills?"

"Yeah."

"OK. You're the doctor. Go and fix him up, for Christ's sake."

He strode away, then turned around and came back.

"And give me some of the goddamn things, will you?"

I tipped a dozen pills into the palm of his hand.

After he'd gone, Eddie said, "Hell, you better give me some of them boogers, Billy."

"OK. Don't do anything silly."

Then I swallowed two myself.

On my way to Marty's dressing room, I saw Ted and told him about the rumble outside.

"They're circling in for the kill," I said.

"Yeah, but they're being careful."

"Careful?"

"They could have used guns, but they didn't. They probably figure that if they cause too much ruckus, then the police will wake up that it's more than just a fight—that there's some real rorting going on. All we can do is keep them away from the gear for the time being. I'll go tell Max. You still got your gun?"

"Yeah, yeah."

"Don't 'yeah yeah' me, Bill, this is fucking serious! Everything you and I have is wrapped up in those fucking trinkets."

"Look, I'll see you soon, I've got stuff to do."

Before I could get to Marty's room I bumped into Richard.

"Bill, ooh my *soul*, but that was very sweet of you, getting those for me. I can't wait to put them on. And here was I thinking you were upset with me an' all, after you caught us, you know, in your room last night."

I said, "Forget it, it's nothing."

Thinking, shit, they're only pyjamas.

Marty was in his room, nodding off in his armchair, a cigarette burning down between his fingers. He had a little portable record player with an LP record spinning, Miles Davis or something like that. There was a half-bottle of scotch on the dressing table. I poured myself a double nip, drank it straight down, then poured another and sipped it. I went over and tapped Marty hard on the shoulder.

"Hey, wake up, man."

"Yeah, Billy, man, it's cool."

"Sure. Listen, Marty, it's show time."

"I'm ready to go." Even before he finished the sentence, his head started bowing, his speech slowed.

"Marty, I think you might need some medicine."

"I already took it, man. Me and the dragon are feeling no pain."

"Here. Take these."

"Are they bennies?"

"Sort of."

"You're full of surprises. I *love* bennies."

He took two pills. "And I thought there wouldn't be any drugs in Australia. How much I knew. How about reefer, Bill? You got some weed?"

"Don't think me a wowser, Marty, but haven't you had enough dope?"

"Man, I've never had enough dope."

"Lee wants you on stage tonight. You better lay off chasing the dragon for a while, eh? I think you've caught him. And maybe you should take a shower, freshen up a little?"

"Yeah, yeah, OK."

"Don't 'yeah yeah' me. You're a shot duck. Time to pull yourself together!"

He started to nod off again. I took hold of his lapels and shook him, hard. "Marty, get your arse in gear or I'll take your dope from you and kick you out on the fucking street."

"Goddamn nazi."

"Take a shower, drop those bennies, drink some coffee, shape up. I'll be back in ten minutes. Make yourself funny."

I found Lee, told him Marty was getting ready.

"OK, good. Now, there's something to do." He reached into his back pocket and pulled out a fat roll of ten-pound notes. "For the stadium staff. The stadium manager insisted on hiring heavies. He still remembers the Bill Haley show." He shook his head, counted out some notes. "He suggested we give a little extra to his people before the show, help keep them happy. They're a bunch of rubes, I don't want *them* starting trouble. There's two hundred there. Here's a list. They've been promised ten quid each. Write out a pay envelope for each of them."

"Like with tax and that?"

"No, fuck that, just write the name on the envelope and put a ten in each one, and make sure they get them."

"All right."

"There's something else. I advertised a dancing competition. The winners get twenty-five pounds each. Can you go out into the crowd and pick a winning couple—then send them up onto the stage as soon as the MC calls for them?"

"Righto."

O'Keefe opened the show again. The feeling in the hall was good, and the bodgies seemed inclined to be tolerant. O'Keefe had changed his act even since last night. He got his band to play louder, a bit like the Upsetters. But it wasn't the same. The Upsetters played really hard and loud but still looked relaxed. The Dee Jays looked like they were playing rugby league. But the crowd seemed to appreciate the effort, and booed them only a little. Alis got a mild response.

Then Cochran came on and went off his nut. The go-fast agreed with his style. He jumped up on the grand piano, rolled over on his back. The crowd began screaming and didn't stop till the end of the show.

Gene Vincent and the Blue Caps did their bit, which was a little tame after Cochran. I picked out a couple of dancers to win the money, two girls from Wallsend, Fay and Janelle. The MC called them up at the end of Vincent's set and gave them the dough.

Then Richard came on. He was wearing a cape, with a suit underneath. A little way into the show he threw off the cape, then his coat, then his shirt, then his dacks. He was wearing pyjamas underneath. The crowd went batshit. He did "She's Got It" and "Heebie Jeebies," then took off the pyjama shirt. He had another on underneath. He threw the shirt into the crowd. A scuffle broke out over it. He did "Long Tall Sally." He took off the next shirt and threw that one into the mob. He shouted to the crowd, "All you pretty girls, I want y'all to get off your moneymakers. Come on now, get up *off* that money and shake them titties!"

He sang "Ooh, My Soul," and kept stripping off layer after layer of clothing till he was bare-chested. I was at the back of the stadium. There were police everywhere, and a couple of plainclothes cops right in front of me. One of them was writing in a notebook. A sergeant approached and asked them a question. The plainclothes looked around at the berserk crowd of bodgies, had a little discussion and shook their heads at the sergeant, who left. I went around to the backstage and found Gordon.

"The Vice Squad are on the verge of stopping the show."

"Oh, Christ, is that right?"

"Yeah, I think so. Even *they* got the 'get up off that money' gag. Far as I can tell, the only thing stopping them is they're frightened of what will happen if they step in right now."

He took out his roll, peeled off a hundred quid, handed it to me. "Why don't you go talk to them, sweeten them up a little?"

"I'll try."

"You know what I like about Aussie police? They work cheap."

I stuck the money in my pocket along with the bouncers' bread. I went back out into the crowd just as the show finished. Richard left the stage, and the crowd abruptly stopped screaming and filed out. The cops were gone.

I went backstage. Lee was talking to Richard, begging him not to repeat the striptease next time. Richard said he was out of pyjamas anyway. Then he looked over at me and said, "But I still got a little something up my sleeve."

Gordon shrugged, saw me, and walked over quickly.

"Did you see the lawmen?"

"Not yet."

"Forget that for now. Go and give some of that crank to Gene and the boys. They sort of feel they were upstaged by Eddie. Goddamn artistic egos."

"I should've been a fucking quack, get some money for doing this. Where are they?"

"In the last dressing room. I'm meeting the press people now. And after you do that, the stadium manager's worried about the piano and the stage lights or some bullshit. Can you schmooze him?"

"Maybe I should stick a broom up my arse and sweep the floor while I'm at it?"

I found Vincent outside his dressing room, gave him a handful of pills. He swallowed them in a gulp.

Charlie saw it, came over and said, "Billy, my man, I hope you're not forgetting your ol' friends here?"

I tipped a few pills into his mitt. "This whole show's completely fucking batshit anyway. Listen, come out to the loading dock, I've got some weed."

I got Max and the three of us went out the back door and lit a reefer. We were outside the main building, but protected from the street by a high corrugated-iron fence. Max had a half bottle of Cutty. We passed it around with the reefer. Richard came out and joined us, but didn't take any booze or weed. He had his cape on, ready for the next show.

It was nighttime now, and the stars were out. I still had to make up the pay packets, bribe the cops, and somehow soothe the stadium manager, but I thought, fuck it. So I lingered where I was, let the whisky and reefer do their stuff. We could hear noises from the street, kids waiting for the show, calling to one another. Then a voice nearby called out, "There it is!"

Another said, "Where? I can't see it."

"There! Look, up in the sky."

Max said, "The fuck are they on about. Superman?"

I looked up, saw nothing, then noticed a brighter light, straight above, moving slowly across the sky.

I said to the others, "It's Sputnik!"

"Motherfucker!" said Charlie.

"Great God almighty!" said Richard.

Max lifted the bottle towards the sky. "*Salut*, comrades!"

Richard said, "Oh, my Lord."

Charlie looked at him.

"That's it!" Richard said. "Signs and wonders. Oh, man, that's it."

"Aw, shit, Richard, that's just some Russian flying saucer, that's all!"

Richard shook his head slowly. His lip trembled. "I can't do it any more. Jesus is calling me. I'm gonna join the Baptist church. I'm through with this life."

Charlie looked across at me and Max, embarrassed. Worried, too.

We watched the Sputnik move across our little bit of sky. Richard went inside, muttering about the "latter days." After he'd gone, Charlie told us to take no notice—Richard had been talking like that for months. "He's from Georgia. They take their religion *serious* down there."

I went back to see how Marty was doing, but was intercepted by Ted Rallis. He grabbed my arm, pulled me aside and said, "Thank Christ I've found you! Better listen to me, now. They're inside."

"The nasties?"

He nodded. "They're out on the floor right now. I've seen them. They came in with the crowd for the next show. Here, put this fucking thing in your pocket, will you?" He handed me the Luger.

"Where—"

"I knew you didn't have it on you. I got it from your bag. Now take it, for God's sake!"

I stuck the gun in my belt, pushed it around to the side under my jacket.

Teddy said, "Where's Max got to?"

"Fucked if I know."

I went on into Marty's room. He was half-dressed for the show, but still barefoot. His bowtie was hanging undone around his collar and he hadn't shaved yet. I gave him a shake. The Luger fell out of my belt and banged loudly on the floor.

"I knew it man, you're a motherfucking Nazi, with a fucking Gestapo gat. What are you gonna do, kill me? Send me to a goddamn gas chamber?"

"Can you do your act or not?"

"You gonna make me perform for you? What will you do, arrest my family, torture me? Send me to a labour camp?"

I was about to speak, but then thought, fuck it, and left him.

I was buttonholed outside his door by the stadium manager, a bloke named Arch. Lee had told him to refer all problems to me. I thought, thanks, Lee. Arch said he'd been out looking at the crowd for the second show. He said he was most concerned about the grand piano on stage, and that he feared a riot could break out if the performers were to incite the crowd again the way they had in the first show. He said the stadium owners would be *extremely* concerned if they knew what sort of show was going on, and it was his responsibility as manager to ensure that standards were upheld. The more he talked the more worked up he got.

He shook his head and said, "I'm afraid, Mr. Glasheen, that unless I get an assurance that there'll be no indecorous behaviour in the next show, I'm going to stop proceedings. I'll turn off the power to the stage if I have to!"

I could hear Marty having a spew inside, over the sound of the record player. Off in the distance, I saw Gene Vincent banging his head against a wall. A couple of Blue Caps and Vic Camellieri were passing around a bottle of Johnnie Walker. O'Keefe was howling like a dog. Eddie Cochran was doing an impression of Elvis Presley for the press guys, and at that moment Richard emerged from his dressing room in his underpants, his pomp pumped up to record heights, reading his Bible. Outside, in the stadium, the crowd had started rhythmically stamping their feet.

I turned to Arch, put my arm across his shoulders, looked him in the eye. "I want you to rest assured, Arch, nothing will transpire in the next show that will be in any way a departure from the artistes' normal professional standards." I took the hundred quid Lee had given me for the coppers and stuffed it in Arch's top pocket.

He said it better not, and strode away.

I found Gordon, told him Marty was off the menu. He said had I given the money to the bouncers yet? I said shit, no. He said do it now. I said, what, out there in the crowd? He said, yeah, out there, where the fuck else?

I found an empty room and lit another reefer and did the pay packets. It took about ten minutes. Then I slipped out and up the back of the stadium, approached every bouncer I could find, got his name, dug out his envelope, thanked him for the great work he was doing, all that bullshit.

O'Keefe came on while I was out there, sang two songs, then Alis did her bit. Gene Vincent came out and went berko. Five minutes into the set, half way through "Woman Love," the drummer's kit started to fall apart—the bass pedal fucked up or something. So he stood up, picked up the snare drum, leaped onto the piano, and stamped his foot to the music. Sorry, Arch. Then he jumped off the piano—right over the footlights into the crowd.

The bodgies and widgies loved it. Somewhere off to the side of the hall, I heard a crash as a door was smashed in. Vincent left the stage looking pleased. The cheering became one continuous roar. Charlie Connors came on stage, fiddled with the drum kit for a while, then Cochran came on. He sang "C'mon Everybody." He mopped his face with a handkerchief and threw it into the crowd. A rumble broke out over it. Charlie was playing drums behind Eddie, and really belting the Christ out of the kit. Bits and pieces were falling off it. Eddie pulled out another hanky, wiped his face again, dangled the hanky in front of the crowd. They pressed forward and I could see the footlights getting all busted up. Cochran laughed, balled up the wet hanky and threw it as far back as he could. Then he did "Cut Across Shorty." By the end of the set, the drum kit was history.

I still had four pay packets to give out. I knew if I turned up backstage, Gordon would send me out to scrounge a drum kit somewhere, so I kept circulating slowly through the stadium.

The reefer, the booze, and the dexes were fighting a three-way skirmish over possession of my brain, but no one of them had the upper hand. They were tearing up the terrain, though. I just kept moving.

Max came onstage and removed the fucked-up kit. A minute later he miraculously brought out another kit, and set it up. The Upsetters came on. The crowd was in a state of barely contained riot. The coppers looked terrified. I knew they wouldn't dare stop the show now. When Richard came on, they sort of drifted away.

Richard was wearing his cape. He started with "Good Golly Miss Molly." When it came to the stops, he threw the cape off, then peeled off his shirt and threw it into the crowd.

One by one, I found the remaining bouncers and paid them off, then moved a little way down the aisles towards the front.

Richard sang "Long Tall Sally." The crowd screamed and whistled all the way through it.

Then he sang, "Lucille." I hadn't looked too closely at Richard since he'd come on. Now, I could see that he was gesturing to the people up front, waving his arms at them. Then he threw something into the mob. There was a wild scramble in front of the stage.

I fought my way a bit closer, pushing down the aisle. I stopped and stood up on a vacant chair, saw Richard twenty yards in front of me, standing there on the stage in all his finery.

He was wearing jewellery on every finger, bracelets on his wrists, earrings, seven or eight watches, dozens of gold chains, strings of pearls—it looked like the whole J. Farren Price hoist, here on the stage of Newcastle Stadium, in front of ten thousand bodgies and widgies who had just crossed over into smash-it-up-and-burn-the-fuckin'-joint-down mode. I put my hand to my head, thinking, there it goes, the whole deal, fucked.

Across the hall I saw Crew Cut, looking just as intently at me as I'd been looking at Richard. He turned to look at Richard, looked back at me, grinned, signalled to his snowy-haired mate.

I pushed my way to the front, not trying to be nice any more. I kneed, elbowed, stomped on toes, snarled my way to within a few yards of the front.

Richard was teasing the crowd. They were reaching out, trying to grab his hands. He was waving his fingers, showing off the jewellery.

Crew Cut and Snow had muscled their way to the front. Behind them, I saw the bloke who'd had the iron bar in the alley. The other one would be around somewhere.

Richard took off his shoes and socks, chucked them into the mob. Another scuffle started. Richard took off his belt, dangled it in front, until one of the people leaning over the footlights grabbed it. The song finished and he made a quick signal to the band, turned back to the crowd, looked up and cried "A-wop-bop-a-loo-bop-a-lop-bam-boom!" and launched into "Tutti Frutti." His eyes rolled back in his head, and he was shaking. When the song got to the stops he dropped to his knees, put his head down, and didn't move, like he was overcome. He stayed that way for twenty, thirty seconds. The band kept comping away, with the sax player, Grady, blowing a spastic solo. Then Richard leapt up and did the "A-wop-bop-a-loo-bop" bit again, took off a diamond ring, and pitched it out into the crowd, way over the heads of Crew Cut and Snow. I got as near the stage as I could.

Richard sang "Send Me Some Lovin'" next. He reached forward to tease the crowd, but somebody grabbed his hand and pulled him forward, wouldn't let go. Richard was kind of laughing, but as he kept getting dragged forward, he turned back to the band, waved for help. Grady and Charlie put down their instruments and rushed forward, grabbed his other arm and pulled him back, like in a tug-of-war.

I edged over just as Richard was yanked right off the stage and into the crowd. He went down, right out of sight. I barged over, got right up next to him, reached under my jacket for the gun. Richard was on the ground.

Crew Cut was leaning over him. He had a couple of rings in his left hand already, was working at the bracelets. I swung the Luger down on his head, as hard as I could. He collapsed on top of Richard, blood running from his skull. A couple of people screamed. I picked up one of the rings—the other had skittered off somewhere—and helped Richard to his feet.

Crew Cut was laid out on the floor. Snow made it to the circle, was bending down to help Crew Cut. I grabbed him by the collar and pulled him backwards, trying to get a biff into him with my other hand. I connected, but only just.

A wedge of bouncers made it to us, Teddy with them, and Richard was shepherded back to the stage. I dived into the crowd and grabbed Snow, wrestled him off his feet, down on top of Crew Cut, and shouted at the nearest bouncer, "Throw these pricks out. They started all the trouble!"

Richard made it back to the stage, and kept going, straight out the back. The band followed him off, the MC came on asking everyone to please be patient and settle down; Little Richard and the Upsetters would return to the stage in just a moment.

Max and Teddy were backstage. "The fuck's going on?" asked Max.

"Richard found the gear."

"How?"

"I don't know. I hid it in his room."

"Why *there* for Christ's sake?"

"Hey, it wasn't that easy to find a safe place."

"So how come Richard's modelling the fucking stuff, for everyone to see, cops included?"

"He must've thought I put it there for him."

Teddy said, "The man's completely yarra. We've got to get it off him. Jesus, if the cops see it."

"Maybe it doesn't matter now."

"Eh?"

"He's wearing only a part of the whole stash, but the thugs wouldn't know that. The bouncers have chucked out Crew Cut and one of his mates anyway. There're a couple more of them still inside, but they're the junior partners. They won't be up to much. I'll just speak to Richard, tell him not to go throwing any more gifts into the crowd. Otherwise, we may as well leave the gear with him for now. It might just be to our advantage. These cops here tonight wouldn't in a million years connect the jewellery Richard's wearing with the robbery."

But Richard had run onstage before I could talk to him. I grabbed Charlie on his way back. "For Christ's sake, Charlie, tell Richard not to throw away any more of that jewellery."

"Say what?"

"The jewellery he's wearing. It belongs to me."

He raised his eyebrows.

"Well, sort of. I'm minding it for someone. The point is, it's real. Tell Richard to hang on to it, for Christ's sake—not to go throwing it into the crowd. I'll explain later."

"Ooh, Billy, something going on here, man?"

He walked away shaking his head, before I could explain. He ran onstage, straight over to Richard and whispered in his ear, gestured back at me. Richard turned around, gave me a smile, nodded.

The rest of the show passed pretty much without incident, apart from scuffles, and a lot of screaming and yelling.

But at the end of the set, Richard stopped the band, reached under his cape, and pulled out a Bible. Fuck me if he didn't start reading from it. The crowd sort of laughed along at first, but Richard kept reading.

He went on for ten minutes. Then he told the crowd that he was quitting rock 'n' roll. There were shouts of "No!" and some hooting and booing. Richard said there were signs in the sky, he'd seen them himself; that fire and pestilence were coming, and that he was going to preach the gospel from now on.

I was standing next to Gordon, who stood watching, shaking his head, smoking a cigarette.

"Fucking lunatic!" he said.

"He says he's had the call."

"I'll give him a fucking call!" He shook his head. "This religion thing. He says he wants to quit the business. I begged, bullied, threatened him. I said finish the goddamn tour." He stubbed out the half-finished smoke with his shoe. "*This* is his compromise." He walked off.

Richard finished his sermon and left the stage. The crowd shuffled out of the stadium, subdued.

I met Richard and Charlie in Richard's dressing room. I took the stuff back off Richard and started to repack it, while Charlie watched, not saying anything.

Richard was changing into street clothes, packing away his gear. He said he was sorry, that he wanted to pay for the stuff he'd thrown into the crowd. I told him not to worry about it.

Richard went into the bathroom, while I wrapped the stuff up in the tissue paper, put it back into the bag.

Charlie said, "Billy, if that shit's genuine, like you say, then those rings must have been worth maybe a couple of C-notes, at least."

"What the hell—easy come, easy go."

Charlie shook his head. "Something's wrong here, man."

I put the stuff down, looked at Charlie. "Listen, Charlie, it's sort of hard to explain."

"Yeah, like, for one thing, you're carrying a rod. I saw you hit that guy in the crowd upside his head."

"Well, yeah, that's part of it."

"That's all right, Billy, you go ahead, do what you do. But, man, I sure would appreciate knowing if there gonna be some kind of *High Noon* situation develop, know what I'm saying?"

"Yeah. It's nearly over now, though, Charlie."

There was a light plane waiting at Williamtown Air Base, twenty miles away. The performers were to take the plane to Brisbane that night, perform there the next day, then fly back to Sydney. For me and the drivers, this was the last leg. We would drive the show to the airport, then turn around and take the cars back to Sydney.

We got loaded up within half an hour. I was at the wheel of the lead car, carrying Charlie and Richard. Lee came over just as we were leaving, handed Charlie a big box of fried chicken from the local Chinese restaurant.

"This'll have to keep you guys going until we get to Brisbane," he said.

Charlie shrugged.

We left the stadium and drove through the city, down to the ferry wharf, where we'd be taken across the Hunter River to Stockton.

The river was wide and black. A few streetlights were showing on the other side, but not much else. A smoky breeze was blowing across the water, but it wasn't cold. There were a dozen cars already queued up waiting for the punt when we arrived. We were the first of our entourage.

We pulled up and waited, Charlie up front, Richard in the back. One by one the others arrived and queued up behind us.

The ferry came in, the kid deckhand opened the gate, signalled the cars on. I drove aboard when our turn came. I looked back, saw the kid put his hand up to signal no more as he shut the gate behind us. We pulled away from the ramp, left the others waiting for the next trip.

Once we'd pulled away, Charlie and Richard got out of the car, went over to the passenger bench, sat down and picked at their chicken. I walked over to the rail and lit a smoke. The stirred-up phosphorescence was making the ferry's wake glow blue-green. I took a couple more puffs of my cig, then joined Charlie and Richard on the bench.

Other travellers were out of their cars walking around. Some had obviously been at the show—they had pegged black jeans, red shirts, brushbacks, ponytails, all that. They were checking us out, but no one approached us.

I looked around. On the other side of the punt, half ducking into the shadows, I saw two blokes looking my way. Snow, and maybe the two who had jumped me. I stretched and yawned, like I hadn't noticed anything.

My heart started playing the Bo Diddley beat, and I broke into a sweat. They must have realized that Max and Ted were still back at the dock, waiting for the next trip across. If they were going to do anything it would be now, while we were separated from the others. My gun was in the gladstone bag, which was in the boot of the car, along with the jewellery. I sat back down, trying to look casual. My legs were shaking. I sat staring at the water, immobilized.

Charlie and Richard were next to me, finishing off their chicken. They'd piled the bones back in the cardboard box.

I glanced back over my shoulder. Snow was closer now, ducking out of sight. I thought through what they would do. Throw me into the river, take the car. Jesus, it was all so easy.

I turned to Charlie, spoke quietly. "Charlie, you know how you said you'd appreciate knowing if anything was about to happen?"

"Yeah?"

"It's about to happen."

"Shit."

"Charlie. Listen to me. How'd you like to earn a bit of over-time?"

He looked at me doubtfully.

"You ever done any acting?"

"You ever see *The Girl Can't Help It*?"

"Right. Well, I've got this idea. We'll need Richard's help."

We were just over halfway across the river. I had my coat collar turned up, sitting slumped like I was on the blink. I could sense movements off to both sides. I waited till I was sure the heavies were within earshot, then I coughed, which was our cunningly chosen prearranged signal.

Charlie stood up and pointed to the sky. "Motherfucker! There it is again, the goddamn Russian Sputnik, man, look over there!"

Richard leaped to his feet. "That's it! The sign! That's the sign!" He turned to us. "I'm through! Mine eyes have seen the glory! I care not for mammon—I'm gonna get on board that train! I'm through with rock 'n' roll! I am *through* with sin!"

He was shouting. People were staring. The hoods were just a few yards away, frozen, not sure what to do.

Charlie put his hand on Richard's shoulder, said, "Settle down, Richard, you know you can't just quit like that, man!"

"I can, and oh, I will. Believe me, I've been called!"

"Aw, Richard, that's bullshit, man."

"You believe me if I throw this ring in the water? You believe that, Charlie? Billy, you believe me if I throw this in?" He took off the ring he had on, one of his own.

I said, "Aw, come on Richard, you can't do that." I could hear my own voice. It was no great performance.

"Well, watch this!" He pitched the ring far out into the water. It flashed briefly as it hit the phosphorescence in the still water. Richard reached over and threw the chicken bones in. They sparkled all the way down. I made a lunge for him, but contrived to trip over Charlie. That gave Richard time to empty his pockets, and throw all of his, mine and Charlie's spare change into the drink, all the while calling out, "Vanities! Snares of Satan! I'm leaving Sodom! I ain't looking back! Oh my precious Lord, how great Thou art!"

It was up to me now. I ran back the length of the ferry, as if trying to stay level with the spot where Richard had thrown the stuff in. I pushed past the thugs who were standing in confusion, not sure what to do.

I got to the end of the punt, put my hand to my brow, looked up to the sky, made a gesture of despair and exasperation, then walked back, running my hand through my hair like I was really distracted.

As I got level with Snow, I turned to him. "It's over. The crazy prick! Did you see that? Jesus!" I walked off shaking my head, turned around and came back. "I'm fucked. The other guys are gonna kill me. I'm dead." I grabbed his lapels. "Who's going to believe *this*?" Snow didn't say anything. I walked back over to Richard and Charlie.

Snow's two mates were looking at the water, looking back at Richard. They seemed to be buying it. Richard had fallen to his knees, praying. Charlie was crying, "Richard, why'd you do that for, man?"

The deckhand came over and said to me, "What's the problem here, mate? Did someone go over?"

"Worse than that. Some*thing*. And now I'm in big trouble. How deep is the water there?"

"I don't know . . . forty, fifty feet. What did you lose?"

"Jewellery."

He shook his head. "The tide's running out. Jewellery?"

I nodded.

He shook his head again, gestured off towards the sea and walked away.

I walked back over to Snow, pulling out my flask of Cutty. I took a big swig and said, "What am I gonna tell the others? What will I tell Lee Gordon?"

I passed the bottle to him. He took a drink. I thought, got you.

"Lee Gordon. Is he involved in this, too?"

"He's gonna have my guts for garters. All that for nothing."

I shook my head, stared out to sea. Then I turned to Snow and put out my hand.

"Billy's my name, by the way. Sorry about decking your mate back there at the stadium. Is he OK?"

"My name's Mick. Yeah, he's all right. Got a headache. The rozzers got him for carrying a concealed weapon, took him back to the cells. He's probably out by now. How come Little Richard had the jewellery in the first place?"

"Mick, you tell me, then we'll both know. It was Gordon's idea to hide the stuff with Richard's gear. But Richard found it, thought it was stage jewellery. Crazy bastard put it on and wore it onstage."

"Jesus."

I thought of the working over this guy and his pal had given Laurie, and for a moment considered smashing him with the bottle and throwing him over the rail. But he was more useful to us as a stooge.

"Listen," I said. "If we want to salvage any of that stuff, we're going to have to work together on it. How do you feel about that?"

"What do you have in mind?"

"Maybe diving for it. I mean even if we only get some of it . . . "

"When?"

"I can't do anything for a couple of days. Then maybe."

"I'll have to think about it." I could see the cogs of villainy turning in his double-crossing mind.

"Give me your phone number," I said.

"Don't worry, I'll contact you. I know where you live."

I said suit yourself, and went back to Richard and Charlie.

We drove off the ferry at the other side. Mick and his cronies took the ferry straight back. They waved goodbye to me like we were old comrades. I pulled off the road a mile past the ferry dock and lit a reefer, smoked it with Charlie.

Richard, sitting in the back, said, "How'd we do?"

"Just fine."

Charlie half-turned to Richard and said, "Man, you had me going there for a while. I thought you meant it."

"I did mean it, Charlie."

"Say what?"

"I really am through. I'll finish the tour, like Lee wants me to. But when it's over, I'm going to the river. I'm going to join the ministry."

Charlie said, "Whatever."

We got to the plane twenty minutes before the rest of the party. The pilot was impatient to leave. I helped him load the gear. Richard and Charlie boarded the plane. I said good-bye, thanks again for saving my arse.

The other cars arrived in a convoy. Ted got out of the car quickly, came up to me and said, "What happened back there? That fair-headed bloke was on the ferry. We were about to give him a thumping, but he said something about it being all over. He said no one won."

"Everything's fine. I'll tell you later."

It took fifteen minutes to get the party aboard the plane. Gene Vincent and the Blue Caps could scarcely walk. Likewise for O'Keefe and the Dee Jays. Eddie Cochran said he was already flying, didn't need no plane.

After the plane took off and the other drivers had left, I told Max and Ted what had happened. I gave Ted the bag of jewellery.

We had a drink, a couple of pills for the ride home, and the last of the reefer. Ted said, "Here, give me some of that loco weed. This rock 'n' roll business is playing hell with my nerves."

I drove back to Sydney in four hours, took the car straight back to my flat at Darlo, walked upstairs. Lights were on, even though it was four in the morning. Del Keene was there, asleep in the armchair. There was a suitcase next to her. She roused the moment I walked in the room.

"Your housekeeping has gone to the shithouse since I left, Billy."

Thursday I slept till noon. Del was still asleep when I woke. The sun was shining into the room and I'd've been happy to stay there forever. I made some tea and toast, took it back to Del on a tray.

We stayed in bed until it got dark outside, then went up to the Cross for a meal at the Belgrade.

We sat in the restaurant, looking out at Surrey Street.

I turned to her. "So what made you come back?"

She said, "You know how when I left, I said I was through with Sydney, through with drugs, and through with you?"

"I sure do."

"Well, at least one of those was a fib."

"Don't go away again." I leaned across the table and kissed her.

"Aren't you just the romantic one these days?"

"It must be love. How was Coffs, then?"

"Same as ever. I was different. I never really felt like I fitted in before, but I was like a Martian when I went back. I went out with a bloke for a while, a dentist. He asked me to marry him. I tried to get into the swing of it all, but I couldn't. Then I read about the Little Richard show, thought it would be fun to see it, then I heard you were associated with it." She took a sip of her drink. "So

I figured if I threw a leg over you, I might cop a free ticket."

"What are your plans now?"

"Do I get the free ticket?"

"We'll see. By the way, O'Keefe nagged his way into the show. Wait'll you see him." The waitress came and took our order.

"What are your long-term plans?"

"Oh, I'll have to get a job. Back to Repat, I suppose."

"There's no hurry for the job. I'm cashed, at least I am in theory."

"Oh? How come?"

I gave her the *Reader's Digest* condensed version of the jewellery rort, told her about the standover hoods, the business with the chicken bones. She took it all in without comment, asked a few questions to clarify a point here and there.

She asked if there was more. I said, yeah, there's more, and told her about Marty Jay and Molly Price, about chasing the dragon. She went pretty quiet at that.

When I finished she said, "You've been busy."

"Yeah. Do you still feel like taking a punt on being involved with me?"

"It's better than being married to a dentist in Coffs Harbour, even *with* the free fillings."

Our *pola pola* arrived. We ate in silence.

When she'd finished, she said, "So what happens now?"

"About the jewellery?"

"That, Laurie, the Lee Gordon Show, everything."

"Ted's arranging to get rid of the stuff overseas, I don't even know where. Lee and the show are back in town tomorrow night, of course. Then they go to Melbourne, without me if I can arrange it. They come back here at the end of next week, do Sydney, Newcastle, and Brisbane again, providing there are sufficient ticket sales. Which, judging by Wollongong and Newcastle, there will be. As for Laurie, I really don't know."

Laurie rang that night. He was still at Perkal Towers. I asked him if he was all right, he said yeah, he was fine, really good, in fact. He said he'd seen Max and he'd heard about the Newcastle business. He said he knew all about the jewellery rort. How did he know? I asked. He said he'd guessed—the standover men, the way I was acting, the fact that the J. Farren Price robbery was unsolved, then the bashing—what else could it be?

"So get honest, Laurie. What do you want from me, *really*?"

"I don't want anything from you, Bill. I wish you could understand that."

I rang Max and Ted. There'd been no sign of anyone watching either of them since they'd got back. Ted said he'd spoken to the crowd he hoped would buy the gear, but they were playing a little hard to get. Then I rang the Hampton Court, to speak to Molly, but she wasn't in the room. The desk bloke said he hadn't seen her for a couple of days.

I met up with Max and Teddy again on Friday, picked up the Chevs, and met the party at the airport. Brisbane had been big. Richard had once again performed a show that all but brought the Vice Squad onstage, then finished up by reading from the Bible for fifteen minutes.

Friday night at Sydney Stadium was huge. Gordon put on two shows, starting at five o'clock, and then three shows the next day, starting mid-afternoon. Every show was a full house. Richard did the pyjama game at each gig. Gordon was prepared this time— he'd ordered thirty assorted pairs from David Jones.

For the Saturday show, Gordon had half the ringside seating removed, and offered a hundred quid this time for the best dancers. Half a dozen bodgies were arrested for brawling over Richard's pyjamas, and the rozzers bounced some girls they deemed to be overexcited. The mesh between the bleachers and the floor seating was torn down halfway through the first Saturday show, and a couple of cops got decked. Eddie pashed off a girl who made it onto the stage, and even Alis Lesley started to loosen up a bit. During her set she jumped up on the piano—it had become almost obligatory since Newcastle—then she lay on the floor and thrashed around with the microphone. Finally, she dry-rooted the double bass. Del was impressed.

In the end, I went to Melbourne with the show. Del came along, too. We saw the same pattern repeated in Melbourne. It was like one of those Hindu or Arab religious festivals, where the believers come from far and wide, then all go rats together, except here it was bodgies and widgies. There was only one show that stiffed. Lee Gordon, for reasons none of us could follow, insisted on flying the show out to Broken Hill. The Barrier Industrial Council called a boycott because of the absence of Australian trade union members on the show. Less than a hundred people turned up. Maybe it was just as well.

But elsewhere the tour was like a mobile uprising. The squarehead world at first hardly knew it was going on. The Sputnik, the bush fires, the freak weather, Tulloch, and the atom-bomb tests at Maralinga all conspired to keep Richard off the front pages. (Reading the morning papers some days, it seemed like Richard might have had it right after all.) But as people watched the newsreels and read the page three newspaper reports, they started to get the idea that this was something different from Bill Haley or

Johnnie Ray. Little Richard went on television in all his bejewelled glory. Gene Vincent and the boys were out of control the whole time, and Gordon did his best to steer the press people away from them and onto Alis and Eddie, who could almost pass as clean-cut teenagers.

By the second week of the tour, music shops were taking out ads in the papers, announcing that they had Little Richard, Eddie Cochran, and Gene Vincent records for sale. People came to realize that this teenage music thing wouldn't fit in with the style of entertainment they were used to. It was a whole lot more than speeded-up boogie woogie.

"Rock 'n' roll" as a phrase entered everyday speech. Jazz groups and dance promoters quickly changed their posters and adverts so that they read "Rock 'n' Roll Dance" instead of "Jazz Dance." A jockey was called up before the stewards at Randwick, for failing to ride out the race. He claimed his horse had "rock 'n' rolled from furlong to finish post" after hitting a gale-force headwind in the straight.

Richard stayed on his religious jag. The audience dug it in a way, took it as part of his weirdness, along with the clothes and the queer act. When he sang, he was kind of like a hot gospeller anyway. Eddie Cochran told me the "a-wop-bop-a-loo-bop" stuff was like the way preachers carried on down home when they worked themselves up—talking in tongues and generally going spaz.

Word got out about Richard's repeated declarations that he was quitting show business. The tabloid press in America ran stories on Richard's religious conversion and his decision to quit rock 'n' roll, which was almost enough to ruin his record company. The reports made a big deal about him throwing his jewellery into the Hunter River. Some of them said it happened at Sydney Harbour, others said the Hawkesbury River, a couple of papers said he tried to commit suicide. People would ask me what happened on the ferry. I'd tell them, Oh yeah, Richard threw thousands of bucks worth of gear into the drink, for sure.

Gordon had hoped to run the tour for nearly a month, but Richard became more and more determined to quit. Gordon brought the tour back to Sydney for a show at the Stadium, billed it as "Little Richard's farewell to show business! His last public performance anywhere in the world!" Then he took the show to Newcastle and Brisbane again, minus Eddie and Alis, for three more last performances, ten bob all tickets. I read later that back in the States, Richard did a couple more last-ever farewell performances, for New York disc jockey Alan Freed, before he really did give it up.

Stories got around about the after-show orgies, which were still going on despite Richard's religious leanings. Del and I had to throw him out of our hotel room on one occasion—he had sneaked in unnoticed while we were between the furlong and the finishing post.

Gordon made Gene and the Blue Caps do an extra show to make up for the one they'd missed at the beginning. He booked the Rivoli Ballroom out at Parramatta, which was bodgie Mecca. They did a Sunday night show, with Del and Max doing the support. It was like the Aloha Milk Bar all over again. Del was great, and the band Max put together played good boogie-woogie, but Max couldn't or wouldn't make his guitar twang like Cliff Gallup in the Blue Caps, or like Eddie Cochran could.

Marty Jay and Molly had disappeared from sight.

During the next-to-last show, at Newcastle, I nipped out for half an hour and went down to the ferry wharf. I was in luck—the same deckhand was on who'd been on the fortnight before. I rode the ferry across. He remembered me. He told me he'd been cadging free beers since that night on the strength of having witnessed what was becoming music history. I thought good for you. I asked him if anyone had come back, any divers. He said, are you kidding, there were blokes there with a diving rig the very next day. He laughed. As if they'd ever find anything, with the current there. Plus the tailor had been running for the last couple of weeks, and as everyone knew, they'd have a go at anything shiny.

Teddy finally got word on the jewellery, arranged with a fence in America, of all places. I never asked him for details, but I figured maybe Lee Gordon had had a hand in it. In the end, Teddy flew out on the same Pan Am Constellation as Richard and Vincent and the rest. I saw them all off together, from Brisbane Airport. Marty and Molly weren't there.

During the second week of the tour, I got a call from Laurie. He'd moved out of Perkal Towers, was taking a holiday in a cabin up at Towler's Bay, on Pittwater, north of Sydney. He said he had plenty of room up there, why didn't I come up, and bring Del, whom he'd never met. We could relax, do a bit of fishing, whatever. I said I'd think about it. Then he told me he'd renewed an old acquaintance while he'd been staying at Max's place, she was with him now. For a wild moment I thought he'd chatted up Max's old mum, said as much. Laurie got embarrassed and then shitty. He said gruffly that he'd like me and Del to come up, we could suit our bloody selves. Then he rang off.

I told Del, and she wanted to go. I had no real reason not to. The five hundred quid I'd invested with Lee Gordon had returned fifteen hundred, the weather was turning warm—the day Richard left was the hottest October day on record—so a few days at a weekender sounded all right.

I stayed in town until I'd heard from Teddy in America. He said everything was looking good, he'd ring me when he got back. I gave him Laurie's number at Pittwater, told him to ring me there.

There were two ways to get to his place, Laurie had said. We could drive in the back way through the bush, out along the road to West Head, then turn off along a rough track that worked its way down off the ridge to within a few hundred yards of the house. If we went that way, there was the risk of not getting the car out again if it rained. Alternatively, we could leave the car at Church Point, take the ferry a couple of miles across Pittwater, and then get out at the little jetty at Towler's Bay, which was what we did.

I'd expected a fibro shack built around a caravan, but Laurie's place was better than what most people lived in full-time: a big old four-bedroom house with a veranda around three sides, set in the trees a little way up the hill from the jetty. There was a large boat shed down on the water.

Laurie's mysterious lady friend turned out to be Molly Price.

I couldn't take it in right away. Molly and Laurie. Molly was wearing shorts, had a bit of a tan, looked about three thousand per cent better than she had a fortnight before.

I made the introductions. I'd lugged over a sugar bag full of bottles of beer, so we opened a bottle of warm beer and drank it.

Laurie showed us around the place. He'd bought it back in 1949, when he was riding high. He'd intended to get up here in his spare time, but he hardly ever did. No one knew about it. An old crony of his lived down in the boat shed, looked after the house, had done so all the time Laurie was in prison.

I didn't pay much attention during Laurie's guided tour. I had a thousand questions, but Laurie gave me little opportunity to ask them.

The boat shed was empty at the moment, the regular tenant

being away, so Laurie said Del and I could have it—to enjoy some time together, he said.

I didn't get any answers that day. Del was at me to find out all she could. I'd told her about the Charlie Furner killing from five years before, and about the rort Max and I had done with the tape recorder, and about Laurie's betrayal of me. I'd told her about Molly, how she went to America in the middle of it all, without a word. She was angling to find out if Molly still meant something to me. What could I say? She meant as much as she ever did. We were friends who used to fuck sometimes.

We slept that afternoon, ate with Laurie and Molly that night up at the main house. The sudden absence of dexedrine in my system left me half-asleep. I turned in before nine.

The birds squawking at dawn woke us. I made a pot of tea and took a cup out onto the jetty and drank it while I smoked a Craven A. It was cold in the shadows, but there was no wind and the sun was warm. Mullet were jumping in the still water. Somewhere out on the bay I could hear an outboard, but otherwise it was still. The old fox had a pretty good setup, I thought.

Molly came down to the jetty and sat there next to me.

"How are you feeling?" I asked.

"A lot better than a fortnight ago."

"You still on the drugs?"

"Laurie brought me up here to dry out. He helped me through the worst part."

"So that's it? It's over now?"

"It's never really over. But it's all right for now, I think."

"That's good. What about Marty?"

"Oh, he's around somewhere."

"You and him finished?"

"Yeah. It was never that serious. We were together for two months before the tour. I just hitched a ride home, really. He knew that."

"But he's still here?"

"Yeah. He thinks he might get into television here."

"Doing what?"

"I don't know. Telling gags. He can sing, too, a bit, Tony Bennett–style."

"Is he still chasing the dragon?"

"I suppose so. He went back to see your pal Louis once or twice."

We were silent for a couple of minutes.

"You've got a nice girlfriend, Billy."

"Yeah. What's with you and Laurie, then?"

"He's asked me to marry him."

"Will you?"

"I just might."

Laurie and I took the boat out that afternoon, an old clinker-hulled thing with a diesel motor in the centre. I didn't ask about his new love affair with Molly, and he didn't offer any explanations.

The next day, the four of us took the boat a few miles up the bay to Flint and Steel Beach. Pittwater is a long inlet running south off the main Hawkesbury River–Broken Bay estuary. Flint and Steel is a few miles to the north, facing into the main channel. The estuary is wider than Sydney Harbour, but not as deep. The land around it is thickly wooded bush, with hills rising steeply from the water's edge, up to a height of five hundred feet. The southern shore of the estuary system comprises the northern boundary of the Sydney area, but you could scarcely see any habitations at all from most of Pittwater and Broken Bay.

From Flint and Steel Point you can see past Lion Island straight out to sea, through the Broken Bay heads. We had a picnic on the sand, then Del and I caught blackfish off the rocks. Eagles flew high above us, and out in the bay flocks of sea birds dived for baitfish. A commercial fishing boat patrolled the area a couple of hundred yards off the beach, where the water running out of the Hawkesbury River meets the incoming tide.

We ate and even swam, though the water was cold, then motored home mid-afternoon and barbecued our blackfish.

After five days of that sort of thing, I was feeling pretty fine. Molly seemed truly recovered, and she and Laurie really looked like they were in love. They were unselfconsciously affectionate—something new to both of them, as far as I could recall. He'd listen to her talk, watch her walk around and do things, as if he were hypnotized. She cuddled and hugged him, laughed at his jokes, seemed to enjoy doing little things for him. After a few days, it stopped seeming to me like such a crazy match. Molly was thirty, Laurie was near fifty, but pretty fit. I thought, gee, why not?

Teddy rang on day seven. He was back and holding cash. I told Laurie we'd be off, it was time to be back in town. He said, why rush off now? I said I had business.

"Is Teddy back, then?"

I didn't answer.

"Because if that's what it is, why don't you tell him to come up here?"

He saw the alarm on my face.

"Look, Billy, I'm not trying to muscle in on your deal, can't you see that? I'm happy with what I have, I mean it. I'm really happy with it, Molly and that, and I hope and trust there are no hard feelings in that area with you." He waited, looking at me.

"No, Laurie, I'm happy for you both. I think it's beaut."

"All right then, don't rush off yet. I mean it, ring Teddy and tell him to come up here. Bring Max up, too, if you like. If you blokes want to settle your business here, I won't stick my nose in. Molly would love you and Del to stay for a while."

I talked to Del. She was for staying a while longer. I rang Teddy, asked him how he felt about coming up, whether he had reservations about Laurie. He said no, not really—after all, Laurie had done all he could to help us out. Yeah, all right, a couple of days out of town would be good, he'd bring Max.

They arrived together on the ferry the next morning. They said hello to everyone, and the three of us adjourned straightaway to the boat shed for the whack-up.

Ted had done well. After taking out airfares and expenses, he'd wound up with nearly twenty-one thousand Australian pounds. Lee Gordon had helped with the conversion, and charged us a thousand for it. My share of the take came to just under eight grand.

Ted counted out my money in ten-quid notes. It was bulky. He'd already paid Max off, and by now Max had managed to blow three hundred of it.

Ted and Max stayed over that night and left the next day. Del and Molly rode back in the ferry with them to get some supplies at Church Point. Laurie and I went fishing.

The fishing was so-so. At four o'clock, we brought back a bream and a couple of tailor. We took the fish up to the main house.

Ray Waters was sitting at the table. Molly and Del were in the room, their faces drawn and tight. Ray Waters, a Chief Superintendent now, sat there in a sports shirt, drinking a glass of beer. I'd never seen him in anything other than blue serge.

"Billy Glasheen! Laurie O'Brien! It does my heart good to see you both. Come on in, gents. The ladies have been entertaining me here while I was waiting for you both."

Laurie said, "What do you want, Ray?"

"What do I want? Oh, Laurie, don't be suspicious. After all, we go back a long way, don't we?"

"Too bloody long."

"Oh, Laurie."

Laurie said, "What are you here for, Ray?"

"Billy, do *you* think I want something?"

"Do you?"

"*Should* I be wanting something?"

Laurie moved in front of him. "Why don't you just fuck off, Ray? I've done my time. You've got nothing on anyone here. Leave us alone."

"Oh, Laurie, settle down. Here I was renewing my acquaintance with Molly Price, who I haven't seen since she was hawking the fork from her flat in Darlinghurst. And now here's you, Laurie, fresh out of the slot. And the erstwhile King of the Bodgies, young Billy Glasheen, with his popsy, banned from television, I believe, for obscenity. Now an unkind person would say that you have all found your true level."

"Seems like you have, too, Ray."

He laughed, nodding. "Look, I'll stop bullshitting. I'm human. I like getting away from it all, just like anyone else. Billy, you and I have matters to discuss, but let's not rush into it. Look, I dressed for the occasion. Let's just take it easy, have a beer, we'll sort out our business. I'd love to do some fishing while I'm here. How does that sound? Here, fellers, I brought some beer, have a drink. Maybe the sheilas will make us some dinner."

I took a glass of beer, sat down and drank it. Laurie sat down, but didn't have any beer.

"How did you find your way here, Ray?" I asked.

"Well, that's a long story. For some time, I've had an association with some young chaps who had a particular interest in your and Ted Rallis's affairs, Billy."

"Mick whatsisname and the bloke with the crew cut."

"That's right, and a couple of others. But those blokes aren't all that bright, are they, Billy?"

"I don't know. I'm told they managed to run a yearlong stand-over operation at Darling Harbour without being caught. But then, maybe you had something to do with the investigation."

He waved his hand, like he was dismissing overly generous praise. "Those galahs needed all the help they could get. Mind you, they did tumble to the fact that you and Rallis had the proceeds of the J. Farren Price robbery, sure enough, but then they let it slip away from them."

"It slipped away from us all, Ray."

"When the darkie poof threw it into the drink?"

"Yeah."

He laughed loudly. "Then why did Rallis go to America? Why did he come straight here when he got back? These are the questions I asked myself. Oh, it's all right, you don't have to keep lying to me, you're not that good at it. Christ, it's a dry ship." He leaned back and spoke over his shoulder to Molly. "Bring us another bottle, sweetheart."

She put it down hard on the table.

Waters leaned back, hooked his thumbs under his belt. "This really is the life, Laurie. When I followed Perkal and Rallis up here yesterday, I was intrigued as to the ownership of this place."

"You followed them over here on the ferry?"

"Well, not quite. I followed them to Church Point. Later I inquired of the ferry driver where the lads had gone. He said it could only have been one of the ten or so places up here. Half an hour spent at the shire council turned up a property belonging to one Lawrence O'Brien. Voilà. Yes, this is a great setup here, Laurie. I have a weekender down south, but it's not a patch on this."

"What do you want, Ray?"

"Don't rush me, son." He poured himself another drink. "You know, I really do work too hard. Lately I've been thinking, what's the point of busting a gut? Isn't it more important to enjoy life? Eh, Billy? Laurie? I like to have a bet, do a bit of fishing, get a suntan, keep a nice bit of fluff about the place to suck my cock, that's the way to live, eh?"

Del walked to the door.

"Not so fast, missy. Where are your manners?"

She stopped. Molly stood by the sink, blank-faced.

"Now tell me, Billy. What did you do to Noel Shoebridge?"

"Nothing."

"Well, he had told me I could expect a consideration from him, but after his dealings with you he resigned, persona non grata, from the Security Service."

"He was just a thief, he deserved whatever happened to him. What *did* happen to him?"

"He's at Surfer's Paradise. He runs a property management, private security, and investigation service."

I thought, Jesus—the Jap, Vi Furner, Petrov, Noel Shoebridge, all at Surfer's Paradise. They're probably running the local council by now.

"So, Billy, my feeling is you owe me something. A substantial something. So tell me, boy, what *was* your share of the J. Farren Price take? But before you answer, I'm warning you, don't bullshit me."

"Eight grand."

"And how much did Rallis bring back, all up?"

"Twenty."

"All right, then, think about this: I should have half of that. I take your eight, you find me another two, sort the rest out between you and Rallis and Perkal. But as I say, I'm flexible. Jesus, Molly's got nice tits, eh, boys? Mind you, I haven't seen them in the flesh, so to speak, for quite a while. Maybe we can rectify that later on." He winked at Molly.

Laurie stood up and walked over to the sideboard, opened it and brought out a bottle of scotch, put it on the table, then went to the cupboard and got some glasses.

"Now, that's more like it. I thought you might've gone off the drink out here at the Bay, Laurie."

"No, Ray, I still have one on special occasions."

He sat back down, poured a double nip for himself and one each for Waters and me. Molly shook her head, but Del had one. Laurie drank his down.

"Well, I'm glad you regard this as a special occasion."

"Oh, I do, Ray. I really do."

He brought his hand out from under the table. He was holding a pistol. He lifted it and aimed it into Waters' face.

"Del, Molly, will you excuse us please? Billy, you can stay or go as you please."

Waters looked amused. "Christ, Laurie, do you think this is the first time some mug has pointed a revolver at me?"

"Del, Molly, please wait outside."

They left. I stayed at the table. Outside, the sun had gone down behind the hill, but I could see the last of the sunshine falling on the hillside over on the eastern shore. A nearly full moon was rising. Rosellas were flitting about outside, a kookaburra was cranking up somewhere off in the bush.

Laurie was holding the gun aimed at Waters, saying nothing.

"For Christ's sake, Laurie, put the thing away or use it, as the actress said to the archbishop!"

"All right, then."

He shot Waters in the right side of the chest. Waters jerked backwards, then slumped forward into his glass, smashing it under his face. Whisky and blood seeped out onto the laminex from under his inert body. Laurie put the gun down and poured another whisky, took a sip. We both sat there for fully three or four minutes. Then I reached over and picked up Waters' left wrist, tried to find a pulse, but there was none.

"I think he's bundied off."

Laurie nodded. He was still sitting there.

After another couple of minutes, he went and stood at the window, then turned back and said, "We'll have to get rid of the body. We can take it out into the bay."

"What if someone knows he came up here?"

"Who would know? He was working a standover."

"The gunshot. It sounded like a Howitzer."

"Illegal shooters back in the hills."

"What about his car, then? It'll be over at Church Point. Plus he said he spoke to the bloke on the ferry."

"We can get his keys and take the car somewhere else."

Laurie took the gun apart, wrapped each part in rags, soaked them in petrol and set fire to them. "These pieces will never fit back together," he said.

We wrapped the body in sugar bags and a bit of old matting from the veranda, carried it down to the jetty and into the boat.

We motored out into the bay, under the rising moon. We didn't have any lights showing, but there were no other boats about.

Every ten minutes or so Laurie threw a piece of the gun overboard.

It took us an hour to reach the Palm Beach settlement, another twenty minutes before we drew level with Barrenjoey Head, the huge rock outcrop which made up the southern head to Broken Bay. There was no trace of daylight left, but the moon was bright enough to navigate by. At the foot of Barrenjoey Cliffs we could see three lights—fishermen settled in for the night, waiting for the tide to change.

When we rounded the headland, we encountered a swell, but the boat rode it easily. We passed through areas of phosphorescence, where the foam at our bow glowed like neon. There was no wind. It would have been a great night for fishing.

Laurie guided the boat straight out for three miles, then stopped. The northern beaches' townships could be seen to the south, right down to Manly Beach. We'd passed a fishing trawler coming back into the bay, and an oil tanker passed by another couple of miles out to sea, but apart from that there was no one.

We'd wrapped the body up with rocks and housebricks. Waters was a heavy man to begin with, and it was awkward manhandling the bundle to the edge of the boat. But we did it. The body slipped into the water and straight down. By way of ceremony, Laurie said, "Let the sharks have him."

We got back to the jetty at Towler's Bay two hours later. Molly and Del were sitting in the kitchen when we arrived, looking grim. Molly got up and put her arm around Laurie. They didn't say anything much. We ate some leftovers, and then Laurie took me and Del across to Church Point. I had Waters' car keys. It took ten minutes of trial and error to find the right car, a newish FC Holden.

I drove back to Sydney, Del following in my car. I took Waters' car out to Mascot Airport, left it in the carpark there, then we returned to Church Point. It was one a.m. when we got back. I rang up and Laurie came across for us. We didn't say much. Del and I went to bed. I fell asleep picturing Ray Waters' body sliding off the boat into the black water. I had one of those dreams where you think something is funny, which in real life isn't funny at all. I laughed in my sleep at the pun, Ray Waters, Ray in the waters, then woke up in a sweat.

Next morning I woke early, before Del, and went up to the main house for some breakfast. Laurie was already up, sitting at the table, same place he'd been sitting when he shot Waters. I cut a slice of bread, toasted it, sat down and poured a cup of tea. The sun was shining in.

"So now what?"

"It's all over. We forget about it."

"What will you do?"

"Me and Molly?"

"Yeah."

"We'll get married. I'll sell this place probably. Do you want to buy it?"

"Seriously?"

He nodded.

"How much would you want?"

"Oh, three grand would do."

"I'll think about it. Where will you live, what will you do?"

"I'm barred from the betting ring for life. I might try something new."

"You and Molly?"

"Yes, that's right."

I nodded. "Laurie, clear something up for me. When did you and Molly first get together?"

He didn't answer. Molly's voice behind me said, "When do you think, Billy?"

"I think back in 1952, when you were seeing me and Jim Swain. You were seeing Laurie, too."

I turned around to face her. She was in her dressing gown. She nodded.

I turned back to Laurie. "That was maybe the real reason you set me up for the fall back then."

He didn't speak.

"So where did Waters fit in?"

Molly sat down. "He came around looking for you the morning Charlie Furner was shot?"

She waited for me to acknowledge, then continued. "He came back again after that."

She stopped speaking.

After a few seconds, Laurie turned to me and said, "He raped her."

I said to her, "True?"

She nodded.

Laurie said, "Molly left the country after Waters told her how we had planned to . . . to set you up."

"Why did Waters blow the whistle?"

"He was trying to turn Molly against me. He succeeded."

"So she went away. But you two kept in touch?"

Molly said, "Yes. When Laurie went to jail I heard about it over there, eventually. I wrote to him. He told me when he was getting out. I was in trouble with the dope by then. I went to America to get away from trouble, but it found me over there. I met Lee Gordon, hitched a free ride back with Marty."

"You love Laurie?"

"Yes, Billy, I do."

Del was standing by the door. I hadn't noticed her come in. I said to her, "You wouldn't believe what I've just heard."

"I think I would. Molly told me all about it last night."

Laurie said, "Billy, we've tipped Waters into the sea. That's the end of it. I'm not saying Waters was the cause of all our trouble. I made my own bad luck. But Waters was the symbol of it. He was my dragon."

He paused, looking at me. I nodded.

He went on, "Molly and I have both done our penance. Now we want to live. And now you know it all."

I didn't tell Max and Ted about Waters. When a policeman disappears, there is a major investigation, and rumours are threepence a hundred, but I didn't want any with my name in them.

Waters was known among villains as being a villain himself, but he was also well known to the public as an outstanding policeman, a Queen's Medal holder. The papers ran stories on him.

The car at the airport suggested one obvious explanation for his disappearance. The file on the J. Farren Price robbery investigation was found to be missing, then turned up at his home. A little later, a diamond brooch from the Price robbery appeared in a jewellery store in San Francisco, identified during a routine check of secondhand merchandise. Soon, questions were asked about why the Darling Harbour standover rort had been allowed to go on for so long. There were reasons for both the state government and the opposition not to press too hard for all the answers.

I bought the house from Laurie. But the times I went, I always ended up using the boat shed rather than the main house.

One evening a couple of months later, in midsummer, Del and I were sitting on the jetty, in the dark, fishing for bream. We were pulling one in every half hour or so. Del asked me about my part in the Waters killing.

"When Laurie sent me and Molly out of the room, did you know he was going to shoot Waters?" she asked.

"I did and I didn't. I knew Laurie could be ruthless, absolutely ruthless. Like he told me once, business is about making the best decision at the time, whatever that may be. But I also thought Waters might back down—or Laurie might."

"You could have bowed out."

"I suppose I also knew I was involved no matter what. If I'd had the gun myself, I really don't think I could have shot him, but I benefited from it happening, just the same. I'm part of it, I suppose. Just as you and Molly are."

"Can we live with it?"

"We'll see."

O'Keefe went on to better things. Max watched his rise with bemusement mixed with envy, and for a while there took to speculating on how he might have planned his run differently. At the end of 1957, Lee Gordon brought Nat King Cole and the Trio out. Oscar Moore, the guitarist, invited Max to sit in on an after-hours jam at the Troc. Cole said Max's playing reminded him of Les Paul. It was enough to put Max back on the good foot.

Del joined his club show. She rocked the act up. Max took to calling it "Hawaiian boogie-woogie." But pop music in Australia then was tied to television, and Del's virtual ban from the tube set a limit on how successful they could be. Still, "Bondi Bop," a record they released on Lee Gordon's Leedon label, went to number two on the top 40.

In January 1958, Igor's travel agency at Kingsford was firebombed. The Federal Liberal government denied it was evidence of right-wing activities among the migrant communities; but they continued to keep a sharp eye on the commos.

Marty Jay got the monkey off his back and landed an appearance on television, came back a couple of times, was finally given a midday program to compere, called *Your Lucky Day*. They'd find some battler, do a bit of quick research into how much he owed and who to, and then right there on camera would present him with a bunch of consumer goods, and a check to cover their debts, or enough to buy a set of leg braces for their crippled kiddie, or whatever. Sometimes he'd reunite estranged family members. The old dears loved it, and Marty made some good brass. He could cry on cue, too.

I kept doing what I did. I road-managed two more shows, one with Jerry Lee Lewis, another with Chuck Berry. Gordon said he liked having me on the team when the touring artiste happened to be "difficult to manage."

Del had asked me if I could live with my part in the Waters killing. It didn't bother me that much. But I had this recurring dream. I was fishing, going after this one kingfish which kept getting away. In the dream, I finally hooked up and it felt like a thirty- or forty-pounder. But when I got it to the surface, the line would go still, and I'd pull out a dead fish that would turn into Ray Waters. You figure it out.

GLOSSARY

This brief glossary of colloquial and underworld language inevitably includes a number of words which refer to native Australian and immigrant ethnic groups in a derogatory and racist fashion. These are listed for reasons of social and historical accuracy, and their offensiveness is understood. Anyone interested in a more detailed resource for Australian slang should consult *The Macquarie Australian Slang Dictionary* (2004), or its predecessor, *The Macquarie Dictionary of Australian Colloquial Language.*

Abo *n, derogatory* : Aborigine
Africa Speaks : cheap fortified wine or illegally distilled alcohol. *Aka* "around the world for a zack," "Abo's blanket," and "overnight bag"
ALP : Australian Labor Party, one of the two major Australian political parties. The ALP was out of power when the conservative Liberal Party dominated, from the late 1940s until the early 1970s
Anzac Day : April 25, a national holiday in honour of Australian servicemen and -women (Anzac = Australian and New Zealand Army Corps), particularly those who served in the two world wars
arvo : afternoon
ASIO : Australian Security Intelligence Organisation

bag *vb* : to criticize or ridicule
Balt : post-WWII immigrant from the Baltic states of Europe. A general term for postwar European refugees
battler : a hard-up working person
Bay, the : Long Bay Prison, Sydney
berko : crazy (possibly from "berserk")
berley *n* : mash thrown into the water by fishermen to attract fish —
berley up *vb* : to attract fish
Bex : a popular analgesic
bit : cadged
bitumen : asphalt (US); tarmac (UK)

bludge *vb* : to live off the immoral earnings of prostitutes, to pimp. More generally, to cadge, or to take it easy — **on the bludge** : intentionally unemployed — **bludger** : a work-shy person

blue *n, vb* : fight, brawl

bob : a shilling (later 10 cents)

bodgie *adj* : fake, ersatz, substandard

bodgie *n* : a juvenile delinquent; originally "bodgie (i.e., fake) American," in reference to young men, often black marketeers, who during WWII and afterwards imitated "American" clothing styles (zoot suits, and later denim jeans) and who favoured jive dancing. Also known as **Cornel Wilde Boys**, after the haircuts they sported

bonnet : hood (of a car)

Bonox : a hot beverage

boot : trunk (of a car)

bot *vb* : to cadge (usu. a cigarette)

brass *n* : money — *vb* : to swindle

browneye, drop a : to insult by exposing the sphincter; to moon (US)

bull : police detective

bumper : cigarette butt

bundy, bundy off *vb* **1** : to clock off work, to leave; hence **2** : to die

bung it on : to behave temperamentally

bunger : firecracker, cigarette

cashed *adj* : variant of "cashed-up"; just paid, having ready money

chat *n* : a particularly dirty person, usu. applied to a hobo

chew and spew : a café of the less salubrious type (US: greasy spoon)

chocko : rhyming slang, chocolate frog = wog = immigrant

chook : chicken

Chow *n, derogatory* : Chinese person

Cochran, Eddie : rock 'n' roll singer/guitarist who toured Australia with Little Richard and Gene Vincent in 1957. Killed in a car accident in 1959 on the eve of a return trip to Australia

Colombo Plan : training program set up by British Commonwealth nations after WWII

come good *vb* : to improve dramatically; to produce

commo : Communist (US: commie)

cop *vb* : to receive, often something not desirable, as in "I copped a parking fine"; related to US "cop" (= "get"), and sometimes used in that sense, too ("to cop for someone" = to procure drugs for them), but usu. suggests passive receiving rather than active getting

crook *adj* **1** : unwell **2** : illicit, crooked **3** : of dubious value

Cross, the : King's Cross, the bohemian and red-light district of Sydney

currency : at this time, the units of Australian currency were pounds, shillings, and pence. Important units were the copper penny; the silver sixpenny coin (zack); the shilling (bob), equal to twelve pence; and the two-shilling (two-bob) piece. Units of paper money were the ten-shilling note; the pound (twenty shillings); and the five- and ten-pound note

In everyday parlance, **zack** indicated a petty, insignificant financial level. **Two-bob** was also used to denote a tawdry scale of affairs, so a foolish person might be described as being "silly as a two-bob watch," or a young, dandyish person might be described as a "two-bob lair." And there was no coming back from the put-down "not worth two bob"

In the mid-1950s, the "basic wage" for unskilled work was between £12 and £20 per week. A basic café meal or a packet of cigarettes cost as little as two shillings.

In the mid-1960s, Australia converted to a decimal currency system, in which a penny became a cent and ten shillings became a dollar

dacks : pants (US), trousers (UK)

daggy *adj* : square, out of fashion — **dag** *n* : one who lacks style

dago *n, derogatory* : an Italian

Davey, Jack : popular Sydney radio personality and notorious bad debtor

dekko *n* : look, glance ("I had a quick dekko at the form guide")

digger, old digger : a veteran, esp. of WWI or WWII; more generally, an Australian soldier; also a common term of address ("G'day digger, how are you?")

dinkum : *see* fair dinkum

dirty *adj* : to be dirty on someone = to be angry with someone

dob *vb* : to dob someone in = to blow the whistle, to inform on someone

dunny *n* : toilet, outhouse

Estapol : a clear wood preservative

fair dinkum *adj* : genuine — also often used as a phatic question, in the sense of "Is that so?"

fair go *n* : a term with a wide range of meanings. To give someone a fair go (or to demand the same) means to treat fairly, reasonably. As an exclamation, "fair go!" means something like "give me a break!"

fibro : fibro-cement, a cheap building material much used in housing construction in the period following WWII

fig : clothing — **in copper fig** : dressed like a policeman

fiver : a five-pound note (*see* currency)

footy *abbr* : football; in Sydney, the term refers to the version of football most popular there—namely, Rugby League

flutter *n* : a small wager

galah *n* **1** : a stupid, ungainly variety of parrot, hence **2** : a foolish person

gee'd up *adj* : excited, highly strung

gen *n* : information

get up *vb* : to win (said of a racehorse)

giddy-up *n* : amphetamines

gin *n, derogatory* : an Aboriginal woman

gladstone : gladstone bag; a carry bag favoured by working men

glass *vb* : to push a broken beer glass into an opponent's face in a bar brawl

go-fast *n* : amphetamines

gone to Gowings : indisposed, deranged; originally an advertising slogan for Sydney department store Gowings

gooseberry : odd one out; an unaccompanied person at a social occasion

Gordon, Lee : charismatic 1950s Australian music promoter, who brought early rock 'n' roll acts to Australia. Died of a drug overdose in London in 1963, after a career marked by spectacular rises and falls

grog : alcohol — **sly grog** : alcohol sold illegally, either after hours or from unlicensed premises

half-stung : slightly drunk

hammer *n* **1** : *abbr* "hammer and nail," rhyming slang for tail ("the police are on his hammer") — **2** : *abbr* "hammer and tack," rhyming slang for back, and more recently for smack, i.e., heroin

hard-earneds *n* : money, wages

hawk the fork : to work as a prostitute

hoon *n* : delinquent, hooligan

hoist *vb* : to steal, "lift"

housie *or* **housie-housie** : bingo

how's-your-father *adj* : indifferent

Jay, Marty : a fictitious character combining elements of Lenny Bruce, who toured Australia in the early 1960s, and several other North American entertainers who settled in Australia in the postwar period and enjoyed successful radio and television careers

jack *n* : detective

jonah *vb* : to bring someone bad luck

kero *abbr* : kerosene — **kero heater** : kerosene burner

kick *n* : pocket

kick on *vb* : to carry on, or celebrate late into the night

king-hit **1** *vb* : to knock someone out — **2** *n* : a knockout punch

lagging *n* : a jail sentence

lag *vb* : to inform on someone

lair *n* : a juvenile delinquent, or show-off — **lairising** : behaving like a lair

Leger *abbr* : St Leger, the mid-priced section at Sydney's Randwick racecourse

Liberal Party : the major conservative political party in Australia, which ruled at the federal level throughout the period of this book; not in any sense a lowercase-*l* liberal party

Little Richard : apart from Elvis Presley, the most commercially successful (and arguably the wildest and most intense) of the first-wave rock 'n' rollers. He famously turned his back on rock 'n' roll in favour of evangelical Christianity after his 1957 tour of Australia

lob *vb* : to arrive

lurk *n* : a racket or scam

lurk artist *or* **lurk man** *or* **lurk merchant** : one who lives by scams, schemes, and rackets; a con man

mag *vb* : to talk (also a noun)

mail *n* : inside information, the real story ("He gave me the mail about . . .") — **late mail** : the most up-to-date information, esp. regarding the fitness of a racehorse

Menzies, Sir Robert : Conservative prime minister of Australia, 1949-1965

mug *n* : a fool — **mug punter** : a gambler characterized by consistent imprudence and financial failure; usu. applied to someone who bets on horses

mulga : Scrub, forest (from the name of a species of wild bush which grows in the arid Australian interior)

neck *vb* : to kill — originally, to kill by hanging

New Australian *n* : a more polite—and in its day (the 1950s) politically correct—term for an immigrant

nicked, get nicked : roughly equivalent to "get fucked," although less impolite

nod, on the nod : on credit; originally racetrack argot ("he was betting on the nod," meaning he had a gentlemen's agreement with the bookie, a mere nod of the head being sufficient acknowledgment of indebtedness)

no risk : certain, for sure

O'Keefe, Johnny : Australian rock 'n' roll/pop singer, arguably the first local rock 'n' roll performer to find favour with Australian audiences. Performed with great intensity, influenced by southern gospel, New Orleans R&B, and Jerry Lee Lewis–style rock. Co-wrote "Wild One" (aka "Real Wild Child"), covered by Jerry Lee Lewis and later by Iggy Pop. His soulful version of "It's Too Late" became an R&B hit in New Orleans. His reading of the Isley Brothers' "Shout" was a huge local favourite. His later career was marked by breakdowns and drug abuse

off tap *adj* : extremely displeased, "off the air," lost in private turmoil; derived from barroom terminology, of the beer being on or off tap; later used in jail slang to mean ostracized, untouchable, but this is not how Glasheen uses the term

old duck : old woman

Paddo : Paddington, then a rough working-class area of inner Sydney

pak-a-pu : an illegal Chinese lottery game

pash *or* **pash off** *vb* : to kiss passionately

Pentridge : a notorious jail in Melbourne, Victoria, now closed down

perve *vb* : to look at lasciviously (also a noun ("have a perv at that!"))

Petrov, Vladimir : a staff member in the U.S.S.R. Embassy in Australia who defected with his wife Evdokia (also an intelligence agent) in 1954 at the height of the Cold War and subsequently claimed that a Russian spy ring had been operating in Australia with the collusion of certain elements in the Australian Labor Party. Many claimed these allegations were baseless, serving only to fuel anti-Communist propaganda about a "nest of traitors" in Australia. Recent research suggests a pro-Soviet mole may in fact have been at large in the bureaucracy during and after WWII, when Labour was in power, but in any case the popular hysteria that was whipped up in the aftermath of the Petrov affair enabled Robert Menzies' Liberal Party to cement its hold on power for the next decade and a half

pianola : a player piano

piss : alcohol

pissed : drunk (as distinct from US usage to mean "unhappy, disgruntled"; in Australia and the UK this sense is denoted by the term "pissed off")

PMG *abbr* : Postmaster General's Department, the government body responsible for post and telecommunications

poof *or* **poofter** *n, derogatory* : male homosexual

Porphyry Pearl : a sweet, sparkling white wine, in more unliberated times regarded as a "ladies' drink"

port : suitcase; *abbr* portmanteau

pro : prostitute

punt *vb* : to wager, esp. to bet on horses — **take a punt** : take a chance

punter *n* : someone who bets on horses

push *n* : a gang

quid : slang term for one pound; *see* currency

ratbag : a worthless, unreliable, possibly fanatical fellow

rats, to go : to go crazy

Ratsack : popular brand of rat poison

Ray, Johnnie : pre-rock 'n' roll singer of the early 1950s, with a strong following among the young

Redex Trials : popular annual car race through inland Australia

reffo *n, derogatory* : a refugee, post-WWII European immigrant

rels : relatives

Rene, Roy : a popular Australian vaudeville and radio entertainer

Repat *abbr* : Department of Repatriation, the government bureaucracy which handled war veterans' affairs

returned man : a veteran of WWI and esp. WWII — **returned man's badge** : a lapel badge denoting that the wearer had served overseas during the war

rollie : a hand-rolled cigarette

root *vb* : to copulate (impolite, but less so than "fuck"; roughly = US "screw") — **root a boot** : exclamation, as, "golly!" — **"go root your boot"** : "leave me alone"

rooted *adj* : exhausted, broken, "fucked"

root rat : promiscuous male

rort *n* : an illegal activity, a scam, a lurk — *vb* : to cheat

roscoe : a pistol, gun

roughy : a racehorse considered unlikely to win, hence at long odds with the bookmakers

rozzer : policeman; usu. used in *pl* **rozzers**

RSL : Returned Servicemen's League, a war veterans' association of unfailingly conservative inclinations

sanger : a sandwich

scab *vb* : to cadge

scarper *vb* : to leave quickly, vamoose

septic *n* : an American (from "septic tank," rhyming slang for Yank)

sheila *n* : a girl or woman (informal)

shilling : twelve pennies, one twentieth of a pound — *see* currency

shoot through *vb* : to leave in a hurry ("he shot through like a Bondi tram")

shunter : railway-yard worker responsible for moving rail trucks

shout *vb* : to buy a round of drinks — also a noun ("it's your shout")

silvertail : a rich person

skite *vb* : to brag

slot *n* : jail — **be slotted** : to be put in jail

sly grog : *see* grog

snag *n* : sausage

SP *abbr* : the business of **starting price** bookies, (illegal) off-course book-makers who took bets and paid winners according to the on-course tote odds. Hugely important in Australian cultural life throughout the twentieth century, esp. but not exclusively in working-class areas. Operated from hotels, private houses, army barracks, jails, etc. Tolerated (and in many cases actively supported) by the massive majority of Australians, SP was always a target of puritanical social reformers.

The huge sums of money that changed hands in off-course betting inevitably led to payoffs to the police, and historians now see a link between the illegal status of off-course betting and the development of strong and enduring ties between organized crime and corrupt police, esp. in Sydney. In the 1960s, the New South Wales state government set up its own off-course betting agency, and the scale of SP decreased dramatically; many criminals, some believe, then turned their attention to importing heroin and other drugs

spaz *adj* : uncontrolled, wildly uninhibited — **go spaz** : to act in such a manner

spew *n, vb* : vomit

squarehead : law-abiding citizen

stand over *vb* : to extort money using the threat of physical violence — **standover rort** : organized standover activity

starting price : *see* SP

stiff *adj* : broke

stiff *n* : a derelict or homeless person; more generally : an old person

stone *n* : weight measurement equivalent to fourteen pounds (fifteen stone = 210 lbs.)

strike me lucky : an exclamation of surprise, bewilderment, or exasperation (made famous by Roy Rene)

tailor *n* : species of ocean fish native to the East coast of Australia

tea leaf : thief (rhyming slang)

techo *n* : technician

tick : on tick = on credit

tiddlers : various kinds of small fish

ton : one hundred, often used to refer to a sum of money (i.e., £100 or $100), but also to doing 100 m.p.h.

tooled up *adj* : armed or otherwise equipped for skullduggery

traps : archaic slang term for the police, used primarily in the great age of Australian outlawry in the mid- and late-nineteenth century, when the public avidly followed the contests between the traps (or troopers) and bushrangers (outlaws) such as Ned Kelly or Ben Hall. Some bushrangers were undoubtedly homicidal maniacs; others (including Hall and Kelly) enjoyed folk-hero status

The Tribune : the weekly newspaper, now defunct, of the Communist Party of Australia

troppo *adj* : crazy — from tropical, i.e., referring to a form of tropical lunacy

turn it up! : an exclamation roughly equivalent to "give me a break!"

two-bob *adj* : a person or thing of little worth; *see* currency

two-up *n* : a game in which two coins are tossed in the air and the players bet on whether they fall heads or tails

2GB, 2KY, 2UE, 2UW : the call signs of popular Sydney radio stations. Broadcast television did not arrive in Australia until the late 1950s, so AM radio remained the dominant electronic medium through most of the decade

Ustasha : Extreme Croatian nationalist secret society. Actively pro-Nazi during WWII and fanatically anti-Communist thereafter. Ustasha was active in Australia in the 1950s and 1960s, and was allegedly given covert aid—in the form of funds and military training—by the ruling Liberal government

ute *n* : pickup truck (*abbr* utility vehicle)

verbal *vb* : to concoct and subsequently present in court an unsworn "confession" allegedly made by an accused person to the arresting policeman, which was frequently sufficient to secure a conviction, even if the accused disputed the statement in court. After reform campaigns in the 1970s, courts gradually became sceptical of "police verbals"

Vincent, Gene : Gene Vincent and the Blue Caps toured Australia with Little Richard and Eddie Cochran in 1957. His hits included "BeBop a Lula," "Woman Love," and "Race with the Devil"

walloper : a policeman (*from* to wallop : to assault)

wedding tackle : male genitalia

Wentworth Park : greyhound racing track in Sydney. The greyhounds chase a mechanical device which (very approximately) resembles a hare.

whack up 1 *vb* : to divide up ill-gotten gains among thieves — **2** *n* : the almost ceremonial process of dividing up the spoils

widgie : female counterpart to bodgie

wog *n*, *derogatory* : an immigrant

wowser : a puritan or killjoy, esp. someone opposed to gambling and drinking

yarra *adj* : deranged

TONY MOTT

ABOUT THE AUTHOR

Peter Doyle was born in Maroubra, in Sydney's eastern suburbs. He worked as a taxi driver, musician, and teacher before writing his first book, *Get Rich Quick*, which won the Ned Kelly Award for Best First Crime Novel. He has since published two further books featuring protagonist Billy Glasheen, *Amaze Your Friends* and *The Devil's Jump*, and is currently working on a fourth. He is also the author of the acclaimed *City of Shadows: Sydney Police Photographs 1912–1948* and *Crooks Like Us*. In 2010 Doyle received the Ned Kelly Lifetime Achievement Award. He teaches writing at Macquarie University, Sydney.